Praise for Ava Miles

NORA ROBERTS LAND
Selected as one of the Best Books of 2013 alongside Nora
Roberts' DARK WITCH and Julia Quinn's SUM OF ALL KISSES.
--USA Today Contributor, Becky Lower, Happily Ever After

"It {NORA ROBERTS LAND} captures the best of what I love
in a Nora Roberts novel..."
--BlogCritics

"...finding love like in the pages of a Nora Roberts story."
--Publisher's Weekly WW Ladies Book Club

FRENCH ROAST
"An entertaining ride...{and) a full-bodied romance."
--Readers' Favorite

"Her engaging story and characters kept me turning the pages."
--Bookfan

THE GRAND OPENING
"Ava Miles is fast becoming one of my favorite light
contemporary romance writers."
--Tome Tender

"The latest book in the Dare Valley series is a continuation of
love, family, and romance."
--Mary J. Gramlich

THE HOLIDAY SERENADE
"This story is all romance, steam, and humor with a touch of the
holiday spirit..."
--The Book Nympho

THE TOWN SQUARE
"Ms. Miles' words melted into
around

D1716018

COUNTRY HEAVEN
"If ever there was a contemporary romance that rated a 10 on a scale of 1 to 5 for me, this one is it!"

AVA MILES

ISBN-13: 9781497398535
www.avamiles.com
Ava Miles

Dear Reader,

DARING DECLARATIONS combines two of my shorter novels in the Dare Valley series, THE HOLIDAY SERENADE and THE TOWN SQUARE, into a reader-friendly anthology.

There's simply nothing like the holidays, and THE HOLIDAY SERENADE, Rhett and Abbie's story, seemed tailor-made for miracles, gingerbread houses, and a holiday serenade. These two are dear to my heart, and I'm so glad they finally came together to make a home for themselves and Dustin. I've included our family recipe for the gingerbread houses Abbie makes in the story at the end; this recipe is from the wife of my great-great grandpa who won our family newspaper in a poker game in 1892. I expect he would hold his own with Rhett at the poker table. If making a house seems too daunting, just make cookies. There's nothing like the smell of gingerbread baking during the holidays—or any other time as far as I'm concerned.

THE TOWN SQUARE holds a special place in my heart because I love Grandpa Hale from The Dare Valley series. I modeled him after my own great-great grandfather, our own journalistic legend. Readers have been begging for his story, so here's what I call my ode to *Mad Men* in a small town with a happy ending. It's been wonderful to visit the 1960s and see what Arthur and Dare Valley were like then. And, of course, to meet the tough and lovely, Harriet, who captures his heart.

I hope you enjoy these two novels. Please stay tuned for an excerpt from COUNTRY HEAVEN, the story of Rhett's best friend in THE HOLIDAY SERENADE, and links to the other Dare Valley books that Arthur Hale is a part of. Thanks for reading!

Lots of light,
Ava

Contents

The Holiday Serenade   7

The Town Square   *141*

THE Holiday SERENADE

AVA MILES

To my brother, Greg, for being willing to share his own creative talents with me and for his unfailing support in this new journey I'm on. Here's to always supporting each other.

And to my divine entourage, who makes my heart sing.

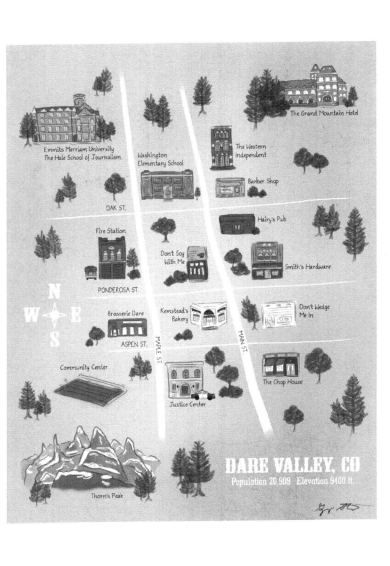

Let your heart be filled with cheer,
Darlin', your Holiday Serenade is here.

It lets me tell you that I want you,
That you're my Christmas dream come true,
That I don't see anyone now but you.

Let the snow fall on your thick, dark hair,
Let the winter wind touch your cheek like I want to.

Come cozy up by the fire with me,
Under the lights of our own Christmas tree.

Let me love you,
Serenade you,
My Christmas dream come true.

Country Singer Rye Crenshaw's Special Christmas
Release, "The Holiday Serenade"
Lyrics by World Series of Poker Champion, Rhett
Butler Blaylock

Chapter 1

Usually Abbie Maven adored the way Christmas allowed her to get her Martha Stewart on by decorating and baking her heart out.

Usually she loved sharing the thirteen different types of cookies she made with family and friends, everything from star-shaped sugar cookies dotted with candy silver balls to grinning gingerbread men.

Usually she didn't have a crazy cowboy and badass poker player named Rhett Butler Blaylock in her kitchen popping cookies into his mouth faster than the Cookie Monster while cracking obscene jokes from a barstool in front of her kitchen island.

"You know, Abbie," he murmured, leaning on the tan granite countertop and waggling his ash-brown brows, "it seems downright chauvinistic of you to make only gingerbread *men*. Maybe you should add breasts to some of these for balance."

Like that would ever happen in her kitchen, with its caramel-colored cabinets and stainless steel appliances, now dotted with vintage Christmas cards of red-cheeked Santas, frolicking reindeer, and luminous angels.

Her sixteen-year-old son, Dustin, hooted with laughter

from his barstool beside Rhett. She even saw her brother, Mac, and his fiancé, Peggy, standing to her right, bite their lips as if they were trying not to join in on the hilarity. Thank goodness Peggy's eight-year-old son, Keith, was in the other room watching the claymation version of *Rudolph The Red-Nosed Reindeer*, which everyone agreed was disturbing. This was so not the PG-rated cookie baking experience she preferred. Especially when everyone was only *watching* her work in the kitchen, the biggest hangout room in the house. They'd complained that making gingerbread men was too hard. Wimps.

The urge to squirt the egg-white gingerbread frosting onto Rhett's red thermal shirt and jeans came over her, but better sense prevailed. Her action might prompt him to strip his shirt off in her kitchen, and frankly, she wouldn't be able to draw a straight line with her frosting if he did that. The man had the best chest she'd ever seen—not that she'd seen many outside of the movies and firemen calendars.

Instead she gestured toward the remaining dough in the bowl, which gave off that special gingerbread scent she loved, redolent of coffee and spice. "Since your poker babes have such remarkable attributes, perhaps you should be the one to shape some female cookies?"

He must have caught the challenge in her eyes. Their ongoing battle over his poker entourage was one of the main reasons why she'd refused to renew their relationship when he moved to her new town of Dare Valley, Colorado, months ago with the sole purpose of getting her to agree to marry him. He'd played poker in overseas venues for a year after she broke off their secret relationship. He'd returned six months ago, declaring his

12

love for her and saying he wouldn't ever leave her again. And, shockingly, he'd stuck by that vow.

Dustin angled his head to the right and flashed a smile at their ongoing banter, and suddenly he reminded her of his father, a man whom she'd believed to be sincere and kind until he'd blown that illusion to smithereens.

Trusting men hadn't been her strong suit since then. Add in the fact that she and Rhett were still ill-suited beyond words, and she hadn't caved to Rhett's dogged pursuit.

If there was one thing Abbie had learned to value in life, it was order. Okay, and control, but that made her sound like a control freak, which she was so not. Mostly.

"I just might do that," Rhett replied, pinching some of the dough out of her holiday Christmas bowl and rolling it into a ball.

"Sweet!" her son cried, jumping up from the bar stool right in front of her kitchen island like he was preparing to make Playboy centerfold gingerbread cookies, a teenager's Christmas fantasy.

Like she would *ever* allow that to happen in her home.

Rhett put a hand on Dustin's shoulder, and he eased back into his chair, about as deflated as an undercooked soufflé.

"Maybe we can just put a dress on them," Rhett said. "That way your mama can still maintain her dignity, Dustin."

The compliment did little to diffuse her. As a poker player, and a flamboyant one at that, Rhett had created a rough-and-tumble image for his act. Every time he played poker, he was accompanied by his poker babes—two women clad in tight, low-cut, often sequined gowns, with death-defying cleavage.

Few knew these women were total brainiacs who worked as his scouts. Frankly, she didn't care that they both had MBAs from Harvard and that he'd never been anything but professional with them.

They were *embarr-a-ssing,* and she didn't want them anywhere near her son.

Plus, how could Rhett expect her to walk into a poker tournament with him if his poker babes were flanking them? Abbie wore conservative Ann Taylor suits most days. She was a single mother. Being respected and respectable was important to her, and she'd fought hard for it. She wasn't about to give it up.

Especially after the horrible way in which Dustin had been conceived when she was just eighteen. Why couldn't he understand that?

Peggy dropped a plastic container filled with the silver balls in front of Rhett. "If you're going to make women with dresses, this might work for sequins."

Abbie gave her future sister-in-law a smile of genuine appreciation. Though there had been some bumps in their relationship, she and Peggy got along pretty well now. True, they didn't always understand one another. As Dare Valley's deputy sheriff, Peggy was a cop to the core, and Abbie really did aspire to be Martha Stewart. But they shared a more important commonality—they were both single mothers.

"What a great idea!" Rhett agreed with his usual aw-shucks ease. "Do you have any of these balls in gold? I don't always like my poker babes to wear the same outfits."

Mac snorted alongside Dustin—a truly horrible

mannerism they'd picked up from Mac's employee and close friend, Jill Hale, who was Jill McConnell now that she was married, but no one remembered to call her that. The Hales were still the backbone of the Dare Valley community, and married names didn't seem to stick.

Abbie shot Dustin a *you'd better stop snorting* look—something that wouldn't work nearly so well with her brother. Her son stood and patted Rhett on the back.

"You're on your own, man. Mom may decide not to feed me, and I'm starving."

"Aren't you always?" Mac asked, wandering over to the refrigerator to pull out a local brew. "Dustin, let's go see what Keith is up to. Peggy?"

She took Mac's hand and gave him an intimate smile, which he returned. It made Abbie's heart sing to see them so happy after everything they'd been through. But it pleased her less that they were doing everything they could to make it difficult for her to ignore Rhett. Granted, he was one of Mac's oldest friends, and had been around for years, but now that he'd declared his love for her, she didn't want him around all the time.

Except when she did.

Call her The Girl Conflicted. It could be an indie film.

The focus of her conflicted thoughts gave her a wry smile as he came around and stood beside her at the kitchen island, his arm brushing hers. Tall, muscular, and as charming as the snake who talked Eve into biting the apple, Rhett knew he had rugged appeal. Sometimes he used it on her. Other times, he simply hung back and waited.

Today he was definitely turning on the charm. Even the brief contact between them was like a match to the kindling—warmth caught from her arm and spread throughout her body.

"It's nice to be in the US of A for Christmas this year," he commented. "Last year's was pretty bad. I was in Monte Carlo playing poker, missing you. I got stinking drunk and went to the hotel's gift shop to buy you a present I knew I'd never send." He dug into his back pocket and fished out a thin box wrapped in shiny red paper.

She edged back, her hands going all clammy. Oh, no. Not this. "Rhett, please, I—"

"I figured that I'd give this to you now since I already have another one for this year's Christmas." When she didn't take it, he set it down on the countertop next to the green sugar sprinkles. "You can open it now or whenever you'd like."

The package might as well have been an airplane's black box, housing information she desperately wanted to know but was terrified of all the same.

"Later, then," he said after a tense moment, forcing a smile. Rhett tapped the box before wandering over to the kitchen table.

What to say? Suddenly she felt guilty. He was giving her a present for heaven's sake, and she couldn't even say thank you. Why did he do this to her manners?

Her arm locked in place. She simply couldn't reach for it. "Rhett, you didn't need to—"

"What else can I help you with?" he asked, cutting off her pitiful statement of gratitude. "Do you need me to glue anything onto those wreaths over there? I can probably manage that if you show me where you want the red flowers and gold bells."

Her newest craft project lay on the kitchen table. Dustin had told her he was too old to be her Wreath Glue Man. Apparently he had an image to uphold. She didn't even want to know what that meant. Funny how he hadn't nixed helping her with the gingerbread houses... She'd see how much he actually ended up doing in the end.

Rhett picked up the fake red amaryllis flowers she'd laid next to the first wreath. The sight of it in his huge hand should have looked silly, but like Dwayne Johnson, The Rock, Rhett combined Alpha male toughness with a softer, playful side. In moments like this, it was easy to imagine them together. Then she would see him playing poker with his poker babes, and she'd remember that his public persona was anathema to her. Even though he was making other modifications designed to show her he was changing his ways, part of her was terrified he'd change on her again, just like Dustin's father had done.

Inside of her beat the heart of a woman who wanted hearth and home.

But she still wanted to be touched by this man—caressed by him, kissed by him.

He'd told her that he wouldn't do that again until she asked.

So far, the duct tape she'd metaphorically placed on her mouth was working...even though the sex-starved woman inside her wanted to beg.

"Do you want all your wreaths to look the same or different?" He set the flower aside and picked up the navy and orange glue gun.

"Rhett, I don't—"

"Just let me help you, Abbie. I won't say anything. We can turn on some Christmas music and work in silence."

For someone who pretty much talked all the time, he'd become a master at simply being in the same room with her without saying a thing.

He reminded her of General Patton in the strategy he was using to pursue her: circling her, laying siege, and then doing something like this. Simply pitching his camp close to hers without doing anything more.

Somehow that meant more to her than anything else. She hadn't expected to find peace with Rhett, but she had. She'd found it in so many ways when they were together—after they'd made love; in the mornings, when she'd wake up first and watch him sleep; at breakfast, when they'd both read the paper. And now this.

She hit the switch to her kitchen radio, and the newest Christmas song from Rhett's close friend, country singer, Rye Crenshaw, filled the room.

"This song is pretty romantic for Rye. Has he met someone?" she asked, listening to the lyrics. *You're my Christmas dream come true.*

Rhett turned his back to her and busied himself with the green floral wire. She'd be shocked if he knew what to do with it.

"Not that I'm aware of," he answered, finally taking a seat at the kitchen table, where a sugar plum spice candle flickered. He was silent for a long moment, and then he said, "I don't mind admitting I'm kinda missing my mama around this time of year, especially with all these things you've been busying yourself with. She likes to bake and decorate like you do. And she makes the finest wreaths in Natchez, if I do say so myself."

She gave the gift box another wary glance, skirted the

kitchen island, and walked toward Rhett, watching with something like disbelief as he arranged the flowers and bells on the wreath. Rhett had decided to spend Christmas with her and her family instead of being with his own mother. Mac had insisted they needed to invite him, and because she wasn't cruel, she'd agreed. He'd be part of their enormous Christmas celebration with the Hale clan, who had become an extension of their family through Peggy, whose brother was married to Meredith Hale.

"How's this?" Rhett asked, gesturing to his impromptu arrangement.

"Pretty good," she said, and she meant it. Who knew Rhett Butler Blaylock had hidden wreath-making talents? Somehow he always managed to surprise her. "You've never told me much about your mother."

His golden eyes finally rested on her for more than a few seconds. The pause in their conversation had her plucking at her green cashmere sweater.

"No, I haven't. When we were *together,* I didn't get the sense you wanted to talk about anything that personal."

Her mind hearkened back to the hours of sweaty, passionate lovemaking they'd shared. They'd laughed together, yes. He'd chanted the Ole Miss fight song, "Hotty Toddy," to her and had given her his Eli Manning jersey to wear to bed. But serious talk had been off limits. Especially since she'd made it clear to him that their secret relationship wasn't going to be about anything but sex. Her first and only foray into that minefield of pleasure.

The kitchen chair framed her body when she sat down across from him at the table. His voice was edged with nostalgia, and since she wasn't close to her own mother, she threw him a bone. "Maybe you can tell me about your mom while we work."

Hope burned in his eyes. "That's a mighty fine idea. So you already know my mama loves *Gone With The Wind* from my name. But what you don't know…"

His words took her on a journey to another world. This was Rhett the man, the doting son. She'd seen so many sides to him: poker player, Mac's friend, Dustin's idol, lover of women, and then her own lover. But the man? His true essence? Well, she'd seen glimpses that had made her want to see more…

He'd been revealing more of himself to her since he'd returned in July, weakening her resolve, making the same darn hope she'd seen burn in his eyes simmer in her own.

But every time she saw him play poker at The Grand Mountain Hotel, Mac's hotel, and her place of employment, her resolve strengthened. She could not become the wife of the wild Cowboy-on-Crack poker player, as Peggy used to call him. And he could not become Dustin's stepdad.

Tonight none of that seemed to matter, though. She listened, enthralled while he told her stories about his childhood Christmases, sticking with the Hallmark Channel version rather than *Oliver Twist,* even though she knew he'd experienced some hard knocks. When he left an hour later, his hands heavy on his hips, the reluctance to leave as plain as day, she murmured her goodbyes as she watched him go.

Then she finally picked up the untouched package from the kitchen island. Everyone was now watching Christmas cartoons with Keith, so she'd have some privacy. When she opened it, her heart stopped. Inside was the most delicate strand of pink pearls she'd ever seen, with a note:

Delicate, beautiful, and elegant, just like you. I miss you. Merry Christmas. Love, RBB

He'd signed it "love" even then? Heavens. Her fingers traced them, a slight tremble in the manicured French tips. She put the necklace on, tucking it under her sweater so no one else would see it.

Rhett had always known what she wanted, what she needed, and given it to her with a generosity that boggled her mind.

What in the world was he planning to give her for Christmas this year?

Part of her couldn't wait to find out.

Chapter 2

For Rhett, curbing wild tendencies had become a new course in the subject of Life. Proving to Abbie that he loved her was harder than winning The World Series of Poker—which was freakin' hard—but proving he could be a good husband to her and a respectable father to Dustin was probably as difficult as climbing Mount Kilimanjaro, something he hadn't done yet.

He sighed as his poker babes—so sexist, he knew—strutted into his house and followed him into his home office. Their oversized Coach purses were filled with files on all the players in Mac's New Year's Eve tournament at The Grand Mountain Hotel. He knew how Abbie felt about them, but he wasn't sure what to do about it. They were like the sisters he'd never had, and they'd helped him become a poker powerhouse.

"Hey Rhett," Raven said, dropping onto the leather sofa—her preferred perch.

"Boss," Vixen called out, easing onto the matching leather ottoman where he was sitting.

Since moving to Dare Valley with him, they'd agreed that the women would go low profile. Legal names and normal dress in town. Poker babe hair, makeup, dresses, *and* aliases at the hotel. This was a conservative small town, after all, and Rhett wanted to be respectful. He also wanted Raven and Vixen to be comfortable in their day-to-day lives since they were staying for the duration.

With her short brown hair and brown eyes, Raven looked perfectly normal when stripped of her jet black beauty pageant wig and add-ons. And her legal name couldn't be plainer: Jane Wilcox. She was as skinny as a rail without all the body padding she had to wear. Vixen's strawberry blond hair and big blue eyes were captivating, and she didn't need any stuffing to turn a man's head. Her God-given curves and the Marilyn Monroe-inspired wig she wore made her a bombshell. But her name, Elizabeth Saunders, was a far cry from her fiery persona.

He'd met them at a poker tournament in Atlantic City seven years ago. Roommates at Harvard, they'd just graduated with MBAs and *loved* poker. He'd bought them a drink, thinking they were cute, fresh-faced, and close to his age.

But all they'd wanted to do was talk about poker and other players—an unusual conversation for him to have with a couple of pretty women. They had blown his socks off with their insights, handle on the players, and ability to keep track of everyone's betting strategies. Being a spontaneous kind of guy, he'd offered them jobs as his scouts on the spot.

They'd agreed, which had kind of surprised him until they'd brought him into the sacred circle of their sisterhood and told them why they were doing it. Jane's father, a state senator in Connecticut, had been pressuring her to return home and campaign for him with the end goal of her working for him. She'd campaigned for him all her life and couldn't take it anymore. Elizabeth had a mountain of debt and an ex-boyfriend who wouldn't leave her alone. Rhett knew there was more to her story, but she'd never told him all the details. For both women, the job had been an escape.

And he'd been happy to help them. Plus there was a reason for the act. Scouting, while totally normal, was best done circumspectly. Plus, Rhett's fame as a flamboyant ladies' man had been growing. Making it a part of his shtick had seemed like the best cover.

His poker babes had traveled to the far end of the globe with him, Elizabeth had paid off her college debts, and they'd all made a lot of money in the process. She and Jane never fraternized with the players, and they only played their bombshell roles in public. Everyone had been very clear on that point early on.

While Jane wasn't prone to much interaction with men, being the more skittish of the two, Elizabeth lived up to her stage name of Vixen, leaving an endless string of broken hearts wherever she went. The women were still best friends, and while they sometimes sighed over the outfits they had to wear for work, they always put their backs into it. Did a man proud.

"So, how's it looking downtown these days?" he asked. "I was thinking about taking Abbie ice skating."

"It's like Happy Town down there, minus Santa and the elves," Jane said, a terse edge in her voice.

Since Rhett knew she was from a small town herself—and had wanted to get as far from her dysfunctional childhood as possible—he patted her hand. "Try and look for the charm. The people here are real nice."

"Yes, they are," Elizabeth agreed, propping her boots onto the coffee table. "Jane is only cranky because she's got a thing for Arthur Hale's great nephew, Matthew, who's moving here to open a law practice. He's been looking for a place to live on the weekends. She can't stand lawyers on principal after her dad, so she's ticked off that she's attracted to one."

Right. Her dad was the kind of ambition-hungry, asshole type who made TV legal dramas popular. "I've heard Matthew's moving here from Denver," Rhett commented. "With his brother, Andy, right?"

Arthur had bragged about it at their weekly poker night, announcing that the younger generation was finally getting a lick of sense and ditching city living to move back to Dare Valley, just like his granddaughter, Meredith, had done over a year ago.

"Someone needs to shut her mouth, Eliz-a-beth, or I'll dish on you," Jane said, pulling a handful of candy canes from her purse and dropping them on the coffee table. She ripped the wrapper off one and started sucking it in a way that would tear Arthur's nephew in two.

"Girls, girls. I tell you, all I hear is bicker, bicker, bicker."

"Sorry, Dad," Jane joked half-heartedly. "So let's talk about the tourney."

And they did, each one outlining their files on the competition. Since most of the high rollers announced their tournament appearances on social media, Rhett didn't have to press Mac for a guest list. He didn't like to trade on their friendship, except when it came to Abbie.

His mind wandered. Would she agree to be with him, marry him if he got rid of the poker babes? Part of him wasn't sure. The other part was a bit pissed that she was insisting he ditch the best damn act in the business, especially when it wasn't hurting anyone. Dustin knew the ladies dressed for show, even though he didn't mind looking at them. Heck, the kid was a teenager, raging on hormones.

Abbie was only using Jane and Elizabeth as an excuse to stop from doing what she really wanted.

She loved him.

He'd literally bet his life on it by moving here.

Maybe it was time for him to call her bluff.

"What would y'all say if I changed your job descriptions?" he suddenly interrupted, reaching for one of the candy canes Jane had set on the coffee table.

"To *what?*" Jane asked, ever suspicious, something he'd always liked about her.

Elizabeth sauntered over to the mini fridge and grabbed a Diet Coke. "This is about Abbie, isn't it?"

"What else?" he asked with a gusty sigh.

"Do you ever wonder if you're wasting your time here?" Jane asked. "I mean, what if she doesn't agree to be with you, Rhett? I hate watching her break your heart like this."

Jane had a heart of gold. He wished Abbie knew her like he did, but he'd never introduced the two of them. She was just about as likely to get chummy with his poker babes as she was to wear sequins for him, something he kinda wanted to see someday. Preferably red sequins.

"It's *my* heart," he told Jane. "But thank you kindly for the thought. Now, seriously, what kind of act could we come up with that would be just as eccentric but more family friendly?"

"You could get a dog like Jane," Elizabeth said. "That's what all the well adjusted people do around here, and you can get pretty eccentric with your pets. I saw someone walking their schnauzer on Main Street all dressed up like a reindeer. With the red nose and antlers and everything."

That poor dog, Rhett thought.

"Rufus isn't like that. He's a chocolate lab." Jane stopped sucking her candy cane and crunched what was left of it.

Rhett rubbed his chin. "You could be my dog walker, Jane, and Elizabeth, you could be my assistant or publicist or something. You already do most of the social media stuff anyway."

Elizabeth set her soft drink aside. "Let me tell you, I wouldn't miss the heels. I consider myself a lucky woman to have never taken a swan dive in those six-inch pumps."

"My physical therapist said they're terrible for my feet," Jane added.

"And all the makeup clogs my pores," Elizabeth said.

"Don't even get me started about the eye infection I got from the fake eyelashes," Jane continued.

"Bitch, bitch, bitch," Rhett joked, even though he sympathized. He'd heard any number of their horror stories over the years, and seeing them soak their feet in his hot tub after a long day of standing by his side at the tables was a regular occurrence. "You work hard for your money."

Elizabeth starting singing the song, making them all grin.

"We need to keep your image edgy, though," Jane said when Elizabeth trailed off. "You're pretty established now, so I think most hotels will let you in with your dog, especially if it's part of the new act. They want the media attention and fan interest as much as we do."

"A slight change to your image probably wouldn't hurt your game now," Elizabeth added. "Everyone knows you come prepared, even if your off-the-table antics are a bit unusual. We just need to find another way to captivate the audience. But you need to see what Abbie says. However much I hate those wigs and heels, there's no use in messing with perfection if it isn't going to change her mind."

That's what he was afraid of. "Right," he agreed. "This is the ante I've been looking for. Research some eccentric dogs. A little one would be a good contrast to my enormous size. Maybe one of those Taco Bell dogs."

Elizabeth—ever the daring one—snickered. Jane simply rolled her eyes.

"We can get you a man purse too. What about matching outfits? Or an itty bitty cowboy hat?" Elizabeth said, enough glee in her voice for him to know she was enjoying this.

He almost cringed. As a man's man, he loved having two beautiful, sexy women hovering around him as he worked, but a small animal dressed like him in matching snakeskin attire? People might laugh...or think he was losing it. Poker players needed to know who the Alpha was at the table. He wasn't sure this change would convey that.

"Okay, let's mock it up and see what we think. Jane, since you know dogs, you can do that research."

"She sure does," Elizabeth snickered.

"Bitch," her friend responded without much heat.

Rhett bit into another candy cane. They were everywhere this time of year, and as irresistible as holiday crack. His dentist was going to have a field day with him after all the sweets he'd consumed. "Elizabeth, find some celebrity's eccentric publicist or assistant or something to model yourself after. We can change your look, and few will be the wiser."

"Except for her figure. That won't change," Jane said with a sigh. "Now me?" She gestured toward her less than ample chest. "There's another story."

"Maybe my skin will finally clear up," Elizabeth said. "And think of all the extra time we'll have, *not* putting on the stage make-up. It takes forever to put that crap on."

Rhett took another bite of his candy. "I say the same thing every morning when I do my face."

They both snorted out a laugh.

"Okay, I think we have a plan. Thanks, girls. We're done for today."

They gathered up their files, and he led them out to the front porch.

"This will make our cover easier in town, too," Jane said. "It isn't always fun telling everyone we meet that we take reservations for the hotel."

Mac was kind enough to help the poker babes maintain their cover. Jane and Elizabeth came and went to the hotel as normal employees and changed into their costumes in a special suite Rhett rented under an anonymous name. It had worked, so far.

"Okay, off with you both. And try and have some fun. You watch more poker games than I do. It's Christmas."

"Yeah, yeah, yeah," they agreed in union and took off in their SUVs, snow crunching under the tires.

The mountains were dotted with white, almost like they'd been topped with whipped cream. Deep inside, he had a sudden urge to pack up his skis and head out for some dangerous trails at The Grand Mountain Hotel's newly renovated slopes.

So, he was going to try and go even more respectable, just like Abbie wanted. Who would have guessed? His friend, Rye, wouldn't believe it. A year ago, Rhett wouldn't have believed it either. Then he'd realized the depth of his love for Abbie and vowed to do whatever it took to fill the hole in his heart he'd walked around with since she'd dumped him.

Being part of this new extended family meant the world to him, but some days the bond felt like a button dangling from a thin piece of thread. He and Abbie needed a stronger piece of thread between them.

God, he hoped this new act would do the trick.

He was running out of ideas.

Chapter 3

Rhett's chortling laughter was booming from the family room when Abbie came home, making her nerves stretch like bungee cords. So, he was here…again. Well, he pretty much came and went from their house as he pleased—after all, he was Mac's best friend and Dustin saw him as an adopted uncle. But deep down, he always came for *her*. That General Patton thing again. He'd circle the embankment she was on, avoiding a direct approach until she was almost sure he wasn't going to charge. And then he did.

While she waited for him to appear, she fiddled with the gingerbread house she was in the midst of decorating. Measured to within a millimeter of its life, the cookie walls had shrunk evenly. She was pretty happy about that since it made everything easier. She'd glued the three by three inch walls together a few hours ago onto the base cookie foundation. The foam padding she'd bought at the craft store had ensured that they'd set upright. Now that the frosting had dried, it was time to add the roof, a tricky business. When *that* frosting dried, she'd add the chimney. Assembling gingerbread houses was a testament to her patience and fearlessness. In cooking she had those traits. Life was another matter.

In the meantime, she arranged the decorations she was planning to use, everything from gumdrops to miniature candy canes. A candy Santa and reindeer would line the white, frosting-lined driveway. Then she'd add red and yellow frosting to the window frames and doors, alternating between colors for dramatic effect.

Dustin thought she had Christmas OCD. Well, he played World of Warcraft and Halo. She played Christmas.

Rhett wandered in, laughing with Dustin, their arms wrapped around each other like old pals. Dustin had loved Rhett since he was a kid, but now that she knew Rhett's intentions, this proof of their camaraderie made her fist clench. She squeezed the gumdrops too hard and felt their sticky insides adhere to her hand. When she opened it, they looked like pulverized colored mushrooms. She hastily cleaned up with a wet paper towel.

"Looking pretty good there, Abbie," Rhett drawled, taking a seat at the kitchen table where the gingerbread house was set up.

Of course, he wasn't talking about the house…

"Yeah, Mom. The only problem is you need to change your gingerbread house rule and let us eat them."

She arched her brow as her son leaned over her and swiped a gumdrop, one she hadn't decimated. "After all of the hours I put into these, *no one* is eating them. Are we clear?" He'd eaten half of one when he was ten. She'd caught him with crumbs around his rosebud lips, the broken house in front of him. He'd gotten an awful tummy ache from the sugar overdose, so she hadn't scolded him.

Much.

"You're the Grinch," her son complained, reaching for one of the pecan sandies she'd set out on a plate.

"Ah, leave your mama alone," Rhett chided, following Dustin's lead and swiping a cookie. "She takes pride in her work, as she should. These houses are things of beauty. I've always loved seeing what new confections she'd whipped up when I visited y'all around Christmas."

His eyes gleamed like the shiny gold wrapping she'd bought from her favorite online paper store. Gosh, she hadn't unconsciously bought it because it reminded her of Rhett's eyes, had she? Oh brother.

"Thank you, Rhett," she managed to respond. "At least someone appreciates my efforts around here."

Teenage sons sometimes didn't. Hers was too busy eating her out of house and home with his hollow leg.

And then Dustin proved her right by bringing out a gallon of milk from the fridge—not a glass—and hefting over six containers of cookies. As if the plate she'd arranged wasn't enough.

"Do you want to go up against me in a Cookie Eat-Off, Rhett?" Dustin asked, pouring milk into the largest glass from their cupboard.

Rhett snagged a piece of peanut brittle, cracking the candy in half with his teeth. "Nah, there's someplace I want to take your mom, if she's at a good stopping point."

Abbie busied herself with rearranging the gumdrops in their bowl by color, red on the left, yellow on the right, and green in the center.

"Mom, you need a Christmas OCD support group."

"Hey, man," Rhett said before she could reproach him. "Be nice to your mama."

The glass Dustin was raising to his lips paused before he nodded. "Yes, sir."

Rhett winked. "That's my boy."

The whole scene made her wring her hands under the table.

Somehow Rhett had managed to become a respected disciplinarian without even asserting himself. Was Dustin doing this because he was trying to show her he approved of Rhett or did he really respect him? Something to think about.

When she glanced through the kitchen window above the sink, all she saw was a sea of darkness. "Rhett, it's pitch black outside."

"Mom, it's only seven thirty," Dustin muttered. "And Uncle Mac is still out there. In the pitch black. Oh no! Rhett, we might need to look for him. He could be in danger."

Her kid hadn't gotten this smartass gene from her, and since she didn't want to think about what other genes he might have gotten from the man who'd fathered him, she tried to laugh it off. "Funny," she said, setting aside the bowl she was still clutching. "What do you have in mind, Rhett?"

His eyes turned molten, like the fire dancing in the fireplace in the next room. She darn well knew she'd opened herself up to that kind of a look.

"Something Christmassy."

"Is that even a word?" she asked to be contrary, part of her not liking how he always maneuvered her into these little outings.

General Patton again.

"Trust me. You'll love it. It's like something out of

34

those old Christmas movies you like."

Dustin groaned. "If I have to watch *It's a Wonderful Life* one more time, I will poke my eye out. No Red Ryder BB gun will be necessary."

His allusion to their other family favorite, *The Christmas Story,* made her smile. "I'll see if I can arrange that. Okay, Rhett." Easier to go than to fight. Dustin would only poke at her until she agreed.

A smile broke out across Dustin's face before he covered it with a fake cough and a hand over his mouth.

"Do I need to change?" she asked, standing up, a little nervous to be going out with Rhett. It always felt like a date when the two of them did something alone, even though there was never a goodnight kiss. She knew there wouldn't be unless she asked for it... He'd made that clear.

His gaze slid down her apron-clad frame, his mouth quirking up to the side. In the center of her apron was a smiling Rudolph with a jingle bell for a nose. She tapped it playfully, and the metal rattle carried across the kitchen.

"Yeah, you might want to change," he said, his face stretching into a full smile now. "Not that I don't like your current look. Wear something warm."

As she turned to leave the room, she could feel his eyes on her and hear Dustin's whispers.

They were plotting. General Patton and his faithful aide, trying to bring her down.

As she spied the mistletoe hanging from the hallway entrance—something that made her think about the last hot kiss they'd shared...way too long ago—she decided she might not mind his strategy so much tonight.

Chapter 4

Situated in the red-brick town square, Dare Valley's ice skating rink looked like a Norman Rockwell painting, complete with the gas lighting. The white lights strung across the various lampposts created a halo effect on Main Street. A sign blinked "Merry Christmas Dare Valley." Sparkly angels with trumpets looked like they were swinging themselves from the lampposts, ready to sing Christmas carols.

Rhett wanted to pat himself on the back when he heard Abbie's sharp intake of breath as he pulled into a parking space someone had just vacated on Main Street. Gotta love parking karma.

"Are we—"

"You've got it, honey. I knew you'd love this." He came around the car to help her out, holding her elbow to make sure she didn't slip on the sidewalk even though Dare was pretty good about keeping its streets clean of all the white stuff.

"I've been wanting to come, but Dustin and Mac said it just wasn't cool." Then she stopped and gave him her trademark suspicious green-eyed look. "They were punking me, weren't they? You guys conspired about this, didn't you?"

The gas streetlights flickered, throwing shadows over her beautiful, frowning face. The cold wind lifted the ends of her black hair out from under her blue knit hat. Without the kid around, he could reach out and swipe a finger across her gorgeous cheekbone, so he did. "I plead the Fifth."

"Fine. I am not going to let your General Patton strategies ruin this for me."

Patton? Well, he considered that a compliment. The guy won the war, after all.

"Just look at these Christmas decorations," she said, gesturing with her hand. "We've lived in some lovely places, but I think I like Dare best of all."

Rhett was starting to feel the same way. "Yeah, it sure has that Christmas magic people talk about."

He looked at the angels wrapped around the lampposts and smiled. *I could use a little help here,* he thought. Even though it had been a while since he'd asked for heavenly assistance, it felt right. His mama had taken him to Sunday school, so he knew how things worked.

Abbie gave a half twirl, surprising him. She looked so young and happy, something he wished he could see more of in her.

When she found her balance, she lowered her arms to her sides. "I'm so glad you brought me, Rhett. Thank you."

God, she was easy to love. He just wished she'd let him do it more fully.

"Come on. Let's have some fun."

Her smile was as bright as that of a two-year-old high

on sugar and presents on Christmas Eve. "Okay," she said, "but I have to say, this is the last thing I'd think you'd ever want to do. You know, what with your image and all."

The snow crunched under their boots as they walked across the brick path to the rink. "Well, I get to be with you, so it doesn't much matter what I'm doing."

Okay, that wasn't quite true. He was as horny as an old coon dog. He kept choosing public places to spend time with her so they wouldn't *truly* be alone. A man could only take so much temptation, and he'd promised himself and her that he wouldn't touch her until she asked.

So far she hadn't, although he'd seen the speculation—and the struggle—in her eyes. It almost comforted him.

"Speaking of images," he said, "I have something to tell you, but let's skate first."

She gave him a wary look, but then again, when didn't she look at him that way? Her walls were strong and well fortified. Her General Patton allusion was apt. He'd managed to breach her walls during the six months they'd secretly been together, but it was like she'd built new ones while he was overseas. Then he laughed to himself as another thought struck him. Abbie was like the gingerbread houses she made. Cute as a button and sweet to boot, but with walls that were nearly indestructible once they were set.

Rhett bought the tickets, and together, they put on their rental skates, sitting in the metal chairs that lined the outdoor rink. Couples skated by—and many times one partner was clearly better than the other, helping their loved one stay upright with each slip and trip. Kids screamed at each other as they skated past, some looking like they'd been born with blades on their feet, others doing a hop-hop-hop, arms flailing before they took a dive and slid across the ice like they were trying to get to second base.

Christmas music boomed over the loud speakers arranged around the rink. Right now, Bing Crosby was crooning "I'll Be Home For Christmas." His mama would have loved it.

Hands pulling at her laces, Abbie said, "I'm really relieved they spray the skates with Lysol. I mean, you don't know what people's feet are like."

Her voice was so serious, he had to bite his lip to keep from laughing out loud. Only Abbie would think of something like that.

All laced up, he took her hand. "Okay, let's go."

The minute he hit the ice with her, his right foot slid out a few inches. Wisely, he released Abbie's hand, his arms flailing out like those little kids they'd watched earlier. And at his whopping height of six foot six, he probably looked like a giraffe about to make a crash landing on the ice.

"Best stay a few yards away until I get the hang of this," he told her, watching as she tucked her hands behind her back, skated forward like a pro, and then did this ridiculously scary turn he knew would make him break a leg if he tried it.

"You're a natural!" he beamed, and then his feet jimmied again on the ice, causing him to hop like an out-of-control rabbit.

The smile on her face was the kind that inspired poets. "I can't beat you at poker, but I'll best you at this. I took ice skating lessons when we lived in Wyoming. I love it."

And when she threw her arms out and did another one of those twirly turns, his heart plopped at his feet. God, she was the most beautiful woman he'd ever seen, and he'd seen a fair amount. He could never get enough of her black hair, green eyes, and porcelain skin…or that wickedly slim yet curvy body.

Then his ankle turned, and he had to fight to stay upright. Shit. Where were his leg muscles? Heck, he worked out, but two minutes on the ice had turned him into Plastic Man. The dumb things a guy did for a girl.

"Go on and skate ahead. I know you want to," he said, being realistic. This wasn't going to be the romantic hand-holding date he'd hoped for.

Mostly because he sucked.

And looked like an idiot. This was not putting him in his best light at all.

She waved and skated off, her feet crisscrossing as she picked up speed on the ice. He tried to follow her, but when he swiveled his head to watch her, his feet did the whole slide-scamper, running-in-place thing again. He'd invented a new skating technique: jogging on the ice like a moron.

The people watching from the sidelines weren't even trying to contain their laughter. Terrific. Normally he didn't mind attention—heck, he invited it—but tonight he'd wanted to lay a metaphorical Christmas cloak at Abbie's feet like a prince.

Instead, he was trying not to crash onto the ice more than those punishing few times he'd fallen in the beginning. Each time he'd get back up, jaw locked, and think, *watch out, kids, I don't want to crush you* as the adolescent skaters zipped past him, guffawing like baboons. When Rhett started complaining to himself about the kids' antics, he realized he was sounding like an old man.

It was a low point, all right.

Abbie would circle him when she reached him, making him dizzy from something other than her perfume. Then she'd laugh and take off again, her blades calling out *swish-swish* as they made grooves in the ice.

"I like seeing you like this," he said as she came to a stop in front of him for what seemed like the hundredth time, a mist of ice from her toe-picks cascading over his own skates.

"I love being out here. The weather is perfect when you wear the right gear, and it's so freeing."

Yeah, she did look free—a word that could rarely be used to describe her.

For as long as he'd known her, she'd been chained to the past—a past she'd finally shared with him—and her responsibilities to Dustin, Mac, and the hotel chain.

How wonderful to see her this way. He would do anything he could to put this look on her face every day.

"Come on," she called, skating way too close to him.

"Stay back," he called.

"No, take my hand. I'll help you."

Yeah, right. All one hundred and fifteen pounds of her.

"No, I'm gonna follow the sucky people, since I'm clearly one of them." Since the skating rink was outside, there were no rails like in the indoor hockey rinks he'd attended for games. "You keep on having fun. When you're ready, I'll buy you some hot chocolate."

And tell her about his plan to give up the poker babes.

Surely that would satisfy her. If it didn't, the next part of his plan would, something he'd begun months earlier with his friend Rye.

Abbie kept skating and skating long after he'd given up. He watched her with a smile while listening to the whining and crying of the kids sitting next to him, who clearly needed to go to bed. Every so often, she'd wave at him. Her wave reminded him of Princess Diana, so royal. So Abbie. She apparently knew a few people on the ice since she stopped and talked to them.

With the moonlight beaming down from above, he could make out the snow caps on the mountains in which the valley was nestled, almost like it was held between their palms. This was a great place. Family-oriented, yes, which he hadn't been sure about, but now he rather liked it.

Would she want to have kids with him?

He shifted in his chair. *Let's not get ahead of ourselves, Blaylock*, he told himself.

But he wanted to get ahead of himself. It was like being at the poker table—sometimes he just wanted to go all in. The rush was tremendous, and the payoff could be huge.

When she finally skated toward him, her cheeks were flushed from the cold. Her green eyes twinkled, her rosy lips were tipped up in a smile.

"You looked beautiful out there," he said, feeling the familiar rush of attraction and warmth for her.

She bowed at the waist, something he couldn't have done on the ice in a thousand years without killing himself. "Thank you."

"You ready for some hot chocolate?"

She settled in close when she sat down to take off her skates. "You bet."

When they were wearing real shoes again—God, he wouldn't ever take those for granted—they made their way over to Don't Soy with Me's beverage stand. Jill Hale, ever the businesswoman, had arranged for her coffee shop to sell holiday-inspired coffees, hot chocolate, and apple cider by the rink. In line with Jill's over-the-top style, the stand was decked out in bold Christmas colors and twinkling red and green lights. Her signature holiday coffee fairies were pinned to the stand's red walls.

"I'll have the raspberry hot chocolate, please," Abbie said to the cashier.

Rhett studied the chalk board, laughing at the hand-scrawled quote. *Christmas isn't for wimps. Drink more coffee.*

"I'll have the Mexican hot chocolate," he ordered, fishing out his wallet.

"You do love spicy things," Abbie commented, humming along to Harry Connick, Jr.'s version of "I Saw Mommy Kissing Santa Claus."

Given their turtle pace toward sex, Santa would probably be kissing Abbie before he would.

"Yes, I do," he said, and then had a flash of her feeding him Tabasco-laced peppers one night after he'd grilled them steaks for dinner.

Their eyes met, and he saw her mouth part breathlessly. Her lashes fluttered as she plucked at some invisible thread on her jacket. She couldn't meet his gaze, so she busied herself by studying the rim of her cup while he waited for his beverage.

"It hasn't gone away, you know," he said.

Best to call out the elephant by the coffee stand.

She didn't say anything for a long moment, blowing on her hot chocolate. "I know," she finally replied, and then turned and walked away.

Dammit, he thought, tapping his boot on the brick sidewalk as he waited for his drink. He took the time to compose himself. Reminded himself that pseudo-dating Abbie was like high-stakes poker. When he finally sat beside her on the chairs she'd found for them by the rink, he was more in command of himself. Like with a big pot, it was time to call her raise.

"So, I know you've objected to the poker babes, and we've had our differences about them."

While other people squealed and laughed on the ice, she stayed quiet, staring straight ahead.

"Look at me," he commanded.

Her head turned inch by inch, her reluctance clear. Then he felt the familiar haymaker-pow of those liquid green eyes.

"I'm changing up my act. The poker babes are out."

Those rosy lips he hadn't kissed for five hundred and eight-five days parted in shock. "What?" Her voice was breathy—like when he'd licked chocolate off her skin.

"I told you I'd do whatever it takes to get you back. If this is a major stumbling block, then consider it gone." He waved his hand as if banishing it. "Actually, I changed their job descriptions because I still need them to scout for me. Raven's going to be my dog walker. I've told her to dress however she likes, even at the hotel. She's even going to use her real name. It's Jane. Can you imagine? Vixen—well, Elizabeth—will take over as my publicist or assistant or something. You know, without their beauty-pageant-grade wigs and makeup, they're pretty normal looking. No one's going to know the difference."

While they were secretly together, he'd tried to tell her about Jane and Elizabeth and their real backgrounds, hoping it would reassure her, but she'd shut him down. He hadn't pushed. He had no idea what she knew about their cover of working at Mac's hotel.

"When did you get a dog?" she asked, her suspicion as clear as the stars shining overhead in the vast winter sky.

So, she still didn't want to talk about his girls. Fine.

Another kid slid across the ice and started to wail, the sound so loud it was distracting.

"We're discussing various breeds. It'll need to be a crowd-pleasing little sucker," he said, trying to tune the crying out, "but nothing too girly. And I'm not putting him in a man purse. That's where I draw the line."

"No toy poodles for you?" she asked, her voice icy.

This was not how he'd expected the conversation to go. He'd hoped she would embrace this idea. But just the mention of his poker babes had clearly bent her out of shape.

"I told you I was changing my act—all of it. I figured having an unusual dog might be entertaining. I can even dress it up." God, he sounded like a total moron. "People love their dogs, right?"

She cringed, and he knew without asking that it wasn't because another kid, a girl this time, had fallen on the ice. "I have this horrible image of you and your 'unusual' breed wearing matching snakeskin outfits."

Hadn't he had the same thought? He didn't mind his poker babes wearing matching outfits, but he was a *man*.

"Not in this lifetime."

"Well, I guess it goes with the whole dogs-playing-poker motif," she said sarcastically, and then sipped her hot chocolate.

Funny how her barbed jibes were just convincing him that this could be the G-rated kind of act that would reassure Abbie while still drawing in crowds. "Yep. Man, I love that drawing." He'd bet the house she hated those paintings.

"Hmm," was all she said.

He knew just what she was thinking: *We're ill-suited beyond belief.* "Of course, I'd never ask you to put one in our house. I know it's not your style. Now are you going to admit you love me and agree to marry me?"

Her hand slipped, and her drink spilled on her gloves. He hastily grabbed her cup, fearing she'd burned her fingers through the blue knitting.

"Put some snow on it," he commanded.

"No, it's okay," she said, her hand trembling.

In that moment, he knew that none of it had changed her mind, not one bit. "Christ, Abbie, you're killing me here."

The chocolate-stained glove fell to her side when she pulled it off. He checked to make sure her hand wasn't red. It wasn't, thank God.

"Don't change your act for me."

His breath could be seen in the winter night when he blew it out. "I'm changing *everything* for you. My whole life. When is it going to be enough?"

Her absolute silence only pissed him off. Jane and Elizabeth had been right.

They weren't the problem.

"Okay, Abbie," he said, leaning closer, crowding her. "I called your bluff about the poker babes, and you show me you've got nothing. It's not about them at all, is it? Then what is it? Even after being here for almost six months, you don't believe I can be a good husband to you and stepdad to Dustin?"

"Let's not talk about it here. We're in public." And she cast a meaningful look at the nearby ice skaters.

"Right, in public, where you didn't want us to be when we were actually seeing each other. You're not making sense."

She stood, and her tight mouth reminded him of Mac when he was cornered at the poker table when the chips are down. "I'm through discussing this."

He stood, both their cups in his hands, wishing he could drop them and reach for her. "Why? Because you say so? I told you I'm never leaving you again, and I meant it. I figure if we have to be like those two tortured cowboys in *Brokeback Mountain*—in love with each other but never together—I'll live with it."

A reluctant laugh popped out. "Rhett, those two were *gay.*"

Maybe humor would humor her. Hah. "Huh… So that explains the fuss everyone made about that movie." He bumped her playfully, but her body was as rigid as a candy cane. "Those poor guys couldn't be together. We can, Abbie. Just say the words."

Leaving him standing was an answer, he supposed. Just not one he liked. He let her stew all the way to the car. Her earlier happiness had vanished like Santa's milk and cookies on Christmas Eve.

She dove inside the minute he unlocked the car. He

had to juggle their drinks to open the door. When he sat beside her, he stuffed their cups into the holders in the middle console and turned to look at her.

"You can't keep running like this. It's time we got to the bottom of what's holding you back. This clearly isn't it."

Even though she was mostly in shadow, the Christmas lights lining Main Street brightened the interior of the car, helping him make out her tense expression. "Please, Rhett. It's Christmas."

Shit. And he was taking away from her enjoyment. He hated that.

"Fine, but I still have your present, remember? Maybe then you'll believe what we have is real."

As he pulled away from the curb, he could only nod to the angel decorating the lantern, praying that it was true.

Chapter 5

The invitation Abbie received in the mail could easily have been sent by Martha Stewart herself. Whoever it was from certainly had class. The gold-leaf monogrammed Christmas tree inlay, surrounded by a swirl of silver snow, held an artful whimsy. There was no return address, and because the envelope was so gorgeous, she located her Waterford crystal letter opener and carefully slit the paper before removing the card. Her letter opener clattered to the desk as she started to read.

Rhett Butler Blaylock graciously requests
Your company at his Christmas Gala
On the nineteenth day of December in the year two thousand and thirteen
At eight o'clock in the ballroom of The Grand Mountain Hotel.
Holiday-themed costumes are encouraged.
To RSVP, please contact The Grand Mountain Hotel.

The invitation somehow ended up pressed against her beating heart. How could she have not known he was hosting a party in their hotel? She was usually part of the planning for events like this one, but no one had said a word to her.

She picked up her cell and called Mac, who was at Peggy's tonight with Dustin. When he answered, she didn't beat around the bush.

"Did you know Rhett was throwing a party at The Grand?" she asked.

"Yes," he replied. "He came to me with the stipulation that you couldn't have anything to do with it. He's the client, so I agreed to his terms. He wants you to enjoy yourself as a guest. I knew you wouldn't be happy about it, but I also think he's right. If you helped out with the planning, you'd spend the whole time fussing like a mother hen. You wouldn't let yourself have fun."

She paced in front of her desk as her mechanical Santa rang his bell in time with her steps. "Dammit, Mac. I don't like this. This is one of my duties at the hotel."

"I'm sure Karen will get along fine without you."

Yeah, Karen would be fine. She had a great eye for detail, but he was missing the point. She shut Santa off. Right now, his incessant cheer was annoying the crap out of her.

"I don't like being kept in the dark. Rhett had no right."

"Well, if you feel that way, why don't you go talk to him? He's at his house tonight. I called him to see if he wanted to join us for dinner at Peg's, but he declined. He sounded pretty low if you want to know the truth."

Probably because his sacrifice of the poker babes hadn't worked.

The tree in her office—one of several she'd scattered across the house—blinked white lights amidst golden and baby blue bows and smelled divine. Yes, it was Christmas, but this whole thing with Rhett was really starting to dilute her enjoyment. Plus, she felt guilty. She wasn't sure why she was still holding back…so how could she explain it to him?

"Okay, let's not talk about it," she said, deciding it was pointless to continue this discussion with her brother. She knew he was becoming frustrated with her tenacity about Rhett. "How's Dustin?"

"He's fine. He and Keith are playing a Christmas video game with deranged Santas and serial-killer snowmen. It's kinda fun. Abbie, go talk to Rhett. You'll feel better."

"Have fun," she murmured and hung up.

The Christmas star she'd chosen for the tree in her office was dotted with gold sparkles. It was the one she'd purchased when she'd started working in Mac's first hotel, a proud moment for her since it had taken her six years to finish college while raising Dustin at the same time. When she brought the ornament out each year, her hands—and some other interesting parts—always ended up covered in glitter, but she didn't care. It was The Universal Law of Glitter, something you couldn't help but learn volunteering at your kid's school, helping with art projects.

The star winked like it was trying to tell her something. She took a deep breath and reached for her inner calm. *Follow the star,* she heard from somewhere inside her.

The whole message thing was a little unnerving and confusing, so she stalked out of her office and grabbed her coat. She and Rhett needed to get something clear. Her job was important to her. Cutting her out of the party planning was disrespectful.

As she drove to his house, turning onto the road that spanned the ridge line above town, she took a moment to marvel at the beauty of Dare Valley. The holiday lights gave it a golden halo, like it was trapped inside a giant Christmas globe. The carpet of plush white snow that covered the valley made it look as though moonlight had broken through the earth's core and was shining out. She took a moment to be grateful for being where she was, for this sense of rightness in her life when everything else seemed off.

She had avoided going to Rhett's house because she didn't want to be alone with him. Correction. She was afraid of what she might do if she *was* alone with him.

Just like he'd observed the other night, she still wanted him. That hadn't changed.

The decorations on his house surprised her as her Subaru crunched its way down the drive. He'd put up Christmas lights, the white strings flickering on and off on the roof and in the bushes lining his front porch. An inflatable Santa swayed in the cold wind, looking as if he might have indulged in too much peppermint schnapps in his hot chocolate.

The front light flicked on as she left the car. She took a deep breath and walked toward the front door, taking note of the classy holiday wreath that was decked out with silver bells and pinecones. The door opened before she reached it. And there stood Rhett Butler Blaylock at home: another thermal long-sleeve shirt—black this time—defining every muscle in his upper body and a pair of well-worn jeans with a hole in the knee.

Again, his wardrobe had done a three-sixty since he'd

returned to her. No more crazy fur coats or gallon-size cowboy hats. While he still wore leather, he'd tailored it back to jackets, which he could still make look sexy, as if he were some reformed bad boy. Which she supposed he was—for now.

"Abbie," he said, a question in his voice.

Right, why had she come again? Her heart was rapping hard in her chest now, long-repressed pleasure receptors begging to be released from the cage she'd stuffed them in.

"Hi, Rhett," she managed, taking careful steps in case there were any icy patches. "Can I come in?"

His eyes slid over her before settling on her face. Even if they weren't physically involved, she still liked knowing he was attracted to her. She was glad she'd taken the time to change into black pants and boots and a snug black wool coat. Black had always set off her coloring well.

"This isn't a social call, is it?" He made a sound, half laugh, half resignation. "You got your invitation in the mail and found out that I asked Mac to keep you out of the party planning."

"Yes," she answered honestly.

When he sighed, his breath could be seen from the warm glow of the yellow porch light. "Well, part of me had hoped you would show up here alone at some point because you wanted to see me, but... Okay, you might as well come in if you're planning on dressing me down."

With that piece of honesty resounding throughout her body, causing tremors everywhere, she crossed the threshold. The urge to look up and see if there was mistletoe got the better of her. She made a quick glance.

His dark chuckle turned the tremors inside her into seismic waves of desire. "I thought about putting mistletoe up, but one, you never come here, and two, even if you did, I don't want you to use mistletoe as an excuse when you finally ask me to touch you again."

That revelation shook her to the core.

"Let me take your coat," he said, moving behind her, his Southern manners on display.

She could feel the heat from his body, sense his tall, strong frame. When they were this close, she barely reached his collarbone. She elbowed him accidentally as she shrugged out of her coat.

"No need for anyone to get hurt," he murmured.

Right. Like that hadn't happened already. They were both hurting, although for different reasons.

His hands brushed the back of her neck, startling her. It had been so long since he'd given her an intimate touch, even if this one was purely G-rated.

"You smell good," he mused. "Like always. When I was overseas, I bought some Chanel Cristalle in your honor. Sometimes when I was missing you, I would just spray it in my hotel room and close my eyes and imagine you were with me. I looked the perfume up online, actually, and one review called it a beautiful, cold stranger. It seemed pretty on point to me."

Isn't that why she'd chosen it? She wanted to be well groomed but aloof, but hearing his confession made her want to hang her head in shame.

And then her mind tracked back to the pink pearls he'd given her, the ones he'd bought for her last Christmas, never expecting to give to her.

She'd never been far from his thoughts, and the

knowledge was as sweet as Christmas plum pudding.

Which reminded her. She hadn't thanked him for the present. "Rhett, I wanted to say how beautiful the pink pearls are. Thank you."

He just stared at her quietly for a moment. "I'm glad you like them. Let's sit by the fire," he said, hanging her coat in the closet.

She handed him her gloves, scarf, and hat, and after he put them away, they walked into the den together. With its tall, timbered ceilings and open spaces, the mountain cabin was more like a ski chalet. She'd only been here once before to drop Dustin off to hang out with Rhett. Usually Dustin drove himself, but he'd been grounded at the time. Plus, her curiosity had gotten the better of her.

The only difference in the decor was the twenty-foot Christmas tree garlanded with silver and gold ornaments and white lights, which was tucked against the back windows. The brown leather sofa and loveseat, earth-tone Mission rugs, and Western art were all as she remembered.

"Do you want some tea? Or do we need something stronger for this discussion?" he asked, his hand curved around the wooden beam that served as the demarcation point between the kitchen and the den.

"Tea would be fine," she replied, folding her hands into prayer position so she wouldn't feel so weird standing in his space.

Then she turned and spotted the gigantic TV on the wall. A poker tournament was on the screen, the action paused. "What are you doing with a tourney on?" she asked. She hadn't heard about any major tourneys, and Mac usually told her about such things.

"Watching tape," he called out.

Of course. Mac put his hours in studying players in old tournaments too.

She wandered into the kitchen. Rhett's big hands covered a silver tea kettle, making her think he could crush it with one squeeze. He was so big and strong. Funny how his size had always made her feel sexy and cherished, especially since her first experience with sex had been getting date raped by Dustin's father.

She hadn't been with anyone else until Rhett... For years, sex just hadn't interested her; deep down, she'd worried that she would have a flashback or something, that a big, strong man would scare her. But she and Rhett had known each other forever. He'd gotten into a few tussles, sure, but she'd never known him to be a violent man. And whenever he came to visit her, Mac, and Dustin—always with a gift for her son—something about him had just called to her...

When he came back from a run all sweaty and manly during one visit, nothing could have stopped her from finally taking what she wanted. Thankfully, he'd been of the same mind.

Deep down, she'd sensed his interest in her over the years, but had disregarded it.

Until that moment.

"What are you thinking about?" he asked, resting his elbows on the blue granite kitchen island.

"Nothing," she said, hoping her cheeks hadn't turned red.

"You're thinking about how it used to be between us, aren't you? Hard not to, I suppose. I think about it all the time, and most days, it doesn't feel so great."

Suddenly it was like a chicken bone had gotten stuck

in her throat. She coughed to clear whatever that was.

"We should celebrate," he continued. "You finally came to my house *alone,* even if you did it with the intention of chewing me out."

She stuffed her hands behind her because wringing them was making her wrists ache. "You shouldn't have stipulated that I couldn't be involved with the party, Rhett. It's disrespectful to me, and sends the wrong message to the staff. What in the heavens are they going to think?" The last thing she wanted was people to talk about her.

"Personally, I don't care, but since I knew it would upset you, I simply told Karen-whatever-her-name-is that I want you to enjoy the party because you're a family friend. She understood. Leave it at that."

Men thought everything was so simple sometimes. She almost wished she lived in their universe. "Rhett, is this party my present? Because if it is—"

Bent over at the waist with his elbows on the kitchen island, his pose beyond relaxed, he looked downright sexy. He was studying her intently. Like usual.

"Abigail, a party with fifty other guests is hardly a present. Please give me a little more credit."

The tea kettle's sharp whistle shot across the kitchen. Unlike most people who would dart forward to stop the sound, Rhett took his time, uncurling from the counter with an ease she envied. He never rushed anything. Even this thing between them. She hadn't expected him to hold out this long.

"Aren't you getting tired of living here, Rhett?" she decided to ask.

"Nope. I love being close to you."

He pulled out a tin decorated with white and gold

crisscrosses with a peach patch on the front. She'd know it anywhere.

"You just happen to have Caffè Florian?" she asked.

"Venetian Rose. It's your favorite brand," he responded with the flick of a hand. "Just because you haven't come over here, doesn't mean I haven't prepared. I also have the Venice kind with jasmine, since I know you prefer green tea at breakfast."

On the few occasions when Mac had been out of town for business and Dustin occupied with a strategically-arranged sleepover, Rhett had flown in for the night from Vegas, his former residence. They would make love from pretty much the moment he shut the door and backed her into the wall. In the morning, they'd make breakfast together, since he was always starving after the hours of sex play. She'd brew her tea and make him a dark roast coffee. Then they'd sip their beverages, read the newspaper, and eat the pancakes or omelets they'd cooked together. It had been eerily domestic.

"I started drinking the Florian Darjeeling," he informed her. "Asia got me hooked on tea. Not a lot of coffee out that way."

Tea seemed too tame for Rhett, too delicate. But he poured two cups of the rose petal tea for them all the same.

"You're having some?"

His shrug almost seemed like an afterthought. "If I can't taste you…"

Thank God she wasn't holding her cup, or she would have burned her hand six ways to Sunday. "Don't talk like that. It isn't proper."

"Well, don't you sound like Scarlett O'Hara right now?" He chuckled, the sound as dark as the loose tea he'd used. "I said I wouldn't touch you until you asked me. I didn't say I wouldn't talk about it. Especially when it's just us around."

She crossed her arms over her chest. "I'm leaving if you do."

The corner of that gorgeous, sensual mouth tipped up. "I believe you just might, so I won't call your bluff. Now, let's go sit down in the den, and you can chew at me all you want."

Since she'd used her teeth on him in some rather wild moments in the past, she knew it was a double entendre. Her toes curled in her boots in a desperate attempt to stay grounded.

He took her tea cup and his and left the kitchen. She trailed behind him, her eyes lowering to his ridiculously firm butt. God, how she'd loved having her hands on it.

When he paused, she followed suit. "Why did you stop?" she asked.

Looking over his shoulder, he said, "I know you're looking at my ass. I wanted to make sure you had your fill."

Had she thought her tremors were like an earthquake earlier? Then surely this was the aftershock. She had to clear her throat before she could issue a comeback. "You're full of it."

The murmur he gave was low and sexy. "I'd rather be full of you. Do you want a glance at the front too? I recall you saying both my front and back sides were exceptional."

She bit her lip at the heated flashes that ran through her mind, one of which involved her on her knees in front of him. "I told you I would leave if you kept talking like this."

"You looked."

How could she not?

"Fine," he said when she focused all her energy on giving him her *Don't mess with me* look, the same one she gave Dustin.

Rhett set their cups on an old Mission-style coffee table in dark mahogany.

She wisely took the loveseat next to the couch, not trusting herself to sit next to him. "Rhett, you know there was no one else but you after…what happened to me with Dustin's father, right?"

Maybe it was because it had been on her mind earlier, but the words just popped out of her mouth. They'd never talked about her past relationships, largely because there hadn't been any. Plus, she'd been embarrassed in light of his reputation with the ladies. Thankfully, it had never been an issue. They'd been so obsessed with each other that she hadn't questioned his faithfulness for the six months they were together. He'd called or texted her every day, telling her he was thinking about her. Trusting him had been easy. Rhett didn't say things he didn't mean.

He carefully lowered the tea cup he'd picked up, and she was shocked to see it tremble in his large hand.

"I didn't know that until now, although I suspected what we had wasn't typical for you. I mean, I knew you had a son, but I'd never seen you with anyone. I'm honored, Abbie. I'm sorry I can't say the same thing about me, but there's no one else but you now."

God, why did he always have to say the sweetest things when she was trying… "I didn't tell you to make you feel bad," she said, not exactly sure now why she'd brought it up. Confusion had become her new normal. "I only wanted you to understand…"

And in that minute, she didn't know what she wanted him to understand. It was like the answer was stored in a lockbox, even from herself.

"Yes?" he said, settling the cup of tea against his thigh, his face impassive.

She shook her head and reached for her tea. The answer was out of reach. "Never mind."

His stillness reminded her of how he kept his body at the table at a tournament when the pressure was crushing.

"You wanted me to understand it's unusual for you to be with a man, and something you don't take lightly. I know that. Always have. Now, if you're telling me because you're plagued with self-doubt and have forgotten how hot and sexy it was between us, then let me assure you. It was. I'd be happy to remind you, Abbie."

"No, I haven't forgotten how it was." And wasn't that her fear? That the fire would rage as hot and all-consuming as it had before, making her do things that were out of character, making her go a little crazy.

"Good. I'd be upset if you had. And now we need to change the subject. My body is responding pretty typically to this line of talk."

She could tell it was, from the tense line of muscles showcased by his thermal shirt to the rigid line in the front of his jeans.

Things unused to clenching in desire were moved as much by the words he'd used as the velvety voice in which he'd said them.

The rose scent tickled her nose when she raised her cup to her mouth with both hands and took a sip of her tea.

"Rhett, why can't you understand? Getting rid of the poker babes isn't going to make us a better match."

He sunk lower into the couch. "That's not true anymore. All of the changes on the outside are meant to convince you that we *are* meant to be together. But you're right. Deep down, the outer doesn't matter diddly unless the inner is there. Wow! I almost sounded wise or something. I'll have to tell my mama. She'll be so proud."

Her raspberry blew out easily. "The inner isn't enough."

"Bullshit," he said, his voice no longer playful. "It's all there is. We either love each other, or we don't. And since we do, the rest is just window dressing. But you clearly don't trust that."

"Rhett—"

He leaned forward. "There's no way you've stopped loving me. You couldn't tell me that you didn't love me when I arrived in July, and you can't tell me now. If anything, you love me more. As I do you. Being this close to you has helped me notice a few things I missed in the past."

Her tea cup suddenly seemed too heavy, so she set it down on the coffee table. "And what's that?"

Those golden eyes seemed to burn into her.

"I knew you were a wonderful mother, a loyal sister, and a kind person. I knew you were creative and passionate about what you do at Mac's hotels and how detailed and organized you are about practically everything."

Yeah, he'd always seen the real her.

He ran his hand through his hair and pursed his lip for a moment, like he was trying to decide whether to speak.

"And I also knew that you made nearly every decision in your life based on fear."

She inhaled sharply at his accusation. Okay, that hurt. And it so wasn't true. Firming her shoulders, she prepared to give him a piece of her mind.

He held up his hand, stopping her.

"Give me a second to explain," he said. "I understand that fear better after you told me about Dustin's father."

Right. The rich college kid who had date raped her and then suggested that the baby she'd conceived wasn't his, that she'd lied about the whole thing.

Rhett set his cup aside, his eyes beseeching. "You're terrified someone might learn about what happened to you and think you're a victim. You're also mortally afraid of what Dustin might think—totally understandable—and have chosen to protect him in ways I could never begin to understand. What I haven't figured out is the root cause of all your fear, because it's not just that. Once I do, I want to help you move forward and live from a place of happiness. I want that for you, Abbie."

Confusion rained down on her like cold, icy sleet, making her shiver. This could not be borne. She shot to her feet. "I do live from a place of happiness," she shot back, and then her breathing shattered, the asthma attack coming on so suddenly it blindsided her.

Rhett's eyes widened for a moment before he raced out of the room. She stood up, fighting for oxygen, clawing at her throat.

She couldn't *breathe.*

God, please let her breathe.

When he ran back to her, her over-sized purse in his hands, he dumped its contents on the rug and sorted through it until he found her rescue inhaler. Then he pressed it to her mouth. Her hands clamped around his as she took that first puff. Then she gave herself a second one just to be sure. The mist coated her mouth, and she closed her eyes to concentrate on her breathing, trying to calm herself.

Rhett pulled her back to his chest and wrapped his arms around her ribs as if willing her to breathe.

It took five minutes for her to stabilize. By then, her head was buzzing, and the deep inner roar of tears was rushing up her throat. She shook her head. No, she would not cry.

This had happened before with him since his return, but never this bad.

He didn't say anything as he held her, his caress as gentle as if he were holding a newborn kitten. The Christmas lights cast a white glow in the den, the only sound her exaggerated breathing. She concentrated on taking another inhale. And then another. Somehow, with his arms around her, she recovered faster, became stronger.

She didn't want to think about what that meant.

Leaning against him made her want to be enveloped in his body heat, his comfort.

She became aware of his cologne, the one she'd bought for him. Narciso Rodriguez Limited Edition. His breath on the back of her neck was what she noticed next—warm and sweet. Moving out of his arms seemed the best approach, and he didn't fight her, although his hands tightened for a second before letting go.

"I'm sorry," he said, edging away from her and shoving his hands in his jean pockets. "Can I get you anything? What can I do?"

Nothing. The problem resided in her, and it was so bad it could steal even her breath away.

She shook her head. "I'm just going to…"

The bathroom seemed to be the safest spot to gather her emotions. When she was in better command of herself, she reemerged to find him pacing in front of the Christmas tree, ruffling his ash-blond hair. He froze when he saw her.

"You're as white as my mama's bedclothes on the clothesline every Sunday, Abbie," he said.

She knew she looked like shit. Hadn't the mirror told her? Plus, she looked defeated. And all because he'd called her out on the very thing even she couldn't put her finger on.

The core of her fear.

"Rhett, I'm going to go," she said in a shaky voice, hating that, hating herself. She walked forward and gathered her things back into her purse.

"Please let me drive you home." His voice was hoarse, and when she gazed at him, his whole body was wound as tight as a wind-up toy soldier.

"No, I can manage," she responded as coolly as she could.

His hand reached out to her. "I know you can, but what if you have another spell and black out? Please, let me take you. Abbie, please."

Three pleases from him in less than thirty seconds? "Okay. Mac and Dustin can pick up my car in the morning."

His fingers stroked her arm before dropping loosely to his side. "Thank you for not fighting me on this."

"I don't have the strength right now, Rhett." And God

if the truth didn't make her look away to hide the tears she felt in her eyes.

"I'll get your coat."

Then he came back and dressed her like she was a little kid. After he'd smoothed her hair away from her face and tucked her hat on, he scooped her up in his arms.

"What are you doing?" she asked as he walked out of the room.

"You said you don't have the strength. Let me do this. It's little enough." He snagged his keys from the entryway and shut the front door behind them.

"But your coat. And you didn't lock the house."

"Doesn't matter," he ground out. "Save your breath."

And so she did...because deep down a part of her always feared another asthma attack would follow an episode this serious.

Fear.

There was that word again.

He drove slowly. The silence between them seemed eerie in the cold night. Even the quaint glow of Dare did little to raise her spirits.

She was in chaos again.

When he pulled into her driveway, he stopped her from reaching for the door. "Let me come around."

"I'm fine," she protested even though her whole body was still trembling.

"No, you're not."

He carried her to the front door and wouldn't set her down until they were inside. The lights came on after he fumbled with the switches. He finally deposited her on the couch in the family room, and a part of her missed his warmth and the comfort when he stopped holding her.

After gently tucking a purple throw around her, he turned on the Christmas tree and made her a fire.

"I'm calling Mac," he told her, his hands tinged black from the newsprint he'd used to make the fire.

"I don't need a babysitter," she told him, even though she knew it was probably a good idea. She didn't want to be alone, and with this incident hovering between them, she couldn't bear to be alone with *him*.

He tapped his phone and put it to his ear. "Hey, Mac."

She couldn't hear what he said since he wandered away. Instead she burrowed under the throw and continued to take deep breaths.

When he came back into the room, he sat down on the loveseat beside the couch. "I'm sorry," he said, swallowing thickly, meeting her eyes. "It's my fault."

The guilt between them hung in the air like a soupy fog.

"No, it's not. It's mine. Rhett…"

And she heard that inner voice again. *Follow the star*.

Her eyes tracked to the silver star on top of their family tree. It winked at her, seeming to radiate a luminous light from another place, a light that uncovered more truth in her heart.

"Don't give up on me," she found herself saying in a whisper, feeling as broken in body as she did in sprit.

He sank to his knees in front of her. *"Never."*

When Mac arrived, he and Rhett conversed for a moment in the other room. Dustin nestled in close and wrapped his arm around her, worry written all over his still-changing face, now dotted with patches of stubble.

When Rhett returned, he walked over to the couch and stood there, shifting from one foot to the other. "You take care of yourself. Do you hear?"

She just nodded, watching as Mac slapped him on the back and he left, his head bowed as if in defeat.

Part of her wanted to call him back. But she didn't.

And dammit if the reason wasn't called Fear.

Chapter 6

For the next ten days Abbie didn't see much of Rhett, although he was frequently at the hotel playing poker or meeting with Nancy to discuss his party. Mac had told her Rhett wanted her to be surprised by the decorations, so she kept out of the ballroom as the staff set up on the day of the party. Mac and Dustin told her they would meet her there, so she changed into her costume alone in their family suite. And made sure she didn't head down until thirty minutes after the party started.

As she checked her makeup in the mirror by the door, a part of her started to worry. What in the heck was he being so secretive about anyway? Because she knew there was something. Wasn't the costume thing an indication that this would not be a normal holiday party? He wouldn't have legions of poker babes dressed up as Santa's helpers, would he? Well, after what he'd told her about giving them up, she doubted it.

Still…

When she finally left their suite and found her way to the ballroom—first using her inhaler preemptively to treat the asthma he often inspired—her mouth fell open at the scene before her.

He'd created a magical winter wonderland. Him. Rhett Butler Blaylock. White netting dotted with miniscule white lights rippled like waves from the high ceiling, creating a magical sense of intimacy. Giant soldiers straight out of *The Nutcracker* flanked a small stage at the front. The servers were all dressed in winter white uniforms dotted with a gold insignia of The Grand Mountain Hotel, carrying silver trays filled with an array of succulent hors d'oeuvres and frosted crystal glasses of champagne. The music drifted through the room like a gentle breeze. Was that from *The Nutcracker,* too? It sure sounded like it, and it made her body want to sway and execute an arabesque.

About fifty people mingled around the ballroom. Some she recognized, like the parents from Dustin's indoor soccer team, whom Rhett had come to know by attending games. Others were harder to identify because of their holiday-themed attire. Like the snowman with the big carrot for a nose and a black top hat. Someone clearly had found an impressive costume online—Dare didn't sell that kind of stuff.

Rhett's suggestion about costumes had raised her guard, so she'd chosen the least sexy outfit possible: Mrs. Claus, decked out in a curly white wig, silver spectacles, padding around the middle, and more blush than usual to create rosy cheeks.

Her new trio of friends approached her as soon as they spotted her, making her smile. Peggy wasn't used to having female friends, but she'd become close to her sister-in-law, Meredith, and Meredith's sister, Jill. They always asked Abbie to hang out on girls' nights, and sometimes she did. Whereas Peggy and Abbie played the "straight man" role, Meredith was pretty down to earth, while Jill had a wicked streak of humor and a larger-than-life personality that was sometimes reminiscent of Rhett. It was nice to have some new friends.

Their costume choices perfectly captured their personalities. Abbie hadn't wanted to talk about the party or what she was wearing, so they hadn't traded notes beforehand. She studied Peggy's outfit first—black pants and a shirt with a silver star on the pocket. It didn't exactly scream Christmas.

"What in the world are you supposed to be, Peggy?" she asked when they reached her.

"The head security elf," she totally deadpanned.

Jill threw her arms up and twirled around. "Guess who I am."

Abbie let her eyes travel over the bright red Santa outfit, which was similar in style to hers save for the thick black handlebar mustache gracing Jill's lip. "I almost don't want to know."

She grabbed her pillow-stuffed belly and laughed in a big boom. "Snicker Claus, 'cause I crack jokes. Wanna hear one?"

"No," Meredith said, stepping forward to give Abbie a hug. "You look lovely, Abbie. The perfect Mrs. Claus."

Meredith was dressed like a super hero, from the white leather pants to the sparkly white bustier and cape.

"Your cape is fantastic," Abbie commented, wanting to run her fingers over the white velvet. "What are you?"

Meredith stuck out her hip playfully. "A Winter Goddess Badass, of course. I had to bring out the La Perla again. I used to wear La Perla every day to give myself a confidence boost, and it's nice to reprise it every now and then."

Abbie wasn't sure she wanted to know about her new friend's lingerie.

"Tanner likes the costume," Meredith murmured, flicking her cape with her gloved hand.

"Please," Peggy pleaded. "Sister here." Then she grabbed a piece of prosciutto-wrapped melon from a passing tray. "This seems more like summer food," she concluded after taking a bite.

And that was when Abbie took a better look at the hors d'oeurves. All of her favorites were making the rounds, from the fig-roasted beef tenderloin in tiny black bowls to the mounds of strawberries dipped in chocolate. Her breath hitched, and her wig started to itch.

"He's done this for me," she whispered, even though he'd said this wasn't her present. She wasn't sure if she should be upset about it. The romantic part of her thought it was incredibly sweet.

Peggy gave a snort. "Well, duh. Do you really think Cowboy-on-Crack would ever have come up with this shindig without romance on the mind? I mean, look at this place, Abbie."

Jill put an arm around her, bumping her with her fake girth. "It's like a fairy tale."

Yeah, no poker babes in Santa's helper outfits anywhere. Thank God.

And then the crowd seemed to part, and her fairy tale prince appeared. He wore gray dress pants and a white dress coat with a white shirt underneath. The gray silk tie had sparkles on it, something only Rhett could pull off. He wasn't truly in a Christmas costume, but it didn't matter. It was the most dressed up she'd ever seen him. And her heart beat rapidly in her chest.

"Don't make the man suffer much longer," Jill suggested, giving her a squeeze. "It's Christmas. Time to make up. Let's go, girls," she said to the others.

"Wait," Abbie called after them, but they just smiled and continued on their way.

Rhett bowed grandly in front of her. When he straightened, he plucked a red rose from his lapel and extended it to her. "Merry Christmas, Abbie."

As she took the rose, part of her wished she wasn't wearing white gloves. She wanted to run her fingers over the velvety petals. Instead, she brought it to her nose. "My goodness, this one is fragrant."

That cocky smile flashed across his face. "What can I say? This hotel carries great flowers."

And since ordering the flowers fell under her purview, she appreciated the compliment.

"So," he continued, his golden eyes as inviting as shiny tree ornaments, "do you like it? I missed you so badly last Christmas that I wanted to celebrate being together this year. And I know you like elegant parties."

She bit her tongue as she struggled with what to say. "Rhett, this is…lovely…more beautiful than I ever could have imagined. But you know we're not a couple."

His smile lost a few watts of its power. "Sure we are. You just haven't realized it yet."

Well, he was just as stubborn as ever.

The music danced around them, rather like her nerves. "Rhett—"

"And since I don't like to beat a dead horse, I'm changing the subject," he said with another bow, this one less grand. "I love your outfit. I wondered what you'd wear, and I have to admit, you look downright fetching as Mrs. Claus. It suits your kindness, your nurturing personality. What do you think of my new threads?" he asked, pulling on his lapels with both hands.

"They're nice." Understatement.

Even she couldn't miss the ridges of muscle beneath his clothes, and just the thought of how she used to run her finger across every one of them when they were naked in bed made her mouth go completely dry. She plucked a glass of champagne from a nearby server, and Rhett did the same.

"Merry Christmas, Abbie," he said, lifting his glass toward hers. "You're my Christmas dream, and I love you. Keep remembering that."

The words reminded her of something, but it was hard to concentrate when he was saying romantic things to her in this Winter Wonderland he'd created. He clinked their glasses together and took a sip.

Her hand didn't seem connected to her body anymore, so she didn't raise it to her lips. She held it loosely in her hand, paralyzed by the sheer force of Rhett's will.

"Drink up, darlin'," he urged. "I hate to leave you, but I need to go and see about something." His hand darted out suddenly, and his thumb rubbed her rosy cheek. "I know I said I wouldn't touch you until you asked me, but God, I want to kiss you senseless right now and make love to you with nothing but those spectacles between us. They're beyond sexy."

His eyes twinkled as much as the Christmas lights above their heads. Then he bowed again and strode off, leaving her with a lump of coal in her chest and desire pooling between her thighs.

***

Rhett downed the rest of his champagne on his way to the back. Exiting through a side door, he opened his arms when he saw his friend.

"Rye, it's great to see you, man. Thanks again for coming."

The country singer propped his leg up on a nearby chair, his hand on his waist. "You knew I wouldn't miss this for the world. You're finally letting me tell the world that the lyrics to my Christmas song were written by the wild poker champ, RBB. The sappiness has been ruining my rep. People think I'm a goner over some chick, like you are with Abbie."

Rhett's aw-shucks shoulder shrug seemed like the only fitting response. His friend was still getting used to seeing him in love.

"Everything is set up for you," he told him, although Rye probably had run through everything since the hotel had brought him in the discreet entrance before the party had started, used for more famous guests. Rye's part in the festivities was so secret that he was staying at Rhett's house and not the hotel.

"I'm going to introduce you."

And damn, if his hands weren't sweating at the thought. A private declaration was one thing; a public declaration was another. But if they were going to have a future, their relationship had to come into the light. Abbie had wanted to keep it secret before, and to his mind, nothing good ever came from that. It was time to show her there was no turning back. By declaring his feelings for her in public, he was telling the world he was different.

The old Rhett with the poker babes, and the *other* babes, was totally gone.

"You sure you want to do this?" Rye asked him, looking every inch a country music legend in the making in his black jeans, white T-shirt, and black cowboy hat. "You do realize it'll change your free-wheeling rep."

"That's what I'm hoping for. Let's do this." And then he clapped Rye on the back and opened the door to the ballroom again.

The buzz of conversation punctuated by raucous laughter blended in with the classical music the hotel had selected. They had done an incredible job all around.

"Folks," he said into the microphone after he stepped onto the stage. "Thanks for coming out tonight. Merry early Christmas," he said, straightening his tie, trying to find Abbie in the crowd. "I'm glad to be in one of my best friend's hotels. Mac Maven, where in the heck are you?"

Hearing his friend's shout, he looked to the right, blinking against the lights. Seeing Mac's wave, he gave one in return. His strategy had worked. He now knew where Abbie was. She was standing with Dustin, Peggy, and the Hales.

"Since moving here in July," he continued, "I have grown to appreciate this fine town of ours. Thanks for your warm welcome. I came here because of the love of a good woman, and tonight, I'm going to have a friend sing the song I wrote for her. Abbie Maven, Merry Christmas."

When he gave the signal, Rye came through the cracked door and took the stage just as Rhett left it. The crowd went wild, even though there were only fifty guests. Rhett's ears picked up only white noise as he tried to locate Abbie again. He skirted the edges of the ballroom until he was directly across the room from where she was standing. He leaned against one of the ridiculously cute nutcracker statues that had cost him an arm and a leg, a few nerves kicking up when he thought about his surprise, and how Abbie would react.

"How are y'all doing?" Rye called out to the cheering crowd. "It's my honor to be here in Dare Valley tonight, and I have to say I'm glad I can finally tell the world that my friend, Rhett Butler Blaylock, wrote the Christmas love song I recorded and released that everyone's been hearing on the radio. "The Holiday Serenade." Ladies, let me set the record straight. I am *not* taken. But my friend, Rhett, is. Abbie, darlin', give him another chance. I can promise you no one loves you more. Just listen to what he wrote for ya."

And then Rye took a seat at the shining grand piano and played the opening melody, the white Christmas lights reflecting off the black veneer. Rhett had gotten Rye to agree to a piano ballad—as opposed to his usual, the guitar—and then his friend had worked his magic, keeping it simple and letting the words shape the music. His instincts were gold. The song had already hit number one on the charts.

Abbie's eyes met Rhett's, and in them he could see the usual struggle between longing and resistance. He didn't approach her, but simply stood with his back to Rye, the crowd all around him enthralled by the song.

As Rye brought the song home with his deep baritone, you could have heard a pin drop in the ballroom.

Let me love you.
Serenade you.
My Christmas dream come true.

When Rye's voice faded, the love of his life turned around and strode out, picking her way through the people behind her. Rhett cleared the door and ran after her, ignoring the hotel staff, who stopped what they were doing to watch him race through the main hall.

"Abbie," he called out, his long legs eating up the distance between them.

And then she did something he'd never seen her do before. She started to run. A red bow from her outfit fell off as she reached the main stairs. Rhett jogged after her, fortifying himself, knowing where she was going: the Maven family suite.

There was going to be a battle.

He could feel it.

And he was ready

Chapter 7

Abbie reached the family suite and threw the door open so hard it bounced against the wall. Once she was inside, she yanked off her wig and heaved it across the room. A sound, part scream, part growl emerged from her throat.

She heard the door click like someone was entering the suite, and she clenched her hands, trying to gather control. She knew Mac wouldn't let Dustin see her like this, but her older brother was probably coming to check on her.

When Rhett cleared the hallway and entered the living area, she couldn't believe his gall.

"How dare you come in here!" she yelled, and for a moment, she thought about picking up one of the embroidered pillows on the gold tapestry couch beside her and throwing it at him.

"I have a key from all the time I've spent in here, remember? Abbie, why are you so upset?"

He was an idiot. "You know why!"

His tie wrinkled when he loosened the knot at his neck. "Okay, let's talk about this. I didn't do this to upset you. I simply wanted to show you how much I care about you, make a public declaration."

Which she had never wanted. She strode over to him and thrust a finger into his chest. "What you did was embarrass me in front of the whole town. What in the world were you thinking?"

His hand covered the finger poking him, and he eased it away from him. "Didn't you listen to the lyrics? I was trying to tell you how I feel about you. *Again.* Dammit, when are you going to finally admit to what's between us?"

The tremble started at her feet. "I can't. Why can't *you* understand that?"

This time his fist punched the air. "Why? Tell me why, dammit. This discussion has been going on for months between us, in fits and starts. I know about Dustin's father now, and I'm prepared to give up the poker babes for you. So make me understand. Why can't we be together?"

The vein pulsed in his neck, and his face was flushed from his passionate retort, rather like it looked after they'd made love. The past year and a half of celibacy she'd endured suddenly began to seem interminable.

"We just can't!" she cried out, not knowing what the heck to say after all this time. "I can't explain it to you any more than I have."

"What are you so afraid of?" Rhett cried, stepping so close she had to crane her neck more than usual, given his towering height.

That accusation again. Fear.

His body radiated heat, warming every part of her that seemed to have gone cold when she'd walked away from him.

"I don't want to talk about this anymore," she said and turned, banging her knee into the coffee table behind her.

He grabbed her elbow and pulled her close. Those golden eyes peered deep into her soul. They were suddenly all she could see.

"I'll ask you again. What. Are. You. Afraid. Of?"

Everything inside her snapped. "You," she cried, shoving away his hands. "I'm afraid of you."

Surely that would make him back up, but he stepped into her line of vision when she tried to circle around him, his outstretched arms keeping her in place.

"Why?"

"Leave me alone." God, all she wanted to do was get out of there.

"No. Why?" he grabbed her arm and held her in place.

"Stop this." And the plea was clear even to her ears.

"Tell me!"

She couldn't stand it. "Because you make me want things, Rhett, and I know it can't last. That you can't keep this up."

"So I make you want things? Good! Because, dammit, I want things too." A bonfire burned in his eyes. "And I can keep it up. Haven't I stayed here for months dishing out everything you could throw out?"

"You make me sound cruel," she whispered and tucked her arms around her padded waist, suddenly realizing how ridiculous her outfit was. She was arguing with him dressed as Mrs. Claus sans the wig.

"You're only protecting yourself," he informed her.

A part of her gasped at his insight.

Then he lowered his head until their gazes clashed. *"No one* knows you better than I do, Abbie. No one. And

I'm sick and tired of you refusing to admit that you love me."

She couldn't admit it. Ever. Once she did, there would be no going back.

"Tell me."

"No."

His hold tightened on her. "Tell me."

"I won't," she said, lifting her chin, and considered kicking him in the shin. Rhett always made her come unglued, but tonight was something else.

"You love me, dammit. Why can't you say it? Just once. Some days I feel like I've been left in the Mojave Desert outside of Vegas with no water. You're killing me, Abbie. I love you, but God help me, I don't know what more I can do. I can't change who I am anymore than I already have. And if the song didn't work…"

His total desolation destroyed her. She'd never seen him this hurt, and she couldn't be the cause of it anymore.

Her arms latched around him before she could stop herself, and she pressed her body into his. "Then take what you need. I won't have you hurt by this."

His pulse beat steadily in his temple. *"You* take what you need. I told you when I arrived that I wouldn't touch you unless you asked me. Ask me, Abbie," he commanded, his voice all rough and dark.

The answer had been inside her all along, and she was tired of fighting it. "Touch me, Rhett."

He yanked her the final inches toward him and slid those large, warm hands over her hips, caging her to him. "Always."

Then his mouth covered hers, and their lips met heatedly, searching for connection, searching for a deeper union. He stripped her red velvet dress off without breaking contact with her mouth, ripping it at the seams when it wouldn't fall as fast as he wanted.

After all this time, the passion between them exploded. The padding was torn off her body to reveal her slender shape, and when she stood in only her black heels and red panties, he slid to the floor in front of her and pressed his mouth to her stomach.

"It's been so long, Abbie. I'll try to make it last, but right now, I can't promise this won't be fast."

His lips cruised over the indention of her hips as he slid off her panties. Her head fell back as she stepped out of them and her shoes.

"I don't want it to be slow. It's been so long. Rhett, please."

He stood hastily and stripped off his clothes, keeping close to her. After he flung every piece of clothing across the room, covering the couch, the coffee table, and the carpet, he removed the spectacles she'd been wearing with a gentleness that shocked her.

"I know I said I wanted to make love to you with you wearing these and nothing else, but I've changed my mind. I want to see your eyes when I come into you."

She almost fell to the floor in a pool of lust right then and there.

His body hadn't changed. It was as strong, muscular, and totally enticing as it had always been before. Even though a part of her still feared what this would do to them, she stepped forward.

"Then come into me."

The slow smile he gave her prompted a full-body shiver. "Not quite yet, but we aren't going to make it to the bed," he murmured and nudged her to the rug beside the couch.

He took her breast in his mouth, sucking strongly and sought out the place between her thighs with his fingers. She drew his face up and lifted her head off the floor, inviting him to kiss her again, and when he did, his tongue sought hers, sliding deep inside her mouth, executing a flawless dance that had her heart pounding in strong pulses all over her body.

Her hands caressed his back, his hips, and slid across his spectacular butt. Then she reached between them and gave him a gentle stroke. He shuddered. "God! I've missed your hands on me."

His eyes closed, and his jaw clenched as she pleasured him.

"Enough," he growled and reached into his discarded pants for his wallet, drawing out a condom. "I'm only using these until we get married. Then, if you agree, all bets are off."

Her passion was too great to correct his assertion. She watched as he rolled the condom down his hard length. Then he took her hands and brought them over her head, holding them in place. Part of her had always been thrilled by the total command he had over her body. When his knee nudged her thighs open wider and he stretched out over her, she wanted to purr.

"Look at me," he commanded, his voice smoky and dark, his eyes gleaming like gold coins. *"This* is what's between us. This and more love than I ever imagined having for anyone."

And then he slowly penetrated her. Her head rolled to the side at the heat, the fullness. She was tight, and he was

AVA MILES

large. Like it had always been.

"Look at me," he demanded again.

When she did, he thrust deep. Her body bucked against him.

"Yes," she cried, feeling the power, feeling the heat surge within her. After so long…

Her vision shrank until all she could see was his golden eyes looking into hers. Their lower bodies came together, met in deep, liquid thrusts, and the heat in her flesh grew until she was sure she would turn to ash.

Being held down only made her more eager to ensnare him, so she clamped her legs around his waist. He rose to his knees.

"Oh, yes," he said, yanking her hips high off the floor. "Give me more."

And she did. Then she came in a rush of power, her body contracting and exploding like a supernova, destroying the old and creating a fragile new world for her existence.

He came with a shout, and lowered himself onto his elbows, stretching out on top of her again. She turned her head to kiss his sweaty cheek, and inhaled the cologne she'd picked out for him. He'd never stopped wearing it, even after all this time.

Tears filled her eyes. This is what they'd had. And this is what she'd missed. All of it.

When his eyes met hers, his face fell. "No crying." Then he rose, discarded the condom, and lifted her off the floor and into his arms. "I'll have you back at your house before Dustin wakes up, but you're mine tonight."

And then he walked into the bedroom and lowered her to the bed.

"I love you," he whispered, cradling her cheek. "I'm sorry I forgot to say it before."

She could no longer deny the truth to herself or to him. "I love you too, Rhett."

His exhale was forceful and heartfelt. He rubbed their foreheads together. "Thank God."

For the rest of the night, they did nothing but make love to each other. Talking seemed too tenuous, as if the words were paper dolls like the ones she'd made at Christmas as a child.

But they loved each other, and for hours and hours, it was as if rest of the world didn't exist.

When he finally fell asleep by her side at dawn, she wished the night could have gone on forever. Making love with him and admitting she loved him—something that had always been true—had changed their world.

And she was still scared of it.

Angry with herself, she gathered up her clothes and left him sleeping, holding back the tears she wanted to cry at the injustice of it all.

Chapter 8

For a second, Abbie considered parking her car at the end of the driveway and walking up. But the wind was howling, and she didn't want to slip on the ice and break a limb. Making the walk of shame at dawn was embarrassing enough. How much more so would it be if she actually injured herself? Not that she'd tell a soul.

She had left Rhett sleeping in the suite, stopping for a shower in the private bathroom attached to Mac's office. Somehow, being cleaned up hadn't made her feel any better. All she'd felt was sadness and shame at leaving Rhett behind. But the urge to flee had been too strong to resist. What was she supposed to say to him now?

The house was quiet when she entered. It was just shy of seven o'clock on a Saturday morning, after all, but she still cocked an ear, listening. If she could make it to her room without being heard, she could pretend—at least to her family—that nothing had happened. Lying was against her code, but withholding information was a different story. She was a mom for heaven's sake. Even if she wasn't being the kind of role model she wanted to be.

Another reason she needed to stop this thing with Rhett.

She tiptoed across the hall into the family room.

"Good morning," her brother's even-tempered voice said.

Jumping in fright was ludicrous, but she did it anyway. Her adrenaline spiked, and she put a hand to her racing heart. Busted.

"Mac, you scared me," she whispered, noting he was already dressed in casual gray pants and a black cashmere sweater.

"Sorry," he responded in a normal voice. "Are you okay?"

The old feeling of paranoia—something she'd felt throughout her secret relationship with Rhett—resurfaced. "Is Dustin up yet?" It was unlikely since he usually slept until noon on Saturdays.

"I had him spend the night with Keith to give you a little space," Mac responded. "Come into the kitchen and have some tea."

The big brother thing was in full force if his patient, assessing glance was any indication. Darn it. Thank heavens she'd kept a change of clothes at the hotel, but she was still carrying a bag with her wig and costume. This situation could not have been *more* awkward.

"I need to—"

"Come along," Mac interrupted. "I've been up most of the night worrying about you. Looking at your face, I can see my concern was warranted. It's time for us to talk."

She was thirty-four years old. She could stand up for herself. "Mac, you have security feeds in every part of the hotel. You know where I was, and even though I'm ashamed of it, you must know what I've been doing. I don't want to talk about it."

Those green eyes, so like her own, flickered for a moment. She couldn't read his face. Mr. Poker Champion was in full force.

"You're right. I know where you were. Doesn't mean I wasn't worried about you after the way you ran out of the party last night. That's something you never do. I think it's past time for us to talk about the main reason you're running."

It took a moment for her to inhale past the blockage in her throat. Why was everyone pushing her all of the sudden? "I don't want to."

He lowered his head, staring at the ground. "Abbie, I love you, and I know you don't want to talk about what's really standing in your way, but you need to." When he looked up, it was like someone had snuck around her and was trying to strangle her. "Let me help you."

"Mac, please," she only whispered, shaking her head, feeling the ever-present fear settle in her solar plexus.

He shook his head and walked toward her until they were inches apart. "I didn't want to do this the hard way, but it looks like that's the only way it's going to happen. I've watched you keep yourself frozen for nearly six months with Rhett. After last night, I figured you might have given a little, but you're already shoring up again. I can see it on your face. Abbie, how is Dustin supposed to believe he can have a fulfilling relationship when he gets old enough after seeing how you're acting?"

She sucked in an uneven breath after that sucker punch, an asthma attack calling her name. "That's below the belt."

She pulled out her inhaler and took a puff. It calmed her breathing—for the moment.

His warm hands settled on her shoulders, and he met her gaze. "I know, but I had to up the ante. Listen, you and I made a promise to tell each other when we're doing something that's not in Dustin's best interest. Dammit, I hate to say it, but that's exactly what you're doing."

All of the sudden she had to bite her lip to keep from crying. *I'm just overtired*, she told herself. Mac gathered her against his chest and hugged her.

"Plus, it's hurting you too. Come into the kitchen and talk to me. We always figure things out that way."

She sniffed when she pulled away. He handed her an embroidered handkerchief, the only thing she ever used when she cried. Since she rarely did, she wanted to use something that deserved her tears, and a tissue just didn't cut it.

"You knew I was going to cry?" she asked, taking it from him.

"I rather hoped you would. You need to, Abbie, and not about Rhett. Come on, I'll make you your favorite tea."

He took her arm and led her into the kitchen. After she'd settled down on a bar stool, he busied himself with filling the kettle with water and setting it to boil on the stove. She was reminded of Rhett making her tea not too long ago.

What was it with the men in her life? When were they going to realize there was nothing to be fixed?

A part of her said, *Yeah, right.*

She tried to compose herself, but fissures were spreading through her heart. Long-held pain was leaking out like water from an old pottery mug with a crack in the bottom.

Mac didn't say anything to her; he just focused on filling her tea ball with her special jasmine tea from Venice, the one Rhett had at his house.

God, why couldn't she stop thinking about Rhett? And why couldn't she stop imagining what he'd look like when he awoke to an empty bed?

Mac caught the kettle before it sang its church organ note and poured the hot water into her Royal Albert Christmas teapot, setting her snowman Christmas cozy over it so it would retain its warmth. Thank God he was all male, or he would have looked ridiculous. After letting it steep for four minutes, he poured her tea into a matching teacup and added a slice of lemon and a teaspoon of honey, just the way she liked it.

Then he grabbed his cup of coffee and sat beside her, still saying nothing. The silence between them grew, and with it, her distress. She traced the rim of the cup with a finger.

"You and I have been together a long time, Abbie," her brother finally said. "If you hadn't gotten pregnant at eighteen, we would have gone our separate ways, living apart like most siblings. Getting married. Having kids. We would have seen each other every once in a while, but we wouldn't have been best friends." He set his hand on top of her free one.

Her brother's huge heart could always be counted on, and she could already feel the first tear slipping down her cheek. "Oh, Mac."

"I've watched you grow up. I've helped you raise Dustin. And I've seen you work so hard to make yourself into the person you wanted to be. Our own mother pales in comparison to the way you love and take care of Dustin.

And you have a hell of an eye with the hotels, from the flowers to the furnishings to the decorations. But after what Dustin's father did to you, you stopped letting yourself be a woman. I know this because I'm engaged to a woman who did the same thing after her divorce."

When she tried to lift her delicate tea cup and take a sip, she burned her mouth…just like her memories of what had happened the night of Dustin's conception were burning through her right now.

"I'm not saying your experience is the same as Peggy's, but I am saying that being with her has made me see you more clearly. And I want you to break free of the past like she finally has. This hesitation you have about Rhett isn't about his flamboyance, dependability, suitability, or even his poker babes. It's about you trusting yourself again."

Her hand suddenly went numb, and the cup clattered to the counter. "What?"

He pushed their cups aside and angled her bar stool to face his. "I finally figured it out. You don't trust yourself to know if a man is going to be good to you in the long run. You blame yourself for not seeing the asshole who hurt you for what he really was. You knew him. You liked him. You thought he was a good man. And then he blew that image to bits and stole your innocence."

The handkerchief felt soft on her lips when she raised it to them, trying to hold back the words that were rushing up to be said. Hadn't that been her strategy for years? To deny, deny, deny? And yet it hadn't worked…

"It wasn't your fault," he said gently, stroking her arm.

She shook her head. "Of course it wasn't." The words

were a harsh whisper, burning her throat.

"If you believe that, then say it," he urged, covering her hand again and squeezing it.

Her lips trembled. "It…"

"Tell me," he said again.

Why couldn't she say it? It was like her throat had become a clogged pipe. She coughed to clear it. "It…" Her speech failed her again as the tremors spread through her body.

"Say it, Abbie." It was a demand this time.

Her head buzzed and any thread of control was singed and snapped by the fire raging through her. She shoved back from him, back from the chair, and stood there panting.

"What the hell do you know? You weren't there. You don't know."

He stood slowly, moving in front of her. "So, I don't know. Why can't you say it?"

Her face started to crumble. She could feel every wrinkle, every line. "Because…it's a fucking lie." She slapped her hand over her mouth at her crass language. She *never* said the f-word.

"Why is it a fucking lie? Come on, Abbie. I wasn't there. Tell me."

And his voice was almost a shout, pushing her to the edge of the deep cavern of her fear. She hovered over the brink and then fell.

"Because…it *was* my fault! I didn't see him for what he was. I didn't think he'd do something like that. I trusted him!"

And that final admission brought her to her knees. "Oh, God," she cried, wrapping her arms around herself.

"He raped me."

Before she knew it, Mac was beside her on the floor, gathering her close. "Let it out, Abbie," he whispered, smoothing her hair as she cried against his chest. "It's time to let it go."

She couldn't respond. She was snowed under by nearly seventeen years of buried pain, pain suppressed by the need to take care of a baby who hadn't deserved to be born under such circumstances.

Mac held her tight while she cried out all the pain, the injustice, the victimhood, and the fear that had been frozen inside of her, closing her off to the love of a good man.

Finally spent and completely hollowed out, she leaned against her brother, head buzzing, body tingling. She felt him kiss her hair.

"I'm so proud of you," he whispered.

More tears welled as she raised a head that seemed to weigh as much as a dumbbell. "Why?"

"Because you just opened the door to your own Christmas miracle."

And as he squeezed her tight again, rocking her into a new center of peace, she realized he was only partially right.

Her Christmas miracle had started right now.

Chapter 9

Rhett surveyed the line at Don't Soy with Me. Everyone was chatting like they had candy canes stuck up their asses. Usually he was of good cheer, but he just wasn't feeling the Christmas spirit. Even though Jill had decorated the coffee shop so thoroughly it ought to be criminal. Stuffed elves hung from the ceiling along with a Santa sleigh and reindeer. Flashing white lights added a soft glow, and a cheerful fire roared in the fireplace.

One unfortunate elf had his whole body wrapped around a Don't Soy with Me coffee cup, with Jill's logo of a man and woman sitting at a table with a cup of coffee between them. The woman was crooking her finger at the man. The black image against the lime green backing reminded Rhett of him and Abbie. She crooked her finger—well, not often—and he pretty much came running…but then she always left.

As he shuffled forward in line, he realized he was sounding like the Grinch. Shit. He'd love nothing better than to leave and return to his brooding, but he'd promised the food-obsessed Rye some of the pastries Don't Soy with Me sold from Brasserie Dare. It was the least he could do after leaving his friend to fend for himself last night, not that Rye ever had trouble doing that.

When he finally picked up his coffee, he heard his name shouted over Mariah Carey's "All I Want For Christmas Is You." Damn, he loved that girl, but he wondered if she'd had to sit on a stick pin to hit those high notes. Tucking his gingerbread latte close, which only reminded him of Abbie's baking, he headed over to join Arthur Hale, who was sitting in the corner with his signature red pen in his hand, likely marking up articles for *The Western Independent.* Rhett had grown fond of the oldest member of his Wednesday night poker group.

"Tried to get your attention earlier, but it's like a zoo in here," Arthur said. "Plus you look like someone kicked your dog."

When Arthur gestured to the chair across from him, Rhett sat down. "Sorry, I have a few things on my mind."

"Women troubles after last night, I expect. I saw Abbie's face when she ran out of your party. She doesn't seem like the type of woman who likes to be pressured into giving an answer."

Rhett's gingerbread latte neither pleased his taste buds nor gave him one iota of Christmas spirit. "I wasn't trying to pressure her," he growled, trying to balance respect for his elders with his annoyance about Arthur's usual directness, something he appreciated when it was targeted at other people.

Arthur drew out two red hots, his second food group it seemed, and handed one to Rhett, which he took to be polite. He marveled at how anyone could eat that many candies and still keep his teeth, especially at his friend's age.

"You don't think you were trying to pressure her?"

Arthur snorted, pushing his wireless glasses up his nose. "Then you're lying to yourself, son. Take it from an old codger like me. Sometimes a public declaration backfires, especially on a woman who guards her privacy like she does her underthings. Just because you want everyone to know you love her, doesn't mean it's smart to tell everyone, particularly in a small town like this one. If you look around, you'll notice people are watching you, and not because you're some famous poker player."

Rhett scanned the room, and this time he saw the speculation in people's eyes. Dare's grist mill ran like clockwork. He'd grown so accustomed to it that he didn't even notice anymore. Was this what Abbie had been trying to tell him?

"I was only trying to show her how much I love her. We kept our relationship in the dark before, so I wanted everything out in the open this time. Hell, I even wrote her that damn song and put my heart on my sleeve, and what does she do? Turns tail the minute we get close again." He coughed, realizing he had revealed more than he intended.

Arthur's age-spotted hand sliced through the air. "Please, just because I haven't had sex for a while doesn't mean I don't know what couples do when they care about each other. Anyone can see that Abbie loves you. She just isn't sure she wants to stand with you while you're rustling up pictures and interviews as Rhett Butler Blaylock. To my mind, that makes her a smart woman."

And yet that wasn't the reason at all. It went so much deeper. Rhett knew it went back to what had happened to her—he just wasn't sure what to do about it.

Hoping some sugar would kick his system into the Christmas spirit, Rhett grabbed one of the cookie samples that Margie, the barista, was bringing around on trays. The Santa sugar cookie melted in his mouth. Arthur munched on his sample alongside him.

"When I have Christmas cookies, it always makes me think of my wife, Harriet. She would bake nearly twelve types of sweets for the holiday. It was a shitload of cookies to consume, but I loved her, so I ate them."

The crumbs on the table flew to the floor when Rhett brushed them aside so he could lean forward on his elbows. "Abbie's the same way, and damn if I don't want to eat whatever she puts in front of me, even if it means more time at the gym."

Arthur snorted. "Yeah, I'm really concerned about my time in the gym."

Since the man was seventy-seven, Rhett laughed, and his first genuine smile of the day spread across his face. "So, you old codger, what's your advice then? I've made a public declaration, which backfired. Now what?"

The process of stirring more cream into his coffee took a minute. Rhett knew Arthur was mulling it over.

"You make a private declaration," he suggested. "A woman always likes to be serenaded. Don't send another man to do your serenading, son. I like Rye Crenshaw's music like everyone else, but he's not the one in love with Abbie. You are."

Just the thought of serenading Abbie made his heart triple beat in his chest. "But I suck at singing. It literally will make the cats cry." Or was it the doves cry? Didn't Prince sing about that?

Arthur pocketed his pen and drained his coffee. "That's all the better." He stood and patted Rhett on the back. "A woman can't help but fall for a man who makes an ass of himself for her sake. Do something that's hard for you. It's a winning idea, son. Trust me. I speak from experience."

"Thanks," he said, as Arthur grabbed his cane and ambled off.

When Rhett took a sip of his latte this time, he could hear the jingle of bells in his ears.

His Christmas dream wasn't over.

Even if it involved him making an ass of himself like Arthur had suggested.

Chapter 10

After leaving Don't Soy with Me, Rhett let himself into his house. He wanted to pat himself on the back for not grabbing one of the hot croissants he'd bought for Rye and consuming it on the drive up.

"You know," said Rye, who was lounging on the couch watching ESPN's Sports Center when he walked into the den, "it's a good thing we've been friends so long or you might have hurt my feelings ditching me like you did last night. I was all scared and lonely out here in the big bad woods."

"Sure you were, Red Riding Hood," Rhett responded, knowing a line of bull when he heard it. "I brought you breakfast like I promised to soothe your shattered heart."

Rye swung his legs onto the floor and sat up, studying him. "From what I'm seeing, you're the one who looks like his heart has been through the meat grinder. I take it our song didn't work its intended magic—even though you're doing the walk of shame this morning?"

Yeah, thank God Arthur hadn't mentioned that. Rhett had shed his coat jacket and tie, but he was still wearing the gray pants, white shirt, and shoes from the night before.

"Shut up," he said and thrust the bag of food in Rye's direction.

His friend opened it and moaned. "Dear God, are these—"

"Fresh croissants? Yes. I also brought you a ham and cheese quiche since you're that kind of guy."

His friend's laugh was dirty when he jumped up to head into the kitchen. "That's because the word quiche reminds me of quickie."

Rhett couldn't help but think of how totally miserable he was after a night of fantastic sex. It was unfamiliar territory.

"Well, Abigail and I hardly had a quickie," he confessed. "We spent all night in bed, but she left me high and dry this morning. Nothing's been resolved."

He knew that while making love with him again had been a huge step for Abbie, she still wasn't ready to give her whole heart to him. And that's what he wanted. Them married. Living together. Forever.

Rye slapped him on the back. "I'm sorry, man. I know how much you love her. Women!"

Yeah, who could understand them?

For a man who didn't really care much for order, Rye arranged his food on one of Rhett's white plates with the flair of a Cordon Bleu-trained chef. Then he carried it over to the kitchen table like it was the ark of the covenant itself, sat down, and bowed his head.

"You praying?" Rhett asked, shocked.

His hands opened like he was blessing the food. "Some things are meant to be honored. Food is one of them."

"Well, color me surprised," Rhett said, taking a seat

across from him.

"Feel free to have some food. You're so pathetic, the least I could do is share." When Rye bit into the croissant, his eyes fluttered shut. "Dear God. It's like being at a Paris cafe."

"You truly are sick, man. Your love of food borders on obsessive." But since his friend's display eased his troubles a bit, he smiled.

"I'm telling you, it's like heaven in my mouth." Then he gave Rhett his full attention. "Now talk. What do we need to do to make Abbie realize the lengths to which you'll go to be with her?"

Rhett decided to sample one of the croissants and realized his friend was right, just like always. It *was* heaven in his mouth. "Well, I ran into one of my Wednesday night poker buddies who's seen a lot of years. He had an interesting idea."

After he'd told Rye what he was thinking, his friend started grinning. "Can I watch? Seriously. I mean, I've heard you sing when you're drunk as a skunk. I love you, but you suck balls, man. Maybe you can lip-sync."

Rhett didn't mind being flamboyant, but he did mind being foolish. "I don't like it any better than you do, but I think he's right."

The quiche was quickly obliterated, and his friend's groans punctuated the silence in the kitchen. "Well," Rye said between bites, "if you really wanted to make an ass of yourself, you could sing Mariah Carey's "All I Want For Christmas Is You." You'll need a really tight jock strap for that one though."

Rhett's balls tightened at the mere thought—and not in a good way. "No thanks. I'm gonna sing her the song I wrote. Can you get me the instrumental?"

Rye's shoulder lifted as he finished chewing. "Sure. You planning on pulling a John Cusack in *Say Anything*?"

"Man, right now, I'm embarrassed to even know you."

"Like you don't get the reference," Rye said, diving into the bag for more food. "I've watched it with a girlfriend or two. Holding the boom box overhead is classic. And, this food just keeps getting better and better."

"I figured that since you like your women to be tarts, a French one might do," Rhett responded with an eye roll as Rye drew out a mini raspberry tart.

"Well, in terms of satisfaction, let's see." Rye bit into it and did the whole moaning thing all over again. "Yep. It comes pretty damn close."

"If your fans could only see you now. I'm going to go practice—in the shower—so you can't hear me."

The tart disappeared into his friend's mouth after the third bite. "Like that's gonna stop me."

Digging his feet into his shoes, Rhett said, "You're sick." And then he raced toward his bedroom full throttle.

The door was latched a few seconds after Rye started pounding on it. "Would you seriously deny one of your best friends a lifetime's worth of entertainment?"

As Rhett headed to the shower for singing practice—*singing practice!*—he called over his shoulder. "Hell, yes."

"Merry Christmas to you too, man," Rye called through the door. "And I've changed my mind. I'm playing the piano for this live event."

When Rhett stepped under the spray of the shower, he leaned his head back and let the water wash away all his worries.

Like his mama used to say when they'd go to church when he was a sprout, he'd have to sing from his heart to persuade Abbie to be with him.

Or everything would be lost.

Chapter 11

Rhett sang a few bars of "Do, Rey, Mi" while he shaved. God, those von Trapp kids had made it look easy, but it sure wasn't.

A knock sounded on the bathroom door.

"You come to tell me the dogs are howling?" he asked Rye.

"No," his friend responded, and his voice was wrong. The fact that he didn't take an easy jab at him was another sign that something was up. "Open the door."

"What happened?" he said, setting his electric shaver aside and turning away from the mirror to unlock the door.

Rye's usually relaxed face was tense around the mouth and eyes. "Abbie's son is here, and he seems really upset."

After the way he and Abbie had left the party last night, Rhett wondered if Dustin was here to give him an ass kicking. The kid had been on his side from the beginning, but maybe things had changed.

"Is he pissed off?" he asked, wanting to know what he was walking into.

His friend shook his head. "No, he's hurting. It's like he's lost his reason for living."

Rhett rolled his eyes. "Aren't you being a little dramatic?"

The hands Rye raised were large enough to palm a football and throw one sixty yards. "No, get dressed and come see for yourself. I'm going to head into town and give you guys some space. Text me when it's clear to come back. Then we'll work on your singing. By Christ, you suck, man."

When the door closed behind him, Rhett tossed his towel aside. Ran the shaver over the last track of stubble. Didn't bother with aftershave. And threw on fresh clothes in record time.

The kid was sitting on the couch, his knee jumping as his foot tapped the ground like he was sending a telegram. Rye hadn't exaggerated. The kid looked like he'd just lost his best friend. The usual sparkle in his green eyes—just like his mother's—was totally gone.

"Dustin," he said as he walked into the den. Not knowing what to do, he dug a hand into his jeans pocket and decided to let the kid tell him why he was here.

"I hope…it's okay that I came over without texting," the kid said with more hesitation than usual.

He joined Dustin on the couch and leaned back, trying to appear at ease even though his stomach felt like the wrung-out sheets his mother had hung on the clothesline growing up, squeezed and twisted to within an inch of their life.

"You're always welcome here, son. You know that." He put his hand on Dustin's shoulder. "Now tell me what's wrong."

His heart broke when the kid covered his face with his hands. "I know why Mom won't marry you."

106

Rhett was sure that if he'd been in front of a mirror he would have seen a crack in his famous poker face.

Then Dustin looked up, his eyes slightly damp, and the sight just about broke Rhett's heart in two. This teenager didn't cry. Ever.

"It's because of me."

Rhett held in the sigh that wanted to escape. The kid wasn't entirely wrong. Abbie didn't think he'd make a good stepfather, but still, he'd have to tread carefully here.

"Dustin, it's not your fault, son. Your mother has high standards when it comes to how she wants you to be raised. She's not sure I—"

The kid jumped up and punched his own chest. "No, it's because of me and the man who fathered me."

A vicious ache spread through his gut, and Rhett stood, trying to stay calm in the face of the boy's anguish. "Now, Dustin—"

"You know who he is and what he did to her, don't you?" he yelled, moving toward him.

Rhett stood still, not wanting to inflame the situation.

"Tell me the truth," Dustin demanded when he made no reply. "You know, don't you?"

This time he couldn't stop the sigh from gusting out, and funny how it didn't give him any relief. "This is something you need to talk about with your mother, Dustin. Not me."

The boy lurched around and stalked away before turning back, fists clenched at his sides. "She never tells me anything. A long time ago I realized how much it hurt her when I asked, so I stopped asking. But I can't take it anymore. Not when it's the reason she won't marry you."

This couldn't continue, so Rhett walked over and put

both hands on the kid's growing shoulders. "It has nothing to do with you, son."

Dustin threw off his hands. "I don't believe you. I know what my father did to her."

The ground seemed to tremble beneath his feet. He shifted his weight to re-balance himself. "What do you know?"

His lip started to quiver, and he shook his head. "My best friend finally told me a few weeks ago."

Fucking teenage punks. Rhett's jaw clenched. "Your friend doesn't know squat."

Those green eyes blazed like a forest fire. "Don't bullshit me. Not you, Rhett. Taylor—my friend—said his parents were at the city council meeting when the vote was made about the hotel. He said Peggy brought up a story about Uncle Mac beating a man up and sending him to the hospital, and Uncle Mac admitted he'd done it, but said it was because the man had taken advantage of his sister. Taylor told me Uncle Mac was in college, and I thought about the timing."

Oh sweet Jesus, Rhett thought, wanting to take the kid into his arms. He'd never wanted to protect anyone from the truth so badly.

Dustin faced Rhett, breathing heavily. "'Taking advantage of' is a nice way of saying raped, isn't it? I've heard that in my English lit class. My father raped my mother, didn't he? And that's why she won't marry you. She's been upstairs resting all day, and I couldn't take it anymore. I knew she was upset after she left the party. And I'm done with this. I don't want her to be miserable because of me."

Rhett couldn't take it anymore. He yanked the kid

toward him and squeezed him in a bear hug. "Your mother gets nothing but joy from you, Dustin Macalister Maven, and I'll be damned if you're going to think otherwise."

The kid's arms fisted around him, and he dug his head into his chest. "But it's true, isn't it?"

Like a tick on a horse, the kid wouldn't let it go. "Leave that for now."

Dustin shoved back, the poster boy for a teenager ready to take the world on with his fists and fire. "I thought you were my friend. I thought you'd tell me!"

"I am your friend, Dustin," he replied calmly. "I always have been, and I always will be. But I love your mother. And your uncle. I can't betray their trust in me."

"I'm sixteen, dammit! I'm old enough to know. I'm old enough to face the truth."

He'd been the same way when he was Dustin's age, thinking he was old enough for anything. Funny how wrong he'd been on some occasions, but learning to be a man was about figuring things out from personal experience. And the kid needed to be heard and comforted. This was one wound that would fester if it wasn't properly treated.

"I know you are, son, and I'm proud of you for coming to talk to me. Now, let me take you home, and we'll talk to your mom and Uncle Mac."

Dustin lifted his chin and crossed his arms across his chest. "No, I'm not leaving here until I know the truth."

Rhett studied him. The kid was dead serious, and he would never resort to dragging him out.

"Fine. They'll come here then. But I can't promise you what they'll say."

Lowering his chin an inch, Dustin said, "Okay."

Rhett wanted to cross the room again and gather the boy up, tell him it would be fine, but that would be pointless. It wasn't fine. And if they weren't very careful, everything they'd built for the boy could be destroyed.

"I'm going to get my phone and call your mother, okay?" he told Dustin. Thank God, he'd left his phone on the bathroom counter.

A nod was all he received before he left the room.

When he reached his bedroom, he closed the door. Headed to the bed and sat for a minute, trying to find the inner place he went to when he was in a high-stakes game and the pressure was bone-cracking.

It wouldn't come. He realized in that moment how different the stakes were in this situation. Rising, he found his phone and rubbed the pain in his chest as he called Abbie. Part of him prayed it would go to voicemail. After last night, he wasn't sure she would pick up his call. If not, he would call Mac.

When she picked up, he closed his eyes.

"Hi, Rhett," she said, her voice soft and hesitant.

His heart thundered for her, like a herd of wild mustangs racing across the prairie. "Hi," he responded, not knowing what to say.

"I'm sorry I left…without saying anything."

Well, this was encouraging. "Me too, but it's not why I called."

"Oh," she replied, sounding deflated.

"But I'm glad to hear you're sorry." He took a deep breath. "Abbie, Dustin's here."

"He is? He said he was meeting his friend, Taylor."

Yeah, some friend, Rhett thought. "Abbie, I don't know how to tell you this in a way that won't hurt you

110

since there isn't one, so I'm just going to say it. Dustin suspects that his father raped you."

Her gasp was audible on the line. "But…how…I mean…God!"

"Taylor told him about the town council meeting for Mac's hotel." And he recounted his conversation with Dustin.

She was sniffing audibly by the end. "Oh God, no."

He'd rather be strung up than hear her cry. "Abbie, I didn't tell him anything, but he thinks it's the reason you won't marry me, and I've told him he's not to blame."

"Oh, Rhett."

"Abbie, I think you and Mac need to come over. Dustin says he won't leave my house until you tell him the truth."

"But…this will break his heart."

Like it had broken hers for over sixteen years.

"Abbie, it already has. Now we need to help it heal."

She cried softly. He gripped his phone in a vice, wishing he could scoop her up and comfort her.

"Abbie, I'm here, and I'll do anything I can to help. You aren't alone." No, he would never leave her. Any leftover bitterness from this morning had faded away. "Do you want me to call Mac?"

"No," she said, clearing her throat. "I'll…tell him. We'll be over as soon as we can."

"Okay, sweetheart. I'll sit with Dustin until you get here."

"I know you will, Rhett." And then she hung up.

His arm lowered to his side, and he rested his head against the wall. He finally understood the phrase of feeling bone-bruised.

After a moment, he threw the phone onto his bed and went out to join Dustin like he'd said he would.

He was hunkered down low in the leather couch. There were tear stains on his cheeks, and his nose was red.

"Your mom and Mac are on their way, son."

He walked over and sat next to Dustin, their sides touching. When the kid leaned toward him, Rhett put his arm around him.

"I wish I was your son," Dustin whispered.

It took a moment for Rhett to speak through the blockage in his throat. "Me too, son. Me too."

And as the light filtered in through the windows, he held the boy and remembered how his mama always told him Christmas was a time of miracles. And even though he was rusty at it, he offered up a prayer for the boy beside him, the woman he loved, and his best friend.

When he heard a car drive up, he squeezed Dustin one last time and kissed his head like he used to do when he was a little kid, all freshly bathed, smelling of Crest toothpaste and Johnson & Johnson shampoo.

Then he rose and walked to the door.

Abbie's face had never looked more ashen, and Mac's was close to green. Peggy held Mac's hand, and Mac held Abbie's.

When they reached the front porch, he said, "He's in the den."

Mac nodded, kissed Peggy's cheek, and started up the steps. Abbie wasn't moving with him, so he stopped.

"I can't seem to make my feet move any farther," she said, and then punctuated the silence with a sound of pain and disbelief.

There could be no jokes today, so Rhett didn't offer to

112

carry her inside. Instead, he said, "Take your time."

Her eyes flew to his, and in them, her fear shone through. "I can do this," she said, as if to herself. She took one step. Then another. "I have to."

And like Joan of Arc herself, she walked up those porch steps. When she passed him, she turned back and said, "Thank you for being with him, Rhett."

He raised his chin in acknowledgement. "I'll be in the study," he informed them.

Peggy followed him, not Abbie and Mac. He let her precede him into his private sanctuary.

She settled onto his leather sofa and crossed her arms over her chest.

"Can I take your coat?" he asked since she hadn't dispensed with it.

"It doesn't matter," she said, her voice monotone.

Dare's no-nonsense deputy sheriff was right. Who gave a fuck about pleasantries when a young man's world had just been irrevocably altered?

So Rhett just nodded and sat in the matching arm chair, and the two of them waited together.

It was interminable. He couldn't take his mind off of what might be going on in the other room. Of how fragile Abbie had looked as she'd walked up his porch. How fierce she'd been making love to him last night.

How could such polar opposites exist in one woman?

He didn't care. All he knew was that he would love her until his dying breath and beyond.

Mac finally came into the office. He walked directly to Peggy, who wrapped her arms around him. His friend lowered his face to her shoulder for a long moment and then lifted his head. He met Rhett's gaze, but didn't say anything.

What the hell was there to say?

The desolation was clear.

Abbie and Dustin appeared in the doorway, holding hands. Dustin gave his mother a long look, and then released her hand and crossed into the room. Rhett opened his arms, and the boy flew into them, crushing his face against his chest.

Dustin started crying, and with that sound, Rhett felt tears gather in his own eyes. He held onto the boy, wishing he could do more, wishing he could erase everything that had happened except for the precious gift of this boy's life.

Had Abbie realized that without what had happened they wouldn't have Dustin? Somehow a new peace entered his heart.

When he looked over at her, tears were streaming down her face. He held out his hand, and she glanced from it to his face. She took a few stumbling steps, and then she was rushing toward them. She pressed her body against Dustin's and wrapped her arms around him, and because Rhett's arms were long enough, he enfolded them both in his embrace.

Like his heart had already done.

Finally Dustin pushed back for air, and they shared a shaky laugh, which eased some of the tightness in his chest.

"I love you, kid," he said, ruffling the boy's sweat-soaked hair.

"I love you too, Uncle Rhett," he responded and wiped his nose with his sleeve.

Abbie reached for Dustin's other hand. "Thank you, Rhett," she whispered, and her eyes held a thousand promises—that they would survive this, that she was strong enough, that they would heal.

He hadn't thought he could love her any more than he did, but somehow it happened.

The smile he gave her wasn't his most charming, he expected, but it was real. The right corner of her mouth lifted in response.

Mac stepped forward and put an arm around him, and they man-hugged before they broke apart. Then he followed Abbie and Dustin to the front door.

"Let's go home, Mom and Uncle Mac," the kid said.

Peggy moved toward Rhett. "You did good," she whispered to him as she trailed after Mac.

He saw them all off, his chest feeling hollow, like he'd been suctioned to within an inch of his life.

As the car pulled away, Abbie gave him a slight wave, and like an eagle flying overhead, he felt the same sense of awe.

She loved him, and he somehow knew that what had happened today would help her break free of the past.

His holiday serenade was still on.

Chapter 12

Abbie threw Paulo Coehlo's *The Alchemist* aside and fell back on her pillows. She fluffed her down comforter and smoothed the violet bedspread.

There was no point in pretending. She couldn't read. She couldn't sleep. She could barely eat.

It was the day before Christmas Eve, and her son finally knew the truth about his father. About how he'd come into the world.

Part of her felt like her life was over, and in some ways, the one she'd grown used to had been blown to smithereens. She felt exposed. And heartbroken for her precious son, who had done nothing to deserve such origins.

Then she had to remind herself what Mac had helped her see. She hadn't deserved what happened either.

She reached out for the angel figurine by her bed—the one holding a star. It reminded her of that whisper from a few weeks ago. *Follow the star.* Christmas was about reclaiming the innocence of a child, and that's what she wanted for both of them.

Dustin would heal with their help and some family counseling.

And so would she. Finally.

Her thoughts wandered to Rhett. He'd checked in with everyone, including her—and he always came whenever Dustin wanted him.

But they hadn't spent any time alone since the party. Hadn't talked about what had happened between them, why she'd run, and why she now regretted it.

Dustin had come first.

After seeing how Rhett had handled Dustin's emotional turmoil, she finally believed he would make a good father. Correction. A great father.

Dustin loved him.

And so did she.

He'd been showing her for months how much he wanted to be there for her, from toning down his behavior to changing his poker babe act to throwing that lavish holiday party. Even writing her a romantic song. Settling down was the last thing she'd expected Rhett to do, and yet, here he was in a small town, attending Dustin's school events, going out for pizza with them, and gluing Christmas wreaths for her.

It was time they talked about *them*, about the future he wanted with her.

The strands of a piano reached her ears. The music was like a faint winter breeze, all dreamy and soft. Her mind identified the song right away—Rye Crenshaw's "The Holiday Serenade." Cancel that. The song Rhett had written, and Rye had sung.

She frowned. Was Dustin playing the song as part of his Cupid scheme? He'd told her to stop fighting her feelings and just marry Rhett. Seeing him in so much pain, she'd almost given in then and there.

But she needed to make the decision for herself, and no one else.

And she had. Now she just needed to talk to him.

Rising to investigate, her feet padded down the hall. The music grew fainter.

Mac's door opened. "Do you hear the music? It's your song, right?" he asked.

"I think Dustin's trying to play matchmaker."

The past few days had cut deep grooves into his face. Peggy had been a big comfort to him, but this business with Dustin had hit him hard. Worse, he and Peggy had to deal with the reality that Dustin might never have found out if not for what Peggy had said at the city council meeting. Families meant forgiveness, though, so that's what they all had done. Everyone had agreed Dustin should know at some point. Having him hear about it secondhand hadn't been ideal, but then again, any way they told him would have been hard.

"At least it's something to raise his spirits," Mac said.

Dustin stepped into the hallway. "Are you playing Rhett's song, Mom?" he asked, a spark of hope spreading across his haggard face. So he wasn't sleeping well either.

They'd turned down the furnace for the night, so the hallway held a chill. She drew her red Christmas robe more securely around her. "You're not playing it?"

"No," her son said. "I was watching TV."

"Abbie," Mac said, his voice gentle, "it's a song about a serenade. Maybe you should look out your window."

The furnace kicked on, warming her feet since she was near a vent. "My window?"

"Yeah." His smile was almost an afterthought.

"Cool," Dustin said, crossing the hall.

118

The hairs rose on her neck as she made her way back to her bedroom, Dustin and Mac's footsteps echoing on the hardwood floor behind her. If the music was outside, it could mean only one thing. She pulled back the white lace curtains. Given the fullness of the moon, she had no trouble making out the culprit and his accomplice.

Rhett stood under her window a few yards from the house, dressed in a sheepskin coat with white wool-out seams. He had a microphone in his hand. His friend, Rye, was seated on a foldout chair in a full-length black leather winter coat at what looked to be a portable piano, his black cowboy hat obscuring his face as he played the ballad of her song.

They were insane. It was *freezing* outside.

She opened the window, and the arctic blast made her shiver. "What are you *doing?*"

Rhett tipped his finger to his forehead even though he wasn't wearing a cowboy hat like Rye. His ears had to be frozen.

"I decided to serenade you like I should have the first time. I'm sorry I upset you by making a public declaration. I was only trying to show you how I felt. Plus, I don't sing worth spit, so having my friend do what he does best made sense. But as a wise man recently told me, never send another man to serenade your woman. So Rye's going to play, and I'm going to sing."

"Brace yourself," she heard Rye say.

"Shut up," Rhett bantered back, putting the microphone to his mouth.

Dustin edged closer to her at the window, and Mac put his hand on her shoulder, leaning forward so he could see.

While Rye played the refrain, Rhett started to sing. His voice cracked, and he missed the notes by a mile, going from baritone to alto at the wrong time. Dustin snorted, and Mac muffled a laugh, but it didn't matter.

The words he'd written for her finally went straight to her heart.

It lets me tell you that I want you,
That you're my Christmas dream come true,
That I don't see anyone now but you.

When he looked up, his eyes shining in the moonlight, her toes curled into the carpet. She believed him. He didn't see anyone but her. Didn't want anyone but her. Didn't love anyone but her.

She leaned against the jamb and wrapped her arms around her body as he continued to sing about how she was his Christmas dream come true.

Tears gathered in her eyes, and she could feel Dustin turn his head to look at her as she wiped them away. When her son put his arm around her, she rested her head on his still-growing shoulder.

Come cozy up by the fire with me,
Under the lights of our own Christmas tree.

As Rhett sang, she could envision the house they would share, his red stocking on the fireplace next to hers and Dustin's; she saw him holding her on the couch as the white lights on their Douglas fir tree cast a mellow glow on them.

Let me love you,
Serenade you,
My Christmas dream come true.

When his voice faded, he lowered the microphone and exhaled loudly, his head tipped up to the window.

He was so handsome that she pressed her hand to her rapidly beating heart.

Rye continued playing the piano, the lingering notes the only sound within hearing save the lone hoot of an owl.

When his friend finished, Rhett held out his arms. "I love you, Abbie. Merry Christmas." Then he gave a dramatic bow and gave her a winning smile.

"Oh, Rhett," she said. "What am I supposed to do with you?"

"Marry the poor guy," Rye suggested, rising from the piano. "Anyone who sings like that and does it out here freezing his—"

"Ahem," Rhett coughed.

"Sorry. Nether parts off. I've known him a long time, Abbie, and trust me, you've got him so tame, even a zoo wouldn't take him."

"You're fired," Rhett called out to his friend and rubbed his boot in the snow. "Abbie, *this* is my Christmas present to you. I'm not expecting anything more."

"Ah, give the guy a break, Mom," Dustin said from beside her. "He's crazy about you."

Rhett waved to him. "Thanks, son."

"You lost your nickname tonight, Rhett," Mac called down. "You're no Liberace."

Slapping his knee with one hand, he said, "I know! I told you I couldn't carry a tune. Thank God you don't have any dogs because I would have set them to howling." Rhett raised his gaze toward her again, her cowboy-lovin' Romeo. "Did you like the song better this time 'round, Abbie?"

What was not to love about his romantic gesture? She

raised a finger to her lips, wanting him to kiss her. "I'm a sucker for a man serenading a woman outside her window."

His grin lit up his whole face. "I'm glad to hear it. I thought about wearing a monkey suit, but I didn't think I could pull it off. Plus, it's like eight degrees out." And the white puff from his breath punctuated the point.

She had to disagree with him. He'd look super handsome in black tie, but she understood his meaning.

Black tie wasn't him.

And wasn't that what she needed to come to terms with? She had to love him for him, not for what she wanted him to be.

And she did.

The North Star seemed to wink at her in the star-studded dark sky, while Rhett stood there waiting. Rye started packing up the piano beside him.

Her heart beat so rapidly it felt like someone was drumming her entire body. "Are you asking me to marry you, Rhett?" she finally asked.

Rye grinned and slapped his friend on the back.

"Are you ready to say yes?" he fired back, the light from the North Star shining in his eyes now.

She'd followed the star, and it had led her to Rhett. Why wasn't she surprised?

She cocked her head to one side, suddenly shy. "Come inside and find out."

Even in the moonlight, she could see his shoulders relax. He gave her a lop-sided smile. "That'd be mighty fine."

"Finally!" Rye called.

Her face pressed against the screen. "I'll meet you at

the door in a few minutes."

His arms extended from his body like he was embracing the entire globe. "Don't rush. I've got all the time in the world."

She bumped into her brother when she tried to turn around. The grin on his face encouraged one to spread across her own.

Dustin high-fived Mac and then grabbed her in a huge hug, lifting her off the ground. "Oh, mom, this is the best Christmas present ever!" And his joy was as pure as when he'd been a two-year-old kid receiving his first fire truck.

When he finally set her back down, she laid her hands on his shoulders. "Are you sure, Dustin? Because I love you and only want—"

"Yes!" he cried. "I want you to marry Rhett. I want you to be happy. You deserve it." And then his eyes grew a little wet. "And I want him to be my dad."

"Oh, Dustin," she said, pulling him into another hug, tears running down her face.

Mac handed her a linen handkerchief—where had he found it? He always seemed to have one ready for her when she needed it. She dabbed at her eyes.

"Uncle Mac, just because I want Rhett to be my dad, doesn't mean—"

Mac pulled him in for a hug. "I know, kid. I'm so happy for you." And then he pushed him back playfully and gave Abbie a much gentler hug.

They held each other for a minute. They had been through so much together, but their relationship was changing. Soon, he would live with Peggy and Keith, and she would live with Dustin and Rhett.

"I'm so happy for you, Abbie," Mac whispered,

kissing her hair. "Now, go open the door for the poor man. It's freezing outside."

Her feet took three steps toward the door and then stopped. She fingered her robe, casting a glance at her closet. There was no way she was going to have the man she loved propose to her while she was in bare feet and a Christmas robe.

"You let him inside. I'm going to change."

Dustin groaned. "Oh, jeez. Full makeup?" he asked like he knew how long that would take.

"Yes," she answered, slapping him on the tush like she used to do when he was little. "Full makeup. Now go."

Mac and Dustin playfully bumped each other all the way out of her room. When the door closed behind them, she rushed into her closet, where she pulled out a red silk shirt and a black pencil skirt. Added thigh-high hose because she was going to somehow find a way to make love with Rhett tonight. Even if they had to use his car to conceal themselves from Dustin's prying eyes.

She laughed out loud as she searched for her black heels. She was clearly demented.

Abigail Maven was thinking about having sex in a car.

Oh, happy day!

Humming her song—*her own song!*—she strode into her bathroom and slowly applied her makeup, knowing the one thing women have known since the beginning of time: a woman can take all the time in the world when the man waiting for her wants her badly enough.

Smiling to herself, she added a spritz of Rhett's favorite perfume. She hadn't used it since she'd broken off their relationship. And she'd never before worn it in public.

It had been too exotic for Abbie Maven's image. Well, not anymore!

She threw her old conservative scent, the "cold stranger" one, in the trash can and gave the new one the place of honor on the counter. What did people say around Christmas? Out with the old, in with the new. Or was it a New Year's saying? *Who cares?* she decided.

They were words to live by.

Taking a last glance in the mirror, she fingered the V of her red silk blouse. Showtime.

She detoured to the kitchen, trying to walk softly in her three-inch heels. Impossible. Still, she hoped they would let her make an entrance. She wanted to set the stage.

"I'm in the *den*," Rhett called out like they were playing hide-and-go-seek.

"*Okay*," she volleyed back, her pulse thrumming.

She didn't hurry to leave the room, and after another moment, he yelled back, "You don't want me to propose in the kitchen, do you?"

It was her favorite room in the house, but no. "Be out in a sec."

"What are you *doing* in there?" Rhett asked like he was completely exasperated.

She selected a full-bodied Temperanillo from Spain from the wine rack and two Vera Wang glasses from the china cabinet with shaking hands. Okay, so she was a bit nervous. It wasn't every day a girl received a marriage proposal. She took a deep breath. It was normal to be nervous.

Straightening her spine, she walked in the direction of the den. Then she remembered Rhett liked beer, not wine.

Well, too bad. This was her proposal too.

He was pacing by the Christmas tree when she emerged—something he never did. Rhett sauntered or strolled; he never paced.

"I thought you were hiding from me."

"No," she said, giving a nervous laugh. The glasses clinked against the wine bottle when she held them up. "I was getting us a drink."

The tense lines around his mouth and eyes relaxed. "Good idea."

She squeezed the neck of the wine bottle, moved by his blatant vulnerability. "I hope wine is okay."

"At this moment, it could be dishwater, and I wouldn't care." Then he kicked at something invisible on the woven Southwestern area rug. "Sorry, that's not very romantic."

But somehow it was sweeter for it.

"Where's the crew?" she asked, looking around.

He stuck out his thumb. "I told them to take a hike. The last thing you want is an audience. I learned that at the party. The guys are staying at my house tonight." And then his eyes finally lifted to hers. "If that's not presuming too much."

He was always a few steps ahead of her. Her lips twitched. "I was considering having sex with you in your car since Dustin was around."

He bit his lip as if to keep from laughing. "Why, you little vixen."

And using that word, the stage name for one of his poker babes, reminded her of what he'd done for her.

"Rhett, you don't have to get rid of the poker babes. I'll come to terms with them somehow. I know how

126

important they are to your image."

His golden eyes looked liquid in the soft light from the Christmas tree. "Images can change. Aren't I going to be a husband and a father? Or is that putting the cart before the horse?"

She'd never understood what that phrase meant, so she just shook her head. "Can we sit down?" It suddenly seemed silly that she was still standing across the room, holding the wine and glasses. Plus, her legs were trembling in her heels.

He walked toward her, the power and size of him stealing her breath away. She realized he'd dressed up for her, in black pants and a navy button-up shirt.

"Why don't we?" he said, taking everything from her hands.

He unscrewed the cap off the wine bottle and poured them drinks with the same fumbling earnestness with which he'd sung. The Christmas tree lights spilled a magical glow over the den. The intimacy of the moment flooded her senses. There was romance here, just like she'd always wanted. She rubbed her arms briskly as a shiver ran through her.

"You cold?" he asked, coming closer to her and handing her a glass.

She shook her head.

He gave that secret, sexy smile of his and raised his glass to her. "To the most beautiful woman in the world."

That did it. She turned, put her glass down on the coffee table, and pressed her hands to her face. "Oh, Rhett."

"Abbie," he said, rubbing her back in even strokes. "How does one simple compliment reduce you to tears?"

"You've been so good to me, and I've given you nothing in return." A gold star winked at her from the treetop. "I'm sorry I ran out on you the other morning. And then how you've helped with this horrible thing with Dustin…"

"Hey! There's no reason for you to beat yourself up, Abbie." He pulled her into his arms, the wine forgotten. "I want you happy, not sad."

She wanted that to. "Rhett, I've been so scared of this, of you."

His large, warm palm cupped the back of her neck, and the comfort of his touch began to soothe her. "How about you try something new and stop fighting what you feel? We need each other, Abbie. Look at me."

His command brooked no refusal. She pressed back and met his golden gaze.

His head tilted to the side as he studied her. And then he lowered to one knee by the couch, reached inside his pocket, and pulled out a black box. With the flip of a finger, he popped it open. The antique square-cut setting of the diamond made her eyes tear. It was exactly the ring she would have picked out. It showed her how well he knew her.

"Abigail Anne Maven, I can't live without you, and don't ever want to try again. Will you do me the honor of marrying me?"

Moment of truth time. Looking into his beloved face, the words came easily. "Yes, Rhett, for better or for worse."

"There will be a lot of the better variety, trust me." The glimmer of a smile played across his face. "I thought you'd *never* say yes."

He rose and fitted his mouth to hers in a long, drugging kiss after putting the ring on her finger. Her tears finally spilled down her cheeks, and her heart burst with joy before settling back into place with a warm fire-like glow. She kissed his cheeks, eyes, and neck, reacquainting herself with all the parts of him she'd denied herself.

"Ah, Abs," he whispered, his voice hoarse as he pressed her closer to him. "There's no one but you."

"Don't go away." She inhaled his spicy cologne, her senses awash in him.

"Haven't you been listening? We're getting married. I'm never leaving."

"Good," she decreed, finally giving herself permission to curl into him, love him. "Dustin's over the moon about us."

His hand made a gentle slide up and down her back. "Me too. I love that kid, Abbie, and I promise to do right by him."

"I know you will, Rhett." And it was true.

"Rhett, would you play the song you wrote for me and just dance with me?"

"So long as I don't have to sing again, I'd be happy to, sweetheart," he said, reaching for his phone and punching in the keys until the opening melody spilled out.

"I love you, Rhett," she said when he took her right hand and guided her left to his shoulder, the perfect frame. "Wait. You took cotillion?"

"My mama insisted."

"I do like to dance," she confessed, especially when it involved brushing her highly sensitive body against his.

"Then we'll do it often. I'll even teach the kid if you want. The girls love it." He coughed and then gave her a wink. "Not that I'd know anything about that."

"Right," she said, rolling her eyes.

For a long moment they were quiet, just swaying in time with the music. Then he peered into her eyes. "I love you, Abbie. Thanks for being my Christmas dream come true," he said, his feet not missing a beat.

She tunneled herself into him, and he wrapped his arms around her. "Thanks for being mine."

And as she looked at the Christmas tree, she was sure the angel on top winked at her.

Epilogue

The brown-sugar ham filled the house with a delightful smell on Christmas day. Meredith Hale had agreed to host everyone for dinner since she and her husband had the biggest house. But she'd made her brother-in-law, Brian, swear on his twin baby daughters that he'd help her cook the meat for the whole crew.

Abbie sat on the couch next to Rhett. Rye Crenshaw was singing Christmas carols as Peggy played the piano, something Mac had encouraged her to pursue. She was really good at it too, or so Abbie thought. Even if she hadn't been, Rye's toffee-smooth voice would have coated over any missed notes. Heavens that man could sing.

Mac and Dustin were sitting on the adjoining loveseat, smiling like two crazy people at her and Rhett.

"So, now that Rhett's going to be my stepdad, you're not going to be able to ground me anymore, right?" Dustin said to his uncle.

Mac put his arm around Dustin. "You think Rhett's going to be a softy, huh? Sorry to ruin your fantasy. The ones who run wild tend to be the toughest."

Rhett leaned across her. "I'm creating a new image for myself, kid," he said, "so let's make a deal. Don't do anything stupid, and I won't have to show you how tough I can be."

"Somehow I think I'm getting the raw end of that deal," Dustin complained. He jumped off the couch when Keith came into the room, gleefully waving around his new remote-controlled airplane.

"We're going outside to fly this baby," Keith said.

His Uncle Tanner had the remote, so the boys crowded him.

Mac strolled over. "Let's show them how this is done."

As they headed outside, Abbie lowered her head to Rhett's shoulder. "He's going to get through this, isn't he?"

"Yes," he assured her. "There's no doubt in my mind. And if there's a few dips in the road, we'll help him out of them."

"I thought this was going to be the worst Christmas ever, and then everything changed." She turned her engagement ring in the soft light, loving the way the diamond sparkled.

"Rhett, why don't you come on over and sing Abbie her song?" Rye called out when "White Christmas" came to an end. "Jill wants to hear the rendition you performed the other night."

"So do I," Peggy said, cracking her knuckles over the black-and-white piano keys.

Abbie started to laugh. She couldn't help it. "Go on," she said with a playful jab to his chest. "Your audience awaits."

"Audience my ass," he said, but he stood and strolled over to his friend, planting his fingers in his belt loops.

"Just you wait. When you fall hard for a woman, I'm going to remind you of this day."

"Never going to happen," Rye said, picking up his glass of bourbon, raising it to Abbie in a toast.

"I recall saying something similar."

"I have better genes."

"And tighter ones," Jill added from her position beside the piano, eyeing his black jeans. "If only I wasn't married."

"And the mother of my baby twin girls," Brian called out from the doorway, wiping his hands on his apron. "Get over here, Red."

She did, and he dipped her and kissed her until she finally gave him a shove.

Arthur smacked his cane on the floor from his seat near the fire. "Now that's how they did it in my day."

All of them burst out laughing.

"Abbie," Mac called from the doorway, staying out of sight.

She bit her lip to hide a smile. "Be right back," she told Rhett and then walked out of the family room to join her brother. "Is it here?"

"Yes, be glad for rush jobs." The crate in his hand dipped as the inhabitant shifted.

Crouching on her knees, Abbie looked inside the metal grate. The cutest Chinese Crested puppy peeked out at her, its pointy muzzle bobbing up and down curiously. With a dark brown hairless body dotted with white spots and streaks, it had fine white hair that resembled a Japanese Anime character's bob and matching hair on its feet, making it look like it was wearing legwarmers. Its alert, sparkling brown eyes melted her heart.

"Oh, she's perfect!" Abbie said. "This dog will be a great part of Rhett's new act."

Rhett wasn't backing down on giving up the poker babes, and she wasn't about to fight him on it. They really were embarrassing.

"I hope this is a good idea," Mac said. He put a finger to his lips when Keith and Dustin ambled into the foyer and found them conspiring.

"Oh my gosh," Keith said.

"Is that a—"

"Shhh, Dustin," Abbie whispered, taking the crate from Mac. "Time to get this show on the road, as Rhett would say."

Thankfully the dog didn't bark when she walked into the room, and she shook her head when Jill's mouth dropped open. As she approached the couch, Rhett leaned back, stretching his feet out.

"And what might that be, Abs?" he asked, an intimate tenor in his voice that never failed to light a fire in her belly.

"This is my Christmas present to you. For your new act. Sans the poker babes."

His eyebrow winged up when she placed the crate on the couch. Fiddling with the door, she drew out the pint-sized puppy. And she'd added to the act, hadn't she, by purchasing the dog a green Christmas sweater and red bow for its hair?

Rye barked out a laugh. "Dear God, that's the strangest looking dog I've ever seen."

Everyone else started chuckling with him.

"Isn't that the dog from *How To Lose A Guy In Ten Days*?" Meredith asked from the doorway.

"It's like you're part of a chick flick," Rye called out.

Thrusting the dog out at Rhett, Abbie grabbed the crate, clenching the handle tight from nerves. "You *said* you wanted an exotic dog, and that's what a Chinese Crested is. They're a really playful breed and don't bark much, which will be an advantage since you play in casinos. Plus, they don't pant."

"There's a joke there," Mac drawled from behind her.

"Dear God," Rhett said, holding the fine-boned, slender dog over his lap in his massive hands.

It squirmed and gave a ruff. Thank God it was potty trained.

Rye came over and sat on the arm of the couch by his friend. "Good thing it's not a cat, or I'd have to call you a—"

"Rye! Not in front of the kids," Abbie chastised.

The bad boy country singer didn't even have the sense to look chagrined. Shaking his head, Rye continued to laugh. "It's definitely going to be a new act for you. Maybe I'll get you matching cowboy boots for your birthday."

"Shut up," Rhett said, and then winced, likely from the lack of fur, as the dog cuddled close to him and rubbed its head against his chest.

"It doesn't shed," she said, trying to sell him on the dog.

"No shit," Rye commented, running a finger over the hairless body. "Oops, sorry." He cast a glance to Keith, who stood looking at the dog like it was an alien.

"It looks like a girl," Keith said.

"You might need glasses if you think that," Mac said, pulling him close.

"Its mop of hair kinda looks like yours, Mom," Dustin said, edging away from her as he spoke.

"Thank you very much, Dustin Maven," she said, putting down the crate and making a move toward him.

"Actually, Dustin, I see what you mean," Rhett said. "It looks like when your mom blow dries her hair. And since I can kinda see the resemblance, I'm going to call her Annie since your mama's middle name is Anne. She can be my—"

"Don't say it," Abbie warned, thinking he was going to say bitch.

His mouth pursed as he fought not to laugh. "I was going to say *second lady* since she's a gift from my soon-to-be wife."

"I already miss the poker babes in their sequined dresses," Rye said, lurching off the couch when Rhett tried to hand the dog to him.

"That's because you aren't the one who's lucky enough to be engaged to the most beautiful woman in the world. Just you wait—"

"Henry Higgins," Rye filled in for him.

Abbie sat next to Rhett and patted the poor dog, who didn't deserve this treatment. "I can return her if you don't like it. I know Rav—"

"Jane, my new dog walker, *was* looking into breeds," Rhett interrupted, reminding her to use Jane's real name.

He'd told her everything about his poker babes, saying it was crucial to their future together. She'd listened, and what she'd learned had surprised her, proving that old adage of not judging a book by its cover, even if it happened to be covered in sequins. For Rhett's sake, she was going to try and meet them after the holidays. He didn't expect them to be friends, he'd said, but he hoped they would be friendly. Hearing they were like his sisters had cinched it for her.

"This dog is perfect. Plus, it's so much nicer since you bought her for me."

"Sucker," Rye said, drinking his bourbon.

"You bet," Rhett responded. "Now, since I'm feeling in the Christmas spirit, why don't you play my song, and I'll sing to my sweetheart?"

"Do I have to?" Rye said, dragging his feet to the piano that Peggy had eagerly vacated.

"Be your punishment for talking so badly about this little lady. Abbie and Annie. My two girls."

"I think I'm going to throw up. In my mouth," Dustin said from beside her.

Then Rhett started to sing, his voice so off-key the adults winced. Arthur put his hands over his ears. "If I didn't like to see two young people finally getting together, I'd shove my cane in Rhett's mouth to stop him."

Rhett didn't miss a beat. He just continued looking at Abbie with those golden eyes, holding the dog to his chest. And when he put the puppy on top of the piano, making Rye shoo her aside when she tried to lick his face, Abbie took the hand Rhett held out and cuddled in close.

His holiday serenade had made this one Christmas she'd never forget.

Gingerbread Houses

Recipe by Ava Miles' Great-great Grandma Miles, circa 1900
Baked by Abbie Maven at Christmas

Gingerbread
1 c. butter
1 c. sugar
Cream these two ingredients.
Add ½ c. hot coffee
¾ c. molasses
5 c. flour
1 tsp. salt
1 tsp. soda
¼ tsp. nutmeg
1 ½ tsp. ginger
½ tsp. cloves
Mix the ingredients. Chill for at least 1 hour. Overnight is best.

Icing
4 egg whites
5 c. sifted powdered sugar
Beat egg whites until stiff and slowly add the powdered sugar. Keep covered when not using since the icing dries quickly.

House Dimensions
Roll dough onto a lightly floured surface. Cut the shapes outlined below:
2 Side Walls: 4x6 inches
2 Roof Pieces: 7x8 inches
Base: 10 inches
2 End Pieces: 6.5x6x4
*You can half the dimensions to make a smaller house if you want to start small and practice as you become more adept at assembling. If so, half the frosting recipe too.

Bake at 375 degrees for 3-4 minutes on parchment paper (less time if you use the half dimensions).

Cook pieces in the oven and let cool on a wire rack. Place the frosting in a pastry bag with a small decorating tip. Anchor the base cookie on aluminum foil or parchment paper and use the frosting to glue it down. Secure the end piece and one side wall with frosting and let dry for 30 minutes after propping up. Remove prop and join other side wall and end piece. Prop up and follow earlier instructions. Add the roof next and secure the walls with additional frosting to secure the structure.

Then use your imagination. Add whatever seems to work for your house: gumdrops, chocolate Santas, etc. You can also dye the frosting different colors to decorate the house if you want to go wild—like Abbie does.

If you have leftover dough, form them into gingerbread men or other shapes and bake at 375 for 8-10 minutes. Rhett suggests you make both male and female gingerbread cookies (sugar sprinkles for sequins optional). Enjoy!

THE

Town SQUARE

AVA MILES

To my grandfathers, one I knew, and one who had passed on long before I was born. To Ray Bosn, for Root beer floats, glazed donuts, McDonalds sundaes, and Easter eggs in his shoes. For his infectious laughter and twinkling eyes and the endless car trips he made to see us and give us joy. I miss you. And to my great-great grandpa, George Miles, who came out West in search of a better life, won our first family newspaper in a poker game, fought vigilantes, stood for justice, and printed the truth. Now I know who I'm from, and I can't wait to meet you in heaven. But one thing I know for certain is that you both will be entertaining each other with tall tales until I get there.

And to my divine entourage, who continues to show me so much more is possible and that I'm on the right track.

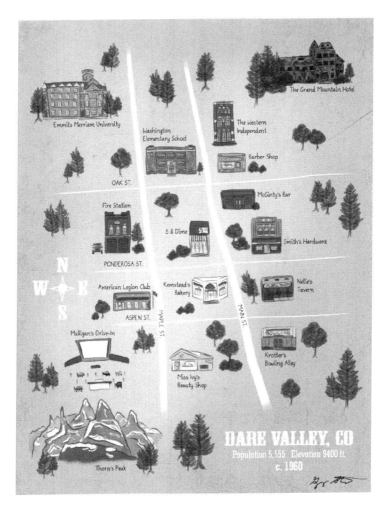

Emmitts Merriam University

Washington Elementary School

The Grand Mountain Hotel

The Western Independent

Barber Shop

OAK ST.

Fire Station

McGinty's Bar

5 & Dime

Smith's Hardware

PONDEROSA ST.

N
W — E
S

American Legion Club

Kemstead's Bakery

Nellie's Tavern

ASPEN ST.

MAPLE ST.

MAIN ST.

Mulligan's Drive-In

Krotter's Bowling Alley

Miss Ivy's Beauty Shop

DARE VALLEY, CO

Population 5,555   Elevation 9400 ft.

c. 1960

Thorn's Peak

Chapter 1

Babies sometimes made Arthur Hale feel as old as dirt, but mostly they made him smile. With his three-month old great granddaughter, Violet, tucked into the curve of his arm, he had to admit it was wonderful to have a baby around again.

And since his granddaughter, Jill, was an overachiever like he was, she'd given him not one, but two great-granddaughters. And they were beautiful, blessed with the red hair that was one of his late wife, Harriet's, legacies. Of course, the babies' hair looked like fuzz on a ripe peach now, but it would grow as they did.

The patter of rapid footsteps sounded in the hall, and one of his other favorite kids skidded to a halt at the door. Keith might be only eight years old, but he knew to be quiet around the babies. His mother, Deputy Sheriff Peggy McBride, had made that clear.

Tiptoeing inside, Keith approached the Amish rocking chair and peered over Arthur's arm. "Grandpa, do you think Violet knows she got christened today?"

Since he'd finally told Keith and Peggy to just call him "Grandpa," he couldn't help but smile. His granddaughters had added to the Hale clan through their marriages, and Peggy was his grandson-in-law's sister. Since everyone lived in Dare Valley, Colorado, the town of his birth and the town he'd be buried in, every weekend was a family fest. Arthur wouldn't have it any other way.

"I think there's a part of her that knows she's been blessed and celebrated today," he answered, wanting to straighten the red bow tie clipped to Keith's white shirt. Funny how bow ties looked cute on boys, but not on grown men. He avoided wearing them except when he had to put on the occasional monkey suit to attend some fancy gala.

Jill danced into the nursery with Mia in her arms, the movement rather like the cha-cha he used to dance with Harriet. Jill's curly red hair, leaf-green eyes, and porcelain skin came from Harriet. His beloved wife and best friend had passed away five years ago, and he still awoke each day hoping to smell the sweet hyacinth fragrance she always wore.

"Is Violet asleep?" Jill asked.

"Out like a light, if the amount of drool is any indication," he replied with a wink, picking up the burp rag to wipe her rosebud mouth.

"Mia too," she said, sinking into the purple arm chair in the corner, which clashed oddly with the explosion of bubble gum pink that decorated the nursery. "I think we can talk in our regular voices now. They're like Brian. When they're out, a passing train couldn't wake them. Do you want me to take her, Grandpa?"

He snorted. "And put her where? On your back? You already have one on the front."

Her curls bounced as she made a face at him, causing Keith to giggle. "I could lay Mia down."

"But you don't want to because she's so sweet. That's why I'm keeping Violet here. Been ages since I've held a baby. I plan to clock as many hours as I can with these two."

Jill's eyes suddenly filled with tears. "Maybe it's the christening, but I really wish Grandma could see them. I think about her all the time since I've had them. Sometimes I even think I smell her hyacinth lotion."

Goosebumps broke out over Arthur's arms. After Harriet's passing, he'd experienced the same thing. Made him believe she was an angel now, watching over them all from her place in heaven. He coughed and had to look away when he spotted the wetness in Jill's eyes.

"She'd have loved these little ones. She had a soft spot for babies. Always wished we could have had more than your dad, but it just didn't happen."

"What didn't happen?" his other granddaughter, Meredith, whispered from the doorway. Peggy was beside her, hanging back a little.

"The girls are out," Jill said in a normal voice. "You don't have to talk like that. How's it going downstairs?"

"Mac's talked the men into playing football even though it's only twenty degrees outside," Peggy said.

"Sweet," Keith said and ran out of the room, ostensibly to join them.

"Where's Abbie?" he asked. It made him happy to see her and her fiancé, Rhett Butler Blaylock, looking so happy together.

"Helping Mom and Brian make dinner. They shooed us out." Meredith propped her hand on her hip. "Said we were in the way. Now what were you two talking about when we interrupted? Jill, I saw tears in your eyes."

"Grandma," she whispered. "I miss her, especially

today, seeing Mia dressed in the christening gown she made for dad."

Meredith came over and touched her sister's shoulder. Still hanging back in the doorway, Peggy looked like she was about ready to join the men. Tears made her squirm.

"Grandma was a softy. She would have melted, seeing these beautiful girls."

And he could tell Meredith was about to tear up too. If he didn't do something fast, this was going to become a pity party, and while he didn't mind tears, Harriet wouldn't have wanted everyone bawling their eyes out on this special day.

"Your grandma was hardly a softy," he told the girls. "You must be thinking of someone else."

His granddaughters exchanged a puzzled look and then gave him their full attention.

"What?" Meredith asked. "Sure she was."

He tucked Violet closer and started rocking, loving the motion. "She was a hard case when I met her. Rather like Peggy."

Now Dare Valley's deputy sheriff was staring at him too. "Like *me?*"

"Why do you think I understand all you tough-as-nails women and what new love does to you?"

"If I weren't so happy, I might object to that bunch of bull," Meredith said, her wavy red hair a stark contrast to her cream-colored sweater.

Arthur shifted the baby in his arms. "Your hair is closer to your grandmother's, Meredith. Jill, yours is a lot curlier, like my mother's."

"Why do you say she was so tough, Grandpa?" Meredith asked, coming forward and sitting on the floor next to him.

Peggy leaned against the doorway. "Part of me is glad you didn't get off so easy in the love department."

"Nothing worth having was ever acquired easily."

"Tell us the story again, Grandpa." Jill said, brushing a tear down her cheek. "I want my girls to hear it, and it seems like the right thing to do today. Like having Grandma here."

"Well, the girls won't understand it," Peggy said, "but I'd love to hear it. I've always wondered what you were like when you were younger."

Arthur decided he might as well tell it. Harriet was already in the room, and this new generation, even small and sleeping, deserved to know how it had all started.

"Well, I met her around this same time of year fifty-three years ago. It was December 1960. Kennedy had just become president, but hadn't moved into the White House yet. I was twenty-three and had just returned to Dare Valley after working in New York at *The New York Times*," he continued, and then started rocking faster in the chair as he took a stroll down memory lane.

***

Arthur spread the newspapers across his beaten-up desk in their proper geographic order with *The New York Times* flanking the right side and *The San Francisco Chronicle* flanking the left. One day he was going to print a paper as respected as they were, but first, he needed a working office space.

"Herman," Arthur called over the incessant hammering in the next room. "When are those bookshelves going to be ready?"

The stacks of boxes spread around his new office building were driving him crazy. Perhaps he shouldn't have hired his high school chum for the renovation job, but having just started a business himself, he wanted to support his friend. Smith's Hardware had opened just last week.

"I'm doing the best I can, Arthur. You don't have a level surface anywhere in this place. No wonder the bank built a new building. It's taking longer to make the boards level than I thought. I don't want your darn books to slide right off the shelves."

Right. He didn't need Herman Smith to tell him he'd bought a building with character. But it had been the only one available on Main Street, and he'd wanted to be situated right in the heart of Dare Valley. *The Western Independent* didn't need to be fancy, as the newly stenciled sign on the front door announced with its simple black lettering. All that mattered was that the paper delivered good content. A quality newspaper sold copies. And his wasn't just going to be good. It was going to be great. There was a niche for this newspaper—he just knew it. The people out West needed news that wasn't tinged with the East Coast bias he'd run across over and over again in New York.

Plus he had the backing of the man who'd changed his life, Emmits Merriam, the oil tycoon who had come to Dare Valley as a young man to gamble at The Grand Mountain Hotel, now abandoned. Darn shame, that.

Emmits had built a summerhouse in Dare in the 1940s, and Arthur had run errands for him in high school until he gave the older man his take on oil exploration in Iran one day, which had made Emmits regard him with new eyes. His parents hadn't understood why Arthur wanted to leave Colorado for college, but Emmits had. He'd even supported Arthur getting what he called a *superior* education, wanting him to "get worldly."

While attending Columbia University in New York City, he'd fallen in love with journalism, and Emmits had managed to secure him a position at *The New York Times*. He'd struck gold with his first story on inner-city crime, rising through the ranks quickly for a young man. And he'd enrolled in Columbia's Graduate School of Journalism, founded by his idol, Joseph Pulitzer, working day and night to become the best reporter he could be.

Emmits had declared the idea of Arthur becoming a journalist "capital" and had opened doors for him when he needed it, calling in favors for interviews with high-ranking officials or the elite.

Yet Arthur had begun to notice that the news in the paper he worked for didn't really represent the opinions of the people he came from. As people throughout the country took to the streets demanding to be heard, from women to people of color, he experienced a proverbial light bulb moment. He wanted to create a newspaper that would represent people's opinions out West. Decision makers in Washington and on Wall Street needed to hear them, and he would be the conduit. He pitched his idea to Emmits one night over Manhattans, and his mentor loved it. Since Emmits had run for the senate, he knew how important it was to learn the pulse of places that were completely alien to New Yorkers.

While Arthur had been the one to secure the main loan, Emmits had been more than willing to heavily invest in the project. He loved knowing there would be a visionary newspaper coming to Dare Valley right as he was building a new university in Dare. Named after himself—so Emmits—it would be opening next fall.

Launching a newspaper might seem like a lofty plan,

but Arthur wasn't intimidated. He was going to be the voice of the West, the *new* west.

He was smart, young, driven, and he had a vision. This new decade was ripe for huge change. Heck, 1959 had shown what kind of path they were on. The first microchip had been unveiled; the Civil Rights movement had gained prominence; and the first casualties in this war in Vietnam had been reported. And now they had a young, idealistic president, who'd captured the imagination of the country with his New Frontier. President Elect Kennedy was going to do great things. He could just feel it.

Arthur picked up the copy of *The New York Times*. Part of him couldn't wait until he held his own newspaper in his hands, the ink leaving a welcome imprint on his fingers.

Now that the 707 had taken its maiden nonstop voyage from coast to coast last year, he could follow stories where they led him. Cuba was so hot politically right now with all of Fidel Castro's hi-jinks, and he was thinking about trying to go there—even if that was pretty damn risky. He was still freelancing as a journalist for other papers while he got *The Western Independent* up and running, writing an article here and there. There was no way he could stop writing about the news. He'd wither like ivy cut away from the mother vine.

He'd arrived only a few weeks ago and was trying to hire his first staff position—a secretary. She'd help him set up the office while he began the process of hiring and training other reporters and staff for the May 7th launch of the newspaper.

Emmits was traveling with his wife, visiting his various companies across the United States. They didn't like the cold much, so they stayed away for a few of the brittle winter months, visiting their grandkids in California. When Emmits returned in March after being a snowbird, there would be a lot to show him.

Arthur had just picked up *The New York Times* when a woman's voice called out over the pounding of the hammer. "Excuse me," she said. "I understand you're looking for a secretary."

He looked up, the newspaper slipping through his fingers onto his desk. The woman's red hair was carefully coiled into that bun-thing women wore, and somehow it made her seem more elegant, like Rita Hayworth. Her green eyes were brighter and more alive than the trees in Sardine Canyon. And her skin? Well, he wouldn't compare it to the heaps of snow covering the ground outside, but there was a coolness to her that told him she liked to keep her distance from people.

"Yes, I am," he said finally, pushing the papers out of the way. Standing, he walked around his desk to her. "I'm Arthur Hale. And you are?"

"Harriet. Harriet Jenkins."

When she shook his hand, he wished she weren't wearing those darn navy gloves that matched her wool coat and pillbox hat. He would have liked to feel her skin against his.

"You're not from around here," he said, and gestured for her to sit while he rested his backside on his desk. She was too coiffed and finished to be a local; plus, he knew everyone here.

There was only one chair in his office besides his own, and it was rickety. She carefully slid into it. "No, I'm not from Dare. I heard around town that you've been pretty particular about typing skills, which is why you haven't found anyone yet. I can type one hundred words per minute and take shorthand at ninety per minute."

"That's pretty impressive," he said. It was true—he'd interviewed a few women around town without success. At best, he'd found a few who could maintain sixty words a minute. "Tell me a little more about yourself. Where you're from and where you went to school. Do you have a resume?"

"No, I don't." Folding her hands in her lap, she regarded him cooly. "I came from Denver, and there's not much more to tell. I'm happy to demonstrate my skills if you'd like."

Her accent suggested back East, but it was the finishing school kind of voice that was impossible to pin down. He stroked his chin. "You know you're talking to a journalist, right? I can't help but ask questions."

Her red-painted mouth tipped up. "What's more important to you? Someone who can type fast or someone who answers questions?"

The hands clenching her clutch purse like it was a life preserver made him wonder if she weren't quite as cool as her expression. He'd bet she was a city girl who was in some sort of trouble. No other reason for her to show up in Dare Valley, population five thousand and a few, and apply for this job.

"How did you hear about the position?" he asked.

"You ran it in several newspapers," she replied vaguely.

He had, but no woman from outside of Dare had applied. It didn't pay well enough for a woman to relocate, and if she were married, her husband would need to find a job here, which complicated the situation.

She scanned his space, and with all the boxes and the mess, who knew what she was thinking? The walls were still blank, but at least they were freshly painted white.

"Can I ask why your office is in the middle of the floor and not in the corner where there are windows?"

"I like to be in the middle of things," he replied.

"I see. So do you want to see if I'm telling the truth about my typing skills and shorthand?" she asked. "Otherwise, I will bid you good day."

Yeah, she was trying to act as cool as a cucumber— and beautiful to boot. He wondered about her marital status, but he wasn't about to ask, and the gloves concealed the answer.

"Fine," he said, gesturing toward the IBM Electromatic typewriter on his back desk. He grabbed an article he'd scratched onto a legal pad this morning. "Let's try this."

She dusted off his chair before sitting down and swiveling around even though he couldn't see a speck of dirt. Off came her gloves, revealing her perfectly manicured nails, which she so wouldn't have gotten in the basement beauty parlors around town.

And no, she wasn't married. Or at least she wasn't wearing a rock.

Sliding the paper he gave her into the typewriter, she propped his legal pad up and took a deep breath. Then her fingers started an intricate dance across the keys. He took a look at his watch as the *chik-chik-cha-chik-chik-chika-chik-cha-chik-Ding-ziiiiiiiiiiiiiiiip* of the typewriter filled the office. Her fingers flew over the letters and before he knew it, she was handing him the paper. He eyed the watch again, then the article.

Okay, she hadn't been bragging, and darn if there weren't a single error. Even with his own typing, there always seemed to be at least one mistake he'd have to blot out.

"I'm impressed," he mused, setting the paper aside.

She wiped her fingers on a linen handkerchief she pulled from her purse. It was embroidered with a single red rose. "So, did I pass the test?"

"Let's try your shorthand. Just for the heck of it." There was no way he wasn't spending as much time with this beautiful woman as he could. He'd been working like a dog, and he hadn't been out much since moving home to Dare.

Dare wasn't New York City. He missed the parties. The gallery openings. Having a drink at Sardi's or going to El Morocco, even though that place wasn't like it used to be.

And he was man enough to admit that he missed women. Not the local Dare variety.

Funny how she rather reminded him of the polished women he was used to meeting in the city. He hadn't been sophisticated, but his charm had allowed him to quickly blend in with those who were.

Harriet looked around for a Steno pad and, not seeing one, said "Your legal pad," holding out her hand. He gave it to her, and she drew a line down the center of the page to cut it in half. She did that on the next few pages also. She poised with one hand holding a pen and the other holding the bottom of the page, ready to flip it when it was filled.

Arthur paced beside his new Panasonic K21-10 color television. The article he dictated was one he'd been playing with for a while. He wanted to dive into what he thought President Kennedy's New Frontier could mean for the nation and how the young leader would face off against the Soviets, something everyone with or without a fallout shelter was wondering. When he finished dictating, he held out his hand for the legal pad. She looked up at him, startled. "Don't you want me to type it up?" He shook his head, no. He could read and write shorthand, and still wrote his interview notes in it. First, because the person he interviewed usually couldn't read it, and second, because he liked the idea of writing in a code. Made him feel like a secret spy.

"Impressive," he said again, wondering if she could have relocated from back East to Denver, which was only two hours away.

No one else around town could offer her skills, and even without a resume or any background information, she was his best candidate. He couldn't stand to do administrative work, and if she insisted she wouldn't answer any questions about herself, he could suck it up. Plus, there were piles of boxes someone had to file, and that someone wasn't going to be him.

"Okay, you're hired."

A secret smile appeared on her lips, and then she stood, pulling her gloves on once again, slowly and deliberately. God, how did women stand the bother of all that fuss about fashion?

"Wonderful," she murmured. "I only have one other request."

He took a step closer, studying her amused face. "Name it."

"I've heard some bosses like to call their secretaries 'sweetheart.' Don't."

Well, she'd just let something slip about her background. She'd never been a secretary, or she would have used the word "seen," not "heard."

"Oh, and I don't make coffee."

That was interesting. Didn't most secretaries do that?

156

To get her goat, he simply said, "So what should I call you?"

"Harriet," she informed him, turning toward the door and walking out. "Or Harry, if it makes it easier to remember not to call me 'sweetheart.'"

As he watched her gorgeous body stroll out of his office, one thought crossed his mind.

There was no way this woman could be mistaken for a Harry.

Chapter 2

Harriet walked down the freshly painted hall of *The Western Independent* and had to wonder again at her success.

She'd done it. She'd given him the fake last name she was using in town, so there was no turning back now.

Jenkins was a name she'd spotted on a mailbox as she and her sister were driving into town. It wasn't like she could use her own. He would have recognized Evangelina Wentworth immediately, and the whole reason she had for being here would have been rendered moot. Evangelina, while a family name, was a mouthful, so she'd gone by her middle name for most of her life anyway.

The sun was stark against the snow when she emerged from the old brick building. Dare Valley was charming with its Christmas decorations of angels and white lights dotting Main Street. Even though the sidewalks had been shoveled, she took care with a few icy patches as she made her way to her blue Buick sedan, mindful of the townspeople's inquisitive stares as she passed, feeling like an outsider. It was not a new feeling, or a pleasant one.

Arthur Hale wasn't at all what she'd expected. Part of her wished he hadn't been so attractive. His thick dark brown hair framed an arresting face punctuated with the keenest blue eyes she'd ever seen. He was tall and lanky, and he seemed to possess plenty of boy-next-door charm.

People said Arthur must have been born under a lucky star given the way he'd landed so many big stories in New York. Granted, he'd had the help of the oil tycoon, Emmits Merriam. People speculated Arthur had left a star-studded career in New York because of some arrangement with the man. Frankly, she could care less.

She eased the car onto the street, trying not to regret being here instead of in New York for the premiere of "Camelot"—where she should have been on this third day in December with her sister, Maybelline, who had some old school chums in the production. Harriet drove to the house she and her sister, Maybelline, were renting as the radio played "Georgia on My Mind" by Ray Charles. She sighed, letting its smooth, slow sound wash over her. It hadn't been easy to convince Burt Kennion to rent his recently deceased mother's house to them without a man's signature on the lease, but the man had finally agreed when she told him their father was dead and they were both unmarried.

Their father wasn't dead, but he might as well be. And Arthur Hale had caused it all.

He'd shot up the journalism ranks with a series of stories about a scientist who hadn't performed adequate testing on a new baby formula, which had resulted in the deaths of seven infants in three different states, the hospitalization of hundreds, and a total recall of the product.

That scientist had been her father. Dr. Ashley

Wentworth had rallied against the bad press, saying he and the company had adhered to the Food and Drug Administration's guidelines. But his protestations hadn't been sufficient in the face of such a disaster. Hale had been tenacious, and the first-person accounts from women who'd lost their children had turned the tide against her father.

He had lost his reputation as a scientist and gone progressively insane in the ensuing months. Since their mother was dead and Harriet was the older sister, the responsibility to commit him had fallen to her. Doing it had broken her heart.

She was here because she wanted to restore her father's reputation.

And to make Arthur Hale pay for his character assassination.

Once she found proof that he'd exaggerated the evidence he had on her father, she was going to discredit him. Her father had to be covering for someone else in the lab. He couldn't have done such a thing. She knew it wouldn't make up for the babies who had died, but at least it would clear her family's name and give them back their old life.

Under the media scrutiny, they'd been shunned by their friends and family in Boston. Wellesley—where Harriet had just matriculated from in May—had recommended that Maybelline take a leave of absence and not return for her sophomore year.

Since June they had been in limbo, barely leaving the house, unsure of what to do. Harriet couldn't find a job. Maybelline hadn't been able to get into another school. Her admissions applications were all politely declined despite her excellent academic record.

They were exiles in their brick townhouse in Beacon Hill.

Until one night three weeks ago, when her inner rage at the injustice of it all had finally compelled her to find a way to change their circumstances. After staring out at the full moon for two hours that night, she decided it was time to take action. She called *The Times* to ask after Arthur, but he had already left New York. The chatty secretary told her of his plans, which most of the people at *The Times* figured would flop. When she hung up, she realized he would need to hire staff, so for the next few days, she kept her eyes peeled on the employment section in *The Denver Post*. One morning she spotted his advertisement for a secretary, and that had set everything into motion.

So here she was, in the smallest place in the world. Amidst all these mountains, she felt even more powerless than she had in Beacon Hill. And even more afraid of doing what she'd vowed to accomplish.

She turned onto quiet Raven Street, where she and Maybelline now lived, pulling up to the simple baby blue A-frame house with its open porch. Some of the paint was peeling, the porch leaned like an old woman resting on a cane, and a few of the screens were missing, but it was home. With the new university being established, housing was scarce in Dare Valley. They'd been fortunate to find this place, furnished with dusty relics of a dead woman's past.

She parked the car in the driveway—one they'd borrowed from Warren Perkins, a cousin of Maybelline's former boyfriend, Eddie, who had promised to set them up with "some wheels" when they made it to Denver because he felt guilty for dumping her. They'd swapped their own car, which was registered under their real name, with

Warren's before making their way to Dare.

The sidewalk was freshly salted to melt the ice—Maybelline's doing—and Harriet headed into the house, the small rocks crunching under her feet with every step.

"Maybelline," she called out as she pulled off her coat and gloves and deposited them in the front closet. Her hat followed them.

Her younger sister didn't approve of Harriet's mission, but she'd opted to come with her rather than stay home alone in their old house.

"How did it go?" Maybelline asked, coming out of the kitchen with a cup of tea.

"I got the job," she said and smoothed a hand over her knotted stomach. "It's a good thing dad had me learn shorthand to help him with his notes."

Her sister's strawberry hair curled at her shoulders, less severe than Harriet's style today. She'd wanted to exude professionalism and cool detachment. Men found her attractive, and the last thing she wanted was for Hale to be interested in her. But despite her best efforts, she knew that he was.

"So, what's he like?" she asked, resting her tea cup against her pink cashmere sweater.

"We should turn up the heat," Harriet said, rubbing her hands together. "It's cold in here."

"You do that then while I make you a cup of tea. Then you can tell me about him."

Minutes later, they sat down with their Lipton tea at the small white laminate table in the kitchen, and Harriet ran her sister through the meeting, leaving out her impression of Hale's looks.

"I'm still not sure this is a good idea," Maybelline said. "Trying to prove he didn't properly investigate the story about father is risky. Everyone says Hale is smart as a tack. What happens if he catches you?"

Rubbing off the red lipstick stain she'd left on her tea cup, she said, "As his secretary, it will make sense for me to look at his files. Plus, from what I could see, there are boxes everywhere. One of the things his advertisement said was that he needed a filing system created for the office. If he has any questions about why I'm not just filing, but reading, I can play dumb. We both know how well that works with men."

Sadly, it had even worked on their father, who had never imagined his girls could be as smart as he was. Scientists had their egos, too.

"What do you want me to do? Other than be here for moral support."

"Just make the rounds. Keep your ear to the ground. Do the shopping—"

"And the cooking," her sister added. "I know the drill. I get to be the wife while you're off playing breadwinner. I should be able to pull that off, since we won't be here too long."

Harriet's mouth quirked up. They'd both lost boyfriends over their family's disgrace. Granted, neither had been serious, but it had wounded their pride. Being the daughters of a man people called The Baby Killer didn't exactly attract men like honey.

Suddenly Harriet wondered if they would need to permanently change their last name to Jenkins to have a normal life and do things like dating again.

"How's the TV reception?" she asked to change the subject.

"Abominable. I'm going to be unhappy if I can't watch *Rawhide*."

Harriet laughed. "Well, maybe you'll find your own cowboy around here. Hale is from a ranching family, after all."

"I'm not looking for a man right now. I just want you to finish this so we can leave. This town is way too small. I've decided to read all my favorite Christmas books while we're here. At least I can have a good holiday season through literature, since we won't be having one in this town."

Harriet threaded her fingers through her sister's and squeezed. "I know it's hard right now, but we'll make the best of it. We can make cookies and—"

"Keep our minds off everything we've lost. I know you keep saying I'll be able to go back to Wellesley, but we both know they might not welcome me back, even if you *can* prove father is taking the blame for someone else."

Harriet stood and walked across the room to the white linoleum counter. Untying the twist cinching the Wonder bread, she took out a piece and popped it in the toaster, taking her time to craft a response. Fortunately, her sister let her. She located the orange marmalade in the ancient white Kelvinator refrigerator and spread it on the toast when the bread popped up. The slightly cracked white dish she carried it on wasn't the Wedgewood china they were used to, but it served its purpose just as well.

"I don't want you to be afraid," she said, praying for the right words. "We'll figure something out."

"What about the money?" she asked, gazing at Harriet steadily.

The toast crunched when she bit into it, and she took her time chewing, searching for the right words. "We aren't poor, Maybelline, but we'll need to make some changes. The full extent of the fallout wasn't immediately apparent until I met with our accountant. Dad had invested everything into the company." Which had gone bankrupt months after Hale's first story broke.

"And his hospital care isn't cheap," she commented.

They both remembered the day they'd installed their father in the hospital. He barely recognized them anymore, having retreated so far into himself that even their pleas could no longer reach him.

The makings of a wry smile broke across Maybelline's face, putting a little of the usual sparkle into her hazel eyes. "Then I guess it's a good thing Hale's paying you."

"Yes," she replied, licking the orange marmalade off the corner of her mouth.

It would take time, but she would find what she was seeking.

She couldn't wait to pay Arthur Hale back for what he'd done to her family.

Chapter 3

Arthur watched as Harriet chatted with Ernest Pinkel, Dare's long-standing postman. From his position at his doorway, he could see that her smile was a lot brighter with the older gentleman than it was with him. He'd turned up the charm, trying to get her to add some warmth to her cool-as-a-cucumber attitude toward him, and when that failed, he amped up his banter. Her tense mouth hadn't moved a millimeter, and he'd started to think he was losing his easygoing effect on people. She was a total professional, he couldn't fault her there, but underneath it all, he could tell she didn't like him.

He hadn't asked her about that. That would have been stupid, and he wasn't a stupid man.

Plus she was the best damn secretary he could hope to find in Dare, so he wasn't complaining. Much.

"Harriet," he called, hating to interrupt their chat, but big news had just come over the teleprinter, and he wanted to start his Sunday editorial for *The Boston Herald*.

Her whole frame tensed up, and he watched as she pasted a fake smile on her face. "Yes, sir?" she asked.

Her formal, icy tone even sent Ernest's brows sky

high. "Sir? Well, if that don't beat all. I seem to recall you getting into trouble for throwing mud pies at the girls at the church picnic when you were in short britches and then having your daddy paddle your behind. Now you're being called sir. My how things change."

Had her mouth twitched for a second there? Well, he could take a jab to his ego if it made her relax around him. "Yes, and I seem to recall I threw one of those mud pies at your daughter. Even at six years of age, I had good aim."

Ernest puffed out his chest. "Why do you think I remember it so well? She fairly screamed bloody murder. That girl still hates getting dirty. Calls me to kill a spider even though she's a grown woman. She needs a husband. Why don't you come by the house tonight for supper, Arthur?"

He'd had many offers like that since returning to town. Fortunately, he'd managed to duck most of them, saying he was too busy getting the newspaper up and running. He wasn't sure how long it would last. He was prime marriageable age, after all, and being home, people expected him to settle down like everyone else did.

"Thanks, Ernest, but I'll be working late tonight. Had a big story come in. We'll have to make it another time."

"Of course," the postman said. "Seems like you're working like a slave here, not even stopping for a coffee break with folks when they stop by."

Because those breaks could take an hour, and he didn't have that kind of time. He'd even turned down his mom and dad when they popped in for a visit.

"It's hard work, starting a business. I'm happy to take a rain check though."

"Good. If you forget, I'll remind you. I'm just like the movie, *The Postman Always Rings Twice.*"

God, he hoped not. That movie had involved murder and betrayal, although Lana Turner had been steamy on screen. "I'll keep that in mind," Arthur said, and waved to him as he departed.

Some days he had to curb his impatience at the slow pace of his life in Dare Valley. Tell himself this wasn't New York. That he was starting up a newspaper, outfitting the old bottling factory outside town for printing and distribution in addition to creating this office as the hive. He had an operation to prepare.

He was more than a journalist now, Emmits had told him. He was an owner. And that made all the difference in the world.

"What's the big story?" she asked, rising from her chair situated perpendicular to his office, allowing him to see her if he angled himself to the left of his desk. Her heels made a tapping sound as she came into his office.

"France just lost another colony. The Ivory Coast has declared its independence. Colonialism is on its last legs in Africa."

"Goodness," she commented. "I wonder what that will do to France's exports and imports."

Not a typical comment from a woman, which made him more curious about her, but she was still tight-lipped about her past. He chewed on a pencil and kicked back in his chair.

"So if you're ready." He started dictating his editorial on how independence was sweeping its way through the former colonies of France and Britain, linking it back to Civil Rights in the U.S.

"Freedom is on the move," she commented when he finished. "I like that. You sound like a regular crusader when you talk like that."

"I am. I believe in justice. In freedom."

She bowed her head and studied the Steno pad in her lap. Since she'd dispensed with wearing her gloves in the office, he could see the whites of her knuckles.

"Harriet?" he asked quietly. "Is everything okay?"

She shook her head, making him wish she wore her hair down. He'd love to see it cascade down her shoulders just once.

Then the fake smile appeared, revealing her perfect teeth. "Of course. Why wouldn't it be?"

He leaned forward and rested his elbows on the desk. "I know you don't want me to ask you any questions, and I respect that. But if you're in any sort of trouble, I'd like to help you."

Every day he saw her confirmed it. Something was wrong, and she was miserable from it. She worked like a fiend, filing more than anyone he'd ever seen in a day's time. She even stayed late like he did.

Her mouth tensed, and the fake smile disappeared. Her green eyes transformed into burning emeralds before she lowered her lids. "Thank you. That's very kind, but everything is fine." And then she rose.

His impatience got the better of him, and before he knew it, he'd sprung out of his chair and cupped her elbow in his hand. Her perfume, something floral—was that hyacinth?—tickled his nose. With a foot between them, he realized she only came up to his shoulder. And he had the almost irrepressible urge to pull her close and make her tell him why she was trying so hard to keep her secrets.

"Everything is not fine," he uttered in a soft voice. "You're in some sort of trouble, aren't you? Let me help you, Harriet."

Her gaze flew to his, and for the first time, he looked

into the part she kept under lock and key. The confusion, the fear, the rage. It was all there, boiling and bubbling inside her like a white-hot inferno.

She put a hand on his suit jacket, right below his shoulder. He didn't know if she meant to push him away or was seeking a connection. Waiting for her seemed like the right thing to do.

"There's nothing wrong with me," she whispered and lowered her head again.

"Bull." He couldn't stand it, so he pulled her close. "You're suffering for some reason, and I hate seeing that. Please tell me how I can help you. I promise you can trust me."

She lurched in his arms, and he pulled his hands away. She stood gaping at him, fists clenched by her sides. "Trust you? I don't even know you."

The outer part of his heart was burning, perhaps from the fire in her eyes. And then he realized the truth. "Yes, you do. And that's what scares you."

Her head moved back and forth in denial, and then she was striding out of his office.

He ran his hands through his hair. He was falling for a woman with secrets.

Funny, that's what scared him too.

Chapter 4

After the worst Christmas and New Year's she and Maybelline had ever had, Harriet threw herself even more into organizing Arthur's files. She was down to fifty boxes, having filed over eighty so far. By God, the man kept everything it seemed, from old magazines to professional journals.

Arthur had scrawled various names and topics on the outside of the boxes, but since he'd stacked the boxes at least three rows deep against the wall, she had to go through them one at a time. She was down to the second row now, and she still hadn't seen her family's name on any of them.

After going through nearly five years of files from both *The Times* and the work he'd done while pursuing his degree, the smell of dust was like an unpleasant perfume in church. Everything from old newspaper clippings to his shorthand interview notes were in these boxes. Then there were the files on people, everything from current members of Congress to the chief executive officers of major corporations—down to what kind of whiskey they preferred.

Every time she cleared another row, her gaze would crest across the outside of the boxes. Hope and dread would burrow in her stomach at the same time. When she saw nothing, desolation would kick in. Today as she cleared the last row and scanned the remaining twenty boxes, her misery was complete. None of them had the name Wentworth on them.

They weren't here.

Having worked so hard these past weeks, hurting her back from all the bending and straightening, suffering through one paper cut after another, she hung her head, sat on a box, and asked herself the one question she'd feared since she'd cleared half the boxes with no luck.

Would Arthur have left his files on her father at *the New York Times*? It had been a huge case, with threads that would have had to be run through the paper's legal department. What if they weren't here?

"Harriet?" Arthur asked suddenly.

She jumped, and the box dipped from the shift in her weight. "Yes, Arthur?" she replied, not turning around, needing a minute to reign in her expression.

"Everything okay out there?"

Gesturing toward the boxes, she finally stood. "Of course. Just taking a break from my friends."

He studied her with those keen blue eyes. "Let's get some air," he said. "We've both been working hard, and it's getting a little stifling in here."

"I'm fine," she said and turned back to the box she'd sat on. "I need to get back to it."

When she felt his hand on her back, she spun in shock. Practically the only time he touched her was to help her with her coat. Except for that insane moment when he'd brought her close, telling her he could help her. When

172

she'd actually thought for a moment that he could, that she could trust him. Clearly insanity ran in her family.

"Harriet, you're exhausted, and who can blame you? In hindsight, I should have hired someone to help you with the filing."

"No, it's fine," she replied. The last thing she needed or wanted was someone's help. Then she took a breath, realizing he'd just given her the opening she'd been looking for. "Please tell me you don't have any more boxes hidden somewhere else, just waiting to give me more paper cuts."

When he reached for her right hand, she inhaled sharply. His palm was warm, and his fingers were gentle as they traced her fingertips. "I'm sorry about these. I hadn't thought."

"I tried to use gloves, but honestly, I couldn't thumb one piece of paper away from the next." She kept her eyes down, looking at their joined hands, avoiding his gaze.

Suddenly the building seemed as deathly quiet as the middle of a forest.

"How about you give the filing a rest for a few weeks? I can have you call and check some references for the advertising candidates I've shortlisted."

Abandon her quest? "No, I'll plough through. And you didn't answer me. Are there more files somewhere?"

He didn't answer for a moment, so she peeked at his face. His brow was knit, and his gaze was far too intense.

"Nah. These are the important ones." His thumb stroked her fingertips once more before he released her hand. "Let's go take a walk in the town square or go over to Kemstead's Bakery and have some peanut butter pie and coffee."

He *never* took a break.

"I don't care for peanut butter, and I want to finish here, Arthur. I don't have time for a walk. Plus, it's freezing outside."

"High of forty-five today," he commented, finally stepping back.

"A regular heat wave," she mused.

He planted his hands on his hips, his white shirt stretching over his strong shoulders. "Okay, Harriet. If you won't take a break with me, then please take one for yourself. How about you head to Miss Ivy's Beauty Parlor and let her do her magic on your hands? It's my treat. I hear they put women's hands in paraffin or something. Maybe it will help with the paper cuts."

Steeling herself against his continued kindness had been hard, like turning down his sweet invitation to join his family for New Year's Day supper. She and Maybelline had been unable to prepare their traditional oyster soup since Dare didn't carry oysters, not even a canned variety. The fact that they couldn't even keep that simple tradition had crushed them both. While Maybelline had curled up with a book, Harriet had resorted to cleaning to keep her mind off their shared misery.

"That's not necessary," she replied, stepping back from him and turning to resume her filing.

His murmur of exasperation was audible. "Harriet, I don't know why you won't let me be nice to you, but I have to tell you, it's really starting to get on my nerves. What have I done to tick you off? And before you deny it, you walked into this office disliking me. Why work for me if you hate me so much?"

Something cold slithered down her spine. She needed to be careful with her words. "Arthur, you misunderstand. I just want to keep things strictly professional." A little prevarication wouldn't hurt. "We're both young and unmarried, mostly working here alone. I don't want there to be talk."

Pursing his lips, he gazed at her with those sky-blue eyes. "And yet, there is talk anyway. It's hard not to have it in a small town. I don't care what people say when I know the truth. Plus, you're not from here, so why should you care?"

Her hands wanted to fist at her sides, if for no reason other than to stop the tingles still running through the fingertips he'd stroked with his thumb. But she controlled the impulse, just as she always did with him.

"I live here now. Please, let's just get back to work. I don't want to discuss this anymore."

"Fine. I'll respect your wishes, but Harriet, I hired a secretary, not a slave, and you're working too hard. More than any secretary I've ever seen. Go home for the rest of the day."

She glanced at her watch. "But it's only four twenty." Was he firing her?

"Go home," he said, pointing a finger at her. "I'm tired of watching you rub your back from bending over all of these boxes and then pasting on a smile and saying that you're fine."

"But I *am* fine," she replied, her heart beating faster. "Okay, I'll go home, but this is a silly argument. I work for you. This is what you hired me to do."

"Yes, but I didn't want you breaking your back like some field hand. Even they take a break for lunch."

And she didn't.

"Harriet, you're the best secretary I could have ever imagined having when I returned to Dare, but sometimes your single-mindedness is too much."

"You're one to talk," she said, her temper getting the better of her. "You're here at dawn and leave well after dusk."

"This paper is my life's blood, and I don't care what you or anyone else has to say about how hard I'm working. I'm building something here, while trying to keep my name alive as a journalist. I don't have time for a long lunch and a nap at home and then a two-hour coffee break at four. That might be Dare's speed, but I'm on a different clock now."

And isolated because of it. Even she had seen that. People had stopped dropping by to try and say hello to him over the last few weeks, even his parents, whom she'd met briefly. He might be from here, but in some ways, he was more alone than she was. At least she had Maybelline.

But she refused to feel sorry for him.

Plus she had bigger worries. What was she going to do now that the boxes weren't here?

"Arthur, I know we're not chummy, but like I told you, I think that's for the best. I'm going to go on home now like you suggested, but I'll be back in the morning to start again."

Time away would give her the opportunity to conceive a new plan.

When she passed him, he grabbed her forearm in a loose grip. His touch pinged up her arm and made her lip tremble.

"You really are the most stubborn woman."

Her chin lifted, and she pulled her arm free. "Take a look in the mirror. I'm not the only stubborn one in this office."

With that comment, she hurried to her desk and grabbed her coat, hat, and purse, not bothering to put them on until she was outside, the cold air dousing her warm cheeks.

A few people strolled by arm and arm, nodding to her as they passed. People finally knew who she was, and while they weren't overly friendly, they no longer stared at her like she was an exotic animal on display at the zoo. Fishing into her purse for her keys, she headed home, their argument replaying in her mind.

There were no files about her father.

She had come for nothing.

A tear leaked out. God, she hadn't considered failing to find what she was looking for when she'd first come up with this plan, but now the bitter taste was like castor oil in her mouth. What in the world was she going to do?

More importantly, what was she going to do about Arthur's continued kindness, his intense regard, and the continued awareness she kept telling herself was only the outcome of proximity? After feeling him hold her hand, she worried it was something more.

Whenever she looked into his deep blue eyes, it was hard to speak. Hard to remember why she was here.

And he felt the same way, but was trying to be a gentleman about it. That much she could tell.

For both of their sakes, she'd better finish what she came here to do and leave Arthur and Dare Valley as soon as possible.

Chapter 5

Harriet surveyed herself in the mirror. Her hair curled invitingly around her shoulders, and her make-up was picture-perfect. The low-cut black slip she wore would have to do.

Without the files, she had nothing tangible with which to prove her father's innocence. But she'd realized she could still make Arthur pay.

Ruining his reputation in his hometown wouldn't alter the stories he'd written, but it would call his character into question, and what better way to do that than to seduce him. People watched neighbor's houses like they were watching a movie at Mulligan's Drive-In southwest of town.

The slip was the sexiest thing she'd brought to Dare, and not intentionally. Who knew she'd decide that she needed to wear it even though her reasons weren't in the least bit sexy? It wasn't like she could buy anything suitable here, and it would take too long to order from the catalogue. Staying in this town any longer wasn't an option. She would destroy him, and she and Maybelline would leave.

The radiator was sputtering again, making the house cold, and her white robe wasn't cutting the mustard. Her bare feet were freezing as she walked to the phone. After all, who wore socks to seduce a man? The glass of brandy she'd poured earlier still had a splash inside, so she downed it. The fire burned from her throat to her belly, but it didn't loosen the knots in her stomach.

Lying to Maybelline had been hard enough, but she still had to get through tonight. Thank God she'd managed to talk Maybelline into going to Denver to withdraw more money from the bank account they'd opened there. Paying cash for everything had reduced the stash she kept in the cereal box in the cupboard. She'd suggested her sister do a little shopping while she was in the city and then spend the night, since it would be dangerous to drive on the icy roads in the dark. Maybelline missed city life terribly, so she had been all too eager to agree.

Harriet poured herself another glass of brandy. The bottle was an unknown vintage from the local liquor store. She snorted at the memory of how the shopkeeper had raised his eyebrows at her while he rung her up. Maybe it would give her the boost she needed to pull off her first seduction attempt. Her stomach fluttered, thinking about kissing Arthur and having him touch her.

It was fear, she told herself. Not attraction.

There was no way she was attracted to the man who'd ruined her father and her family. She just couldn't be.

Would Arthur really go for what she had in mind? And when it came right down to it, could she go through with it? Could she really have intimate relations with the man who'd destroyed her father?

If it would hurt his reputation as a community leader in his hometown, then yes, she could. He had to pay for what he'd done to her family.

Another bead of arousal quickened in her belly, and she told herself again it was only fear.

For heaven's sake, she just needed to call him already. The clock's short hand had just ticked past nine o'clock.

The phone beckoned, so she dialed the numbers for Arthur's party line. This would be her first step in setting him up. People gossiped all the time about what they heard on the phone. Since his house was out of town, she wondered how many people were on his party line. Six? She and Maybelline shared theirs with four neighbors, and even though they'd been assigned a unique ring like everyone else, they never heard it. There was no one to call them.

"Arthur?" she asked when he answered.

"Harriet?"

A palpable pause.

She waited to hear a click from someone else picking up on the party line. This was one time when she hoped her neighbors would snoop, especially since she and Maybelline never received any calls.

One click sounded and then another, and she smiled. Inquiring minds…

"Is something wrong?" Arthur asked. "It's a bit late to be calling." Even on the phone he sounded gruff.

Right, and she had never called him. "I know, and I'm sorry. There's something moving around in the attic, and I'm afraid an animal might be up there. Can you come check it out? I'm scared to look myself."

There was another pause, and for a minute, she was sure he wasn't buying it.

"Might be a raccoon," he finally said, "or a squirrel."

"Or bats," she added. She'd overheard a man telling a

story about finding three of them in his attic the other day in the American Legion post while she and Maybelline were eating hot roast beef sandwiches.

"Great. So, my choices are something flying at me or biting me if I come and check."

Yeah, when she thought about it, who would show up for that? "Don't worry about it then. I'll just..."

And she let her voice trail off like she'd heard her mother do time and time again to get her father to agree to something.

"No, it's okay. Does it sound like it's really big?"

Laughing seemed inappropriate, but she still felt like it. Heck, what a question.

"Small, I think," she said, not wanting him to be too alarmed.

"Let me call a buddy and have him come over and help me."

"No, wait," she said, and then stopped herself from rushing. It hadn't occurred to her that he might ask for backup, and her heart sped up just at the thought. "I don't want you bothering anyone at this hour. I just want to know what it is. I can lock my bedroom door once you leave tonight, and if you find something, you and your buddy can come over to take care of it in the morning."

Silence again.

"Where's your sister?"

"She had to go to Denver for some shopping and didn't want to drive home at night." Her heart pounded in her chest as a few seconds ticked by without a response.

Then a terse, "Fine. I'll be there as soon as I can. Go into your bedroom and lock the door until I get there if you're scared."

"Okay, and thank you, Arthur. I just...didn't know

who else to call." Fortunately, he didn't ask why she hadn't called her landlord.

"That's fine, Harriet. We're all neighborly around here. See you soon."

And with that, he clicked off. Three more clicks sounded after his.

She hung the phone back on the receiver and moved into the family room. Took another drink.

Well, the trap was set, and the only person getting trapped in it was Arthur.

She didn't care what happened to herself anymore.

***

Arthur rapped on Harriet's front door for a minute, but when she didn't answer, he realized she might be too scared to leave her bedroom. It wasn't like a raccoon, squirrel, or bat could open the attic door. But fear wasn't a rational thing.

He turned the knob and found the door unlocked.

"Harriet," he called out as he entered.

She didn't appear, so he walked into the mostly dark house and decided against hanging his coat on the brass rack on the wall since the attic would be freezing. When he entered the family room, the hardwood floor squeaked in places as he moved. He'd never been in old Mrs. Kennion's house, but the soft glow from the antique brass lamp was kind to the house's age. Still, the plaster walls had a few cracks, the lace curtains were brittle and yellowed, and the mauve settee looked faded from too much use. Fortunately, the house didn't smell. He'd heard tall tales about the many cats she'd owned when she died, anywhere from ten to twenty, and how she'd regularly served them red Jell-O as a treat.

He called her name again, and finally heard, "Up here."

So she was holed up in her bedroom after all. Funny how the knowledge tightened every muscle in his body and swept a wave of heat from head to toe, making him wish he'd chucked his coat. Knowing it was a stupid idea, he headed toward her room. It was on the way to the attic, after all. Part of him, the unprofessional part, wanted to see where she slept. See if the hyacinth fragrance he always smelled on her skin was more intense there.

He'd tried not to fantasize about her and failed miserably.

The floor squeaked as he walked up the stairs. The red floor runner was also worn in spots.

The door to her bedroom opened when he appeared on the landing, but he didn't see her. Just saw the faded brass frame of a bed in a yellow-painted room, a pink velvet bedspread pulled back like at a fancy hotel.

He moved to the doorway and froze.

She stood on the other side of the bed by the window, dressed in a black slip that highlighted her creamy shoulders and pert nipples. Her red hair was down for once, curling around her shoulders. Those slumberous green eyes didn't blink as their gazes met.

His heart fell like a downed tree in his chest, and he felt the impending crash reverberate throughout his body.

She was every man's fantasy, and it took a moment for him to dial back the lust slamming through his body. After the way she'd acted toward him since the moment they met, this situation couldn't be more confusing.

"I should have known something was off the minute I found your door unlocked," he commented, trying to find his balance. "Charlie from across the street said you always lock it.'"

She licked her blood-red lips, and a punch of arousal shot straight into his gut. "Right, and no one locks their doors in Dare."

"No," he replied, not taking another step into the room. "Harriet, what are you doing?"

The hand she raised to her chest was shaking. "I would think that's obvious."

He looked at the floor and stared at the seams in the hardwood. Anything to keep his eyes off this goddess with fiery hair and moss-green eyes. If he looked at her, he'd never be able to resist her.

"I don't know *why* you're doing this. You don't even like me, and you sure as hell don't want me," he said.

"You're wrong," she said, and the floor squeaked, signaling she was making her way toward him from across the room.

When her slender bare feet appeared in his vision, he shook his head and met her gaze. "There's nothing in the attic, is there?"

"No."

For hell's sake. She was acting like some Mata Hari, and he was just a regular guy.

He ran a hand through his hair. "Harriet, I'm going to leave now, and we won't speak of this again."

When he turned to leave, she flew in front of him, her hand cutting off his exit like a rail bar at the railroad track south of town. "No. Stay."

Part of him wanted to stay, wanted it more than he'd ever wanted anything, but he had too much respect for her to let this play out. "If you really do like me, then we'll go out on a proper date. I'll take you to Nellie's Tavern, and we can get to know each other better, but I am not just going to be with you like this. I have more respect for you than that, and frankly you're too much of a lady to be acting this way. Plus, we work together."

She ducked her head to her shoulder and gazed at him with pouty lips. "Don't you wonder why I acted like I disliked you so much? I was attracted to you from the first, Arthur, and I'm tired of pretending otherwise."

His body corded with tension. "Well, this is one heck of a switcheroo, and I'm more than a little embarrassed to say it's too fast for me." Even if he'd been in New York, he would have been surprised by a woman acting so forward.

She slid close to him, and the hand she'd used to prevent him from leaving fell to his chest. "I want you. Don't you want me?"

He closed his eyes for a moment, fighting the temptation, but also listening to his gut. He'd been with a few women in New York, and their voices hadn't sounded all business-like when they told him that they wanted him.

Harriet's did.

He opened his eyes, trying to disconnect from the situation, to use his powerful observational skills. Yes, her pulse was hammering in her neck, and her breathing was rapid, but her eyes looked a bit too wild. And then he smelled the liquor on her breath. Okay, so she was nervous.

"Why, Harriet? Why now?"

"Because I'm leaving soon, and I want to be with you before I go."

Her green gaze didn't falter, so he knew there was truth in what she said. Well, he'd known she was only passing through. She wasn't meant for these parts, as out of place as fancy Italian gelato at an ice cream church social.

"You're giving me your notice now? Like *this?* I told you before that I'd help you with whatever you're running from. You can trust me, Harriet."

Her lip started to tremble, and he could see how vulnerable she was now. Her fear reached out to him.

"I can't," she whispered, and then she rose on her tiptoes and crushed her mouth to his.

He didn't take their kiss any further for a moment, but then she gasped, and he knew that sound for what it was. Proof that she *was* attracted to him, just like she'd said, confirming his hunch about those few powerful moments in the office when he'd felt her watching him before she pretended otherwise and turned away to file.

Succumbing to the feel of her in his arms was the most natural thing in the world. He bent his head so their lips could meet more easily. God, her body was all soft and curvy and more sensual than he'd ever imagined. Her hyacinth fragrance curled around him like fog as he took her lips in a deeper kiss, changing the angle of his mouth. When his tongue parted her lips, she went rigid in his arms, like she hadn't kissed too many men. Which is what he'd thought from the start. This was no experienced sexpot. This was a deeply conservative lady. The realization brought him back to his senses.

"Enough," he said and gently pushed her away, his hands on her shoulders, the bones small and delicate under his touch. "I don't know why you're doing this, but you're not this kind of woman. Tell me right now that you've been with a man before, and remember that if we make love, I'll damn well know."

Her eyes flickered back and forth like she was thinking. "Fine, I haven't been with a man before, but I want to be with you."

He thought about touching her intimately to test her words, but that would be crude. His hands lowered to his side. "No, you don't want to be with me. I don't know what you think you're doing, but I'm not going to be part of the biggest mistake of your life. And mine. Did you even consider pregnancy? For cripes sake."

Her eyes widened, and he fought the urge to curse something really shocking. "Get dressed. I've stayed a little too long for this time of night, but we can stick to the cover story you've so conveniently spun. I'm going to get Charlie from across the street and *pretend* to have him help me catch the squirrel I saw in your attic. When I knock on that door downstairs, you'd better be dressed. Do you hear me?"

His voice was gruff, but he didn't care. He was aroused and being lied to by a woman he cared about, one he was attracted to, pissed him off.

"Don't you want me?" she finally said, crossing her arms over her chest as if suddenly ashamed of herself.

"I would think that's fairly obvious. Now, I'm going to get Charlie. You have about two minutes to get dressed and get your butt downstairs."

Then he turned around and rushed down the squeaky steps. As he walked across the street to Charlie's house, the curtain fluttered. Yeah, the old bachelor had been watching Harriet's house all right. He knocked on the door. Charlie opened it slowly, his eyes disapproving.

As Arthur went through the story about the squirrel, which Charlie probably knew about from listening in on the party line, the old man started to relax, laughing right along with him about the animal's made-up antics. He even slapped Arthur on the back as they walked across the street.

"Thanks for the help, Charlie. Harriet's all woman when it comes to vermin, so she's no help."

"Glad her sister's not here to be worried. She left earlier today. Denver, she said."

"Harriet mentioned that," Arthur commented, thinking about how well she'd laid her trap. The party line listeners would have been enough to spread the gossip, and his late night visit would have been all the more damning since the neighbors knew her sister was out of town. He was dealing with a calculating Black Widow gowned in nothing but a lacy black slip, and he didn't like the web she was weaving for him. No, not one bit.

"Are you sure you don't want me to bring my BB gun?" Charlie asked.

"Nah," he said, wanting to roll his eyes at this charade. "We can catch it in a bed sheet and knock it on the head with Harriet's rolling pin."

As they walked up to the door, he prayed Harriet was dressed and ready to put on a show. She knew how to act, that was for sure.

When he knocked, he heard the hardwood squeak and braced himself. Surely she'd have enough respect to come to the door dressed. She'd be a branded woman for sure if she answered the door in that black slip.

"Come back in, Arthur," she said when she opened the door, dressed like she was receiving guests for a late supper. "And Charlie. Thanks so much for coming to a lady's aide. Arthur said you would be the perfect person to help. But before you head up to the attic, would you like a piece of pie or a cup of coffee? I just brewed some for Arthur since it's cold up there, but I hadn't served the pie yet. It's banana cream."

Her smile was picture perfect. As were the lies spewing out of her mouth.

He met her gaze. Oh, he was going to get to the bottom of this, all right. He would find out who she really was, why she was here, the whole shebang. That was for damn sure. No holds barred.

"Pie would be nice," Arthur said, and stepped inside like the fly to the spider web.

Chapter 6

Harriet didn't come to work the next morning.

Not really a surprise.

He called in her license plate number to an old source from his days at *The New York Times* and discovered it was registered to a Warren Perkins from Loveland, Colorado, age twenty-one. Maybe a friend of theirs? He didn't doubt that a man would give his car to the pretty sisters if they batted those rust-colored eyelashes just right.

His friend hadn't found a Harriet Jenkins with a Colorado driver's license, which meant she wasn't a resident, just like he'd thought. So, he'd need to get a look at her license. He wouldn't have looked in her purse before, but last night had helped him overcome his scruples.

Since it was too early to pay a social call to her house, he headed over to Kemstead's Bakery. Over coffee and a donut with Herman and a few of his old school chums, he recounted the fake story about the squirrel in Harriet's attic, telling them about how it had eluded him and Charlie. Everyone had suggestions on how to trap the critter. He told people Harriet was feeling poorly today, likely due to her fear of the squirrel, and that he was taking her a Bavarian cream pastry to cheer her up. And check on that darn squirrel again.

For cripes sake.

As he drove to her house, he realized he'd just lied for her, and that didn't exactly sit well. Elvis sang "Heartbreak Hotel" on the radio, which seemed fitting. Charlie was at work at the gas station when he arrived, but Harriet's other neighbors were home. Likely watching the show from their kitchen windows.

Coming here twice in less than twenty-four hours looked strange, but he hoped the story he'd planted at the bakery would be believed. People already thought something was going on, what with them both working such long hours.

And she'd confirmed it by calling him to help her last night.

A few of his friends had given him a knowing wink. A couple of guys had said she was a stunning broad, so who could blame him? Even if she wasn't from around these parts.

He'd tried to set the record straight every time it had come up, but his assurances had fallen on deaf ears. Since he wasn't keeping the company of any women right now, people weren't inclined to listen.

The sidewalk leading to the sagging white porch was covered with a thin layer of snow that had fallen during the night. Someone hadn't shoveled it yet, and he wondered if they had to do it themselves or if old Mrs. Kennion's son had hired someone to take care of it. Shoveling snow could be back-breaking work when there was a lot of it, which there often was. Then he realized he was worrying about

Harriet and her sister and put a lid on that.

He knocked on the door, holding the white pastry bag. Realized he should have bought two pastries when her sister opened the door.

The car must be in the garage. "Hi, Maybelline." They had met briefly a couple of times when she came to pick Harriet up from the office. "You're back from Denver?"

"Yes, I got an early start," she replied.

Her red hair was a lighter shade than her sister's, and she had blue eyes, not green ones, but it was easy to see the resemblance in the wide mouth and patrician nose.

"Ah, did Harriet, forget to call you? She wasn't feeling… Ah, she had an…errand to run today and won't be able to come in."

Right.

"Well, then, it's your lucky day. You can have her Bavarian cream while we have a cup of coffee and visit."

He handed her the bag, which she reluctantly took. And she had no choice but to step back when he crossed the threshold.

No need to delay his investigation. He could already tell that Harriet's sister would be an easier nut to crack. If nothing else, he could search her purse.

"So, did Harriet tell you about calling me about the squirrel in the attic after nine o'clock last night?" he asked, wanting to see if her sister had made herself scarce last night on purpose.

Her face muscles tensed. "No, ah…she didn't mention it."

He decided to probe. "It was rather late, but she sounded scared, so I came by. She's new to town, so perhaps she didn't realize it wasn't the smartest thing to call a single man over to her house so late—even over a critter."

The hands pouring the coffee into the cups jerked, and the brown liquid spilled over the counter.

"Here," he said, taking pity on her. "Why don't you let me help?"

The pink dishrag looked like it was one of Mrs. Kennion's old hand towels, cut up for rags when it was too worn to put out for company. He mopped the mess up and poured the coffee.

She took over after smoothing her hair back. "Here. I'll bring them over. Please, take a seat."

The white table in the breakfast nook had a few cigarette burns on it, but otherwise, it was clean. She sat stiffly across the table from him, not touching her coffee.

He gestured to the pastry bag she'd left on the counter. "Please, have the Bavarian. Mr. and Mrs. Kemstead make the best pastries in town."

"Thank you. I had a big breakfast, but I'll save it for later."

Horseshit, he thought, not smelling any eggs or bacon in the kitchen or seeing any dishes drying on the rack.

With her hands folded in her lap, he couldn't see if they were shaking, but her pulse drummed in her neck, and she couldn't meet his gaze. He'd interviewed enough people to know when he could go with the direct approach.

"So, I expect you know why I'm here," he began.

Well, that brought the eye contact he wanted. The whites of her eyes made him think of Tandy, the frightened horse they'd had on the ranch growing up.

"No, I…"

"I'm here to find out why you and your sister are really in town. I know when a woman is out to get me. Last night was proof of that. What I don't know is why."

Maybelline reached out for her cigarettes and fumbled with the package until she could take one out. Harriet didn't smoke, he knew, since she'd turned down Herman's offer of a cigarette, saying it made her cough. Arthur drew out his lighter and lit it for her, seeing the telltale shake in her hands. She took a long drag, as if it would give her the fortitude she would need for their conversation. People who had something to hide always smoked when he interviewed them. He didn't join her. Just bided his time.

"I suspect Jenkins isn't your real name," he began, even though he didn't know for sure.

Her eyes went wide, and the cigarette ash fell in a zigzag when her hands shook.

"That car you have is registered to a Warren Perkins from Loveland. I know you pay cash for everything in town and don't have a bank account here, which is odd. After seeing what Harriet is willing to do to herself and me, the gloves are off. I *will* find out why you're here, but since you're her sister, and you love her, I'm going to ask you straight out to tell me. I don't want to get the law involved or embarrass you both."

He let the threat hang in the air.

She tapped her cigarette in the ashtray. "Calling in the law would embarrass you too, and you strike me as a prideful man, Mr. Hale."

So she had spine like her sister. And her animosity was as clear as a summer day in Sardine Canyon. Just like Harriet's had been.

"I came here planning to search your purse when you were out of the room, but I don't want to do anything like that now. Just tell me the truth."

"Why not peek? Isn't that how you usually conduct yourself as a journalist?" she said, her tone as bitter as the smoke wafting between them.

The way she said "journalist," she might as well have been drinking poison, not coffee.

"You don't like me, do you?" he asked.

Instead of answering, she took another long drag. Then she stood. "After what I suspect Harriet tried last night, we won't be staying in Dare much longer, so let me show you what you were planning to steal a look at."

He followed her into the family room. An expensive blue handbag was tucked away on the brown side chair in the corner. She picked it up and brought it over to him.

"Here. I don't want to stop you from being nefarious."

Pursing his lips, he studied her. Somehow her giving him access to her purse made him feel like a jerk.

"Fine," he finally said, remembering Harriet's fake seduction scene last night. Answers were the only way he would understand what the hell was going on with these two.

He grabbed her pocketbook and opened it, drawing out her license. Maybelline Wentworth. Massachusetts.

Wentworth.

Oh shit.

He'd never met her father in person, but he'd seen pictures of him. Dr. Ashley Wentworth. Given those pictures to his editor along with his series of articles about what the man had done. The nose was the same. And then he remembered the scientist had two daughters, both college age.

His stomach dropped, and with it came the utter devastation of realizing Harriet had lied about everything from the day she had walked into his office. He cared about a woman who hated him for doing his job.

"So you and Harriet are here for what? Revenge?" he

asked her.

Maybelline retrieved her license and set that and her purse down on the small side table by the mauve settee. Then she put her hands on her hip, ashes falling to the floor. "We came for the truth, for evidence that you exaggerated your findings on our father. But since the files are still in New York, I guess she decided to try something different last night. She didn't tell me what she had in mind, or I would have stopped her."

They weren't in New York. He just hadn't been able to tell Harriet there were more boxes of filing that day. She'd seemed so darn dejected. Now he knew why.

"By ruining herself in front of the whole town with me?" he scoffed.

"By showing Dare Valley you aren't the Favorite Son everyone thinks you are." Her words were as cutting as a chainsaw through a downed tree.

"This town knows *me*. They don't know you. Trust me. When it comes down to it, they'll believe me over you two."

She crushed her cigarette out in the brown glass ashtray on the lamp stand, twisting it and twisting it until all smoke disappeared. "But you've been gone for five years, and in the big bad city, no less. People have been talking about how different you seem. Working long hours with an attractive woman like my sister, who's working long hours too. Unusual that. And then there's all your big ideas. You've set yourself up as a new leader in the community. That changes things. People think you've gotten pretty big for your britches already. Even *this* outsider has heard the talk."

Well, he knew there had been talk, but he hadn't considered how it could be used against him. If he'd

196

AVA MILES

thrown his integrity aside last night, it would have tarnished his reputation and his place in the community. Sure the woman always got the brunt of the censure, but he would have felt the heat too, particularly as he tried to launch his business.

"Tell Harriet that if she wants to see the files on your father, she can come to the office and ask me herself."

"They're here?" she whispered, her face suddenly losing all color.

"Yes."

Part of him was sad they'd be hurt by the final knowledge that their father was guilty. His evidence was airtight.

"Our father was a good man, and you destroyed him."

He walked to the door, the floor squeaking in spots, and heard her heels click on the hardwood as she trailed behind. When he shrugged into his coat, he turned to her.

"I expect your father was a good man and a good father, but he made an enormous mistake that killed seven infants. *That's* what destroyed him, Ms. Wentworth. Not me. You and your sister would be wise to understand that."

Her face fell.

And with that he let himself out into the cold day.

Chapter 7

Harriet parked the car in the driveway as the sun was dipping below the mountains. Escaping down the highway for a while hadn't helped. She was ashamed of what she'd almost done, and she felt a newfound, begrudging respect for Arthur. He'd kept his head when other men might not.

What *had* she been thinking? Had she become so blinded by anger that she'd been willing to throw away her first moments with a man like that? These were some of the serious questions she'd had to face on her car ride, and she hadn't liked the answers. The one that had scared her the most was how much she'd enjoyed being kissed and held by Arthur, a man she'd sworn to destroy.

Even though part of her hated to admit defeat, she was ready to get the heck out of town and put this whole terrible episode behind them.

Maybelline met her at the door and told her about Arthur's visit. A bucket of cold water to the face couldn't have been more shocking.

"How could you have done something like that?" her sister raged at her. "I know you're upset, but it *scares* me that you'd risk yourself that way, Harry."

Her heart shattered, as much from the honesty as from Maybelline's childhood nickname for her.

"It won't happen again," she pledged as she watched Maybelline storm out of the parlor rather than acknowledging her promise.

She sat on the settee and folded her hands over her face. Shame blossomed inside, but rage quickly followed. Arthur Hale still had the gall to cling to the illusion that he'd been doing his job by destroying her father and their family. How dare he?

She *knew* he must have misrepresented something.

Her father was not guilty.

He couldn't be.

Well, Arthur had said she could look at his files, and so she would. She drove to *The Western Independent* and walked into the place like she owned it. It was after five o'clock, but she knew he'd be working. His typewriter was clacking along as she strode down the hall to his office.

He spun around in his chair the instant she reached his door, almost like that sixth sense of his was working in overdrive.

"I knew you'd come for the files," he said, his tone flat and unfriendly.

She was so used to kindness and warmth from him that it took her a moment to make her way into his office. His eyes didn't remind her of an endless blue sky now, but rather the churning Atlantic Ocean in the middle of a storm.

"Where are they?" she asked.

He tossed something toward her. A rubber-banded stack of papers fell to the floor, and she had to go through the indignity of bending over to pick it up. All his courtliness was gone now.

The file was small compared to what she'd expected, but she had what she wanted, so she turned to walk out.

"Do you *really* think that's all there is?" he asked her, stopping her at the door.

She turned and cocked a brow. So he wasn't going to make this easy. Why hadn't she expected that?

"I figured the size only proved what I already knew. That you didn't research your series of articles on my father worth squat, which is why you got everything so wrong."

His mouth thinned into a bitter smile. "And here I thought you would have realized how wrong *you* are after all the boxes you've filed."

The swipe reminded her of an angry lion she'd seen at the circus. "Well, aren't we a cute sight? After all this time together, both of us are showing our true colors." Her throat tightened after she spoke the words, and she realized part of her was sick that they'd come to this.

"You lied to me from the beginning, and I was starting to care about you. Which you used to your advantage last night." He rose and planted his hands on his hips. "Harriet, if all you wanted when you arrived was the goddamn files I had on your father's case, I would have given them to you."

Because she'd worked with him, because she knew him, she believed that. "Where are the rest of them? You told me the other day that there weren't more boxes."

He fished out his keys, came around the desk, and walked out, leaving her to trail behind him. "My brother helped me move the boxes in here. But we didn't finish before he took off to do some field work, so I got lazy and left them at my house."

"You lied to me." Why would he do that?

He looked over his shoulder. "Well, you looked so tired and worn down that day that I decided not to tell you. I was planning to hire someone to help you once my brother, George, got back, and we brought the rest of the boxes over."

He'd been planning to hire someone to help her? She looked down at her feet, feeling more shame.

"You'll have to follow me. Frankly, I don't want to give you a ride back into town, and after your crap last night, I don't plan on feeding the gossip."

The hard tone of his voice made her clench her teeth. "Fine."

He strode out of the office ahead of her, not bothering to open the door for her, and headed toward his car without a backward glance. Tension radiated through her body, and she realized her shoulders were knotted too.

This side of him intimidated her, and part of her missed the easy going man she'd come to know.

He slammed the door to his Thunderbird and waited until she was in her car, ready to follow him. Then he drove down Main Street.

She'd heard he'd bought an old house on a hill overlooking the valley rather than moving in with his parents. It was a good fifteen minutes out of town, and if her mind hadn't been spinning like her stomach, she would have stopped to appreciate the towering pines rising up the mountain on her left while the valley flowed out below her like a large salad bowl.

His house was a white A-frame and had a porch boasting a gorgeous view of the mountains and the valley. She pulled in behind his car. He didn't wait for her to reach him, his legs eating up the distance to the front door.

Part of her wanted to hurry after him, but she held herself back. Remained in control.

Though she was used to him holding doors open for her, he didn't this time, and she had to open the front door herself. Because of her upbringing, she rubbed her feet on the rug before setting foot on his gleaming hardwood floor.

She wandered into the living room. It could use some furniture, she thought, but it held a lot of promise with its fifteen-foot high white plaster walls and white crown molding with fleur de lis in the corners.

She heard his steps off to the right and followed the sound. He was hefting boxes onto an old partner's desk when she found him. The room had three big windows, one with lead glass panels in the shape of a peacock's tail, and was filled with boxes.

"You can start here," he said.

The lone overhead light didn't provide sufficient light without a table lamp. "Where?" she asked.

He gestured to the two boxes he'd hauled over and spun them around. The name Wentworth was written in black marker in his handwriting, and somehow the starkness of seeing her family name like that made her tummy spasm. Her father's work had boiled down to these papers sorted into a box, nothing to identify them but the careless scrawl of letters.

It hurt, seeing that.

"You can start with these two boxes, and if you get through them in the next two hours and want more, you can start on the next ones."

"Which ones?"

He pointed to the back of the room, and as she looked deeper into the room, she saw her family's name scrawled across at least seven more boxes that were facing front.

Her throat clenched at the sheer volume of it all, and she couldn't speak.

He crossed his hands on his chest, his mouth tight. "You didn't think I'd give the parents of those babies false hope, did you, by throwing out an unconfirmed cause? Or that I'd ruin a respected scientist without doing my research?"

Unable to meet his gaze, she looked down at the rug. It was an uninspired Aubusson with a blue background and faded yellow flowers. "I don't know what to say."

"The file in your hand is a summary of everything in the boxes by number."

"How many boxes are there?"

"Twenty-five," he said, walking toward her. "Do I need to take your purse?"

Clutching it was an automatic response. "Why ever would you say that?"

Those blue eyes held a hint of danger. "I don't want you taking out a matchbook and burning the evidence. It won't change what happened. *The New York Times* has copies of the key documents."

He thought she was capable of arson?

A tick in his jaw made her realize he was angry, and who could blame him?

"After last night, I'm assuming there's pretty much nothing you wouldn't do."

Right. Even she had discovered there were things she didn't know or like about herself. "You don't have to worry about that."

"Good," he replied. "I like this house. Wasn't glad Mrs. Pokens passed, but was glad I could have a place of my own like this one. Be a shame if it burned down before

I got the chance to move in properly. There'll be coffee in the kitchen if you get thirsty."

And then he headed toward the door.

"Arthur?"

He paused, the muscles of his back shifting when he placed his arm on the doorframe, not turning around.

"I'm sorry," she said, clutching her purse to her side. "For last night. I went too far."

His head lowered, but she couldn't see his face. "Yes, you goddamn did."

He left her alone then, in the room filled with the twenty-five boxes organized by number and marked with her family name.

Chapter 8

Watching her go through his files about her father was like being a spectator at a funeral. She came and went from his house for the next two days, stubbornly sifting through the papers in the boxes after telling him that she needed more time to go through all of them.

All of them.

She wasn't going down without a fight. Her face might look ashen, but the chip on her shoulder could take down a small army.

The story he spread around town was that they were working at his place, with her sister acting as chaperone, while a water leak was fixed at the office. He hired Herman to fix the imaginary leak and swore him to secrecy, saying they were working on a big case that required total privacy.

While he was protecting both their reputations, he realized he was lying for her again and wondered what that said about him.

Maybelline was out for a walk when he walked past his home office. Harriet sat on the floor in a pink sweater set and black skirt with one leg bent at the knee. Her hand was pressed against her forehead, and she was clutching some papers to her stomach. Boxes surrounded her like a maze.

He would have walked by, but he heard a sniff and then the unmistakable sound of a woman crying softly.

Cripes, he thought, and ran his hand through his hair. Why wouldn't she give up? Then he realized she couldn't. It was her father, and because he loved his family too, he could understand.

"Harriet?" he called out softly.

Her head jerked up, and she dashed a hand at the tears streaming down her face. "I'm sorry," she said. "I'm almost finished."

He walked forward, his hesitance making him drag his feet. Being nice to her was the last thing he should do, wanted to do. Yet, here he was, fishing out his handkerchief and handing it to her. "It's clean. So, what box are you on?"

The dainty way she wiped her nose reminded him what a city girl she was. "Eighteen," she whispered and extended the file she was holding to him.

Ah, God, he thought. The medical reports on the babies who'd died. He'd gotten drunk after reading through those the first time.

"He lied," she said in that soft tone. "My father *lied.*"

He sat on one of the boxes encircling her, the cardboard giving a bit. He'd been wondering when this moment would come. Part of him had dreaded it.

Her father had fallen off his pedestal.

"Yes," he said, wanting to reach out and stroke the lock of fiery hair that had come loose from her bun.

The file fell to the floor. "Those poor babies," she said. "I keep reading the mothers' statements about how healthy they were, and how they sickened and died so quickly after drinking the formula."

He hung his head. Interviewing the four mothers who had agreed to speak to him had been the hardest experience of his life. The other women had been too inconsolable to talk to him, and their husbands too angry.

"Let's get you a cup of coffee, and when Maybelline gets back from her walk, you can go home."

He pulled her up and helped her step over the boxes. She leaned against him for a moment when she stumbled. Putting his arm around her, he waited until she found her footing, trying to ignore the thrill of touching her. Once she steadied herself, he stepped back. Like he'd been doing since he discovered who she was and why she was here.

She followed him to the kitchen and sat at his farmer's table. Since he drank coffee throughout the day, there was already a pot of it on the stove. He grabbed mugs from the cabinet and poured them both a cup. She didn't reach for hers when he set it in front of her. She just stared unblinkingly at the table, which he'd covered with one of his mother's old plaid green tablecloths.

"Arthur," she said, shaking her head like she was shaking off a daze. "I owe you an apology. I came here…thinking…" Her fingers feathered her brow. "I don't know what…"

"Let's leave it at that." Knowing she was sorry did a lot to abate the anger he felt, but he still didn't want to see her suffer.

"You're letting me off too easy," she murmured, reaching for the cup.

Probably, and he didn't want to think about that either. His mouth quirked up, likely his first smile in days.

"What do you want me to do? Tie you to ol' Bessie in the barn and have her drag you down Main Street?"

Her mouth changed and then fell flat again. "They used to do that around here, right?"

"My granddad told tales." He took a sip of coffee. "So what are you going to do now?"

He hoped she wouldn't go through the rest of the boxes. It only got worse from there.

Her finger traced the plaid squares on the tablecloth. "I don't know. I'd hoped to restore my father's reputation, if not his sanity, but now… Our family is in disgrace. We don't have anything to go back to. I couldn't find a job back home, and Maybelline was asked to leave college."

Jeez, he hadn't imagined anyone other than their father reaping the consequences of his actions, and he hated that Harriet and Maybelline were paying for his mistakes. It was unjust. "Why don't you stay here?" he heard himself say. "You already have a house. Give yourself some time to figure out a long-term plan."

She laid her palms flat on the table and then patted it, like she was trying to play the piano, searching for the right notes. "You surprise me. Just a few days ago, I tried to ruin your reputation in your hometown."

Like he could forget. The memory of her in that black slip kept running through his mind. "And yourself. Since you brought it up, would you really have gone through with it?"

Her hands flexed, and she lowered her eyes. "I don't know. Maybe I'm more like my father than I thought." Her scoff didn't quite come off. It was more like a soft sob.

He took her hand when she patted the table again. "Maybe it will help you forgive him."

"Forgive him?" she said, her voice breaking. "He

killed seven babies and lied about it."

When she tried to yank her hand free, he held firm. "He didn't intentionally kill those babies, and while that doesn't bring them back, it *does* make a difference. I won't excuse his lies about the faulty batch of formula, but I'm a bit more cynical after living in New York. The lies change as often as the headlines out there."

"Whereas the people out here are pretty much what you see is what you get."

"Yes," he responded. "Another reason I'm glad to be home."

Her fingers pressed against her temples like she had a headache. "I should go find Maybelline and get out of your way. We've encroached for too long as it is." She stood, leaving her coffee untouched. "Thank you for letting me go through…"

"You're welcome." My God, how could she drag out pleasantries when her whole world had been destroyed? "If you want to keep working for me until you figure out your next steps, you're welcome to do so." He still needed a secretary, right?

Her mouth parted in shock.

"It might keep the talk down," he reasoned. "People are already wondering what's going on between us. Two days to fix a water leak after a late-night visit to your attic? Well, folks around here aren't stupid, and we're pushing the limit, even with your sister acting as chaperone."

"A water leak?" she asked. "I hadn't realized you'd created…a cover story. Thank you, Arthur."

Well, he'd done it to protect himself, and maybe her a little, too. He didn't like thinking about that. But if she thanked him one more time, looking like a white bed sheet, he was going to lose his temper.

She wandered to the front of the house and went out the door without putting on her coat. Grinding his teeth, he grabbed her navy wool coat and rushed after her. The wind was brisk and had already loosened more strands of red hair from her bun. She was weaving in place like she was lost.

"For God's sake, get into the house where it's warm. I'll go find your sister."

Why her sister loved walking outside in the winter still baffled him, but he'd learned that the Wentworth sisters marched to the beat of their own drum.

After depositing her inside, he grabbed his own coat and headed out to find her equally feckless sister.

The Wentworth sisters were more trouble than they were worth. Hah. Terrible pun, he realized.

And if he didn't feel a little guilty—and dammit, still attracted to Harriet—he would have never suggested they stick around Dare Valley.

They weren't done complicating his life.

Chapter 9

The *chik-chik-cha-chik-chik-chika-chik-cha-chik-ding-ziiiiiiiiiiiip* of Arthur's typewriter greeted Harriet when she arrived in the office the next morning.

As usual, he'd started working before she arrived. People had commented that he was still keeping city hours, but deep down she knew he was a man who liked his work.

Like her father had.

The very thought made her unbearably sad and angry, so she firmed her shoulders and walked over to his office, pausing in the doorway to watch him work.

His back was to her, and she watched with fascination as the muscles in his back shifted as he went through the rhythm of typing. Arthur demonstrated beauty and grace as he swept his hands across the machine and started again. With every press of the keys, it was like he was imprinting his vision of the newspaper story he was writing, one letter, one word at a time. So focused on telling the truth. Sharing what his senses had detected.

The back of his neck gleamed, likely from a trip to

Dave at the Barber Shop. The faint aroma of his cologne permeated his office, all forest and spice. Powerful shoulders filled out the open-collared navy shirt he was wearing.

She could finally admit to herself that she was attracted to him. It might not sit well, but she was tired of the lies. The ones she'd told others. And the ones she'd told herself. It was time to turn over a new leaf.

After talking it over with Maybelline last night, they'd agreed to stay in Dare for a while and sort out what to do next. Both of them were too tired to try and start over again somewhere else right now. Plus, Harriet felt like she owed Arthur a debt of gratitude. Staying to help him start up his newspaper was the least she could do.

"I brought you a jelly donut," she finally said, walking into his office. "Alice at Kemstead's said you like the apricot ones best."

He finished the current section of his news symphony and then swung around in his chair. The smile he normally gave her didn't appear.

Funny how she missed it.

"There's been a cave-in at the mine in Blisswater Canyon. Twenty-one miners are trapped. I was just finishing up the initial story and was going to call it in before heading to the site."

"I can do that," she replied, setting his coffee and pastry on his desk.

He grabbed the pastry and devoured it in three bites, took a gulp of coffee from the cup on his desk, and then sat back down. "Thanks," he muttered before turning to resume his typing.

She busied herself with some filing, but her mind was elsewhere. The tension between her and Arthur could be cut with a knife.

Fifteen minutes later, Arthur dropped the story on her desk. "Some of the townspeople are heading up to help. A few local women have volunteered to cook for the Rescue Team and families keeping vigil. I don't know how long I'll be gone—"

"I want to come," she interrupted, standing up, realizing she wanted to help. She'd ignored the tragedy of the families who'd lost their children to the defective formula to protect herself, her family. Perhaps this was her chance to make amends.

He scratched his cheek. "There won't be much for you to do. I'll be interviewing people, taking pictures."

Picking up her white gloves, she tugged them on, smoothing out the wrinkles. "I can take photos for you, or cook, or take care of any children who are there."

"Trust me, there won't be any children there. It's not a place for anyone with a soft stomach."

"I can take it," she said, infusing her voice with steel even though part of her knew he was right. She had no idea what she was getting herself into.

His blue eyes studied her. "You'll need to dress warmly. Perhaps change into something you don't mind getting dirty. If they have to blow part of the mine to clear out the rubble, we'll be covered in dirt."

Her nod was crisp, a contrast to her wobbling stomach. "Fine. I'll call in your story and then drop by the library to tell Maybelline. I can be back here in twenty minutes."

"Great. I'll have Alice over at the bakery make us up some lunch. These things often take a while."

"You've been to a cave-in before?" she asked, a little breathless in the face of his intensity and the thought of

213

what she'd agreed to do.

"Yes," he replied, putting his hands on his hips.

"What is it like?"

His eyes narrowed. "Gut-wrenching chaos."

***

If there was one thing about Arthur she'd come to appreciate, it was that he never exaggerated.

So when he told her to expect gut-wrenching chaos, he meant it.

Harriet surveyed the cluster of about a hundred people in what had been deemed the safe area or the Rescue Camp, as Arthur called it. The miners' wives and mothers were being comforted by a scattering of older men, probably the miners' fathers. The women were inconsolable, and she found herself brushing aside her own tears.

She couldn't imagine what they were feeling right now, with their men either dead or trapped in the mine that had put food on the table for their families. How horrible it must be to fear your children would never see their father again. And part of her realized she knew exactly how that felt, even if their situations were different.

Staring at the entrance to the mine was ghastly, but she couldn't seem to look away. A pile of rubble and dirt had slid out of the man-made hole, and men were digging to make a path into the heart of the mine.

Arthur kept her close to him, introducing her with her fake name, saying she worked at *The Western Independent* with him. He asked each interviewee the same general set of questions, adding in a few new ones when the person went off on a useful tangent.

As the day progressed, they learned more about the

men who were trapped in the mine. How Bill Powers was only twenty-three, the father of three girls, and helped out at his church. How Mathias Baconey was thirty-four, the father of five kids, and the best third baseman on the community baseball team. How Irving Walters was fifty-eight, the oldest miner in the group, the father of six kids, and the grandfather to twenty.

The stories were told in halting voices, the interviewees' fear-glazed eyes never looking directly at their faces, but always at the entrance to the mine where the Rescue Team was frantically working.

The effort to dig the men out was slow and tedious because the rubble had frozen and was as hard as concrete.

Her nose ran from the blistering cold. Up this high on the mountain, the wind was brisk and icy. Her teeth chattered a few times, prompting Arthur to nudge her toward the coffee station that had been set up by a handful of women.

The coffee was stronger and more bitter than any she'd ever drunk, but she thanked the women and asked who they knew in the mine.

Arthur was teaching her how to talk to people in these situations.

And making her realize that sometimes the only comfort left to a person was to share his or her story and have someone listen.

She brought him a cup of coffee too, the white cup nicked at the top from use.

"Thanks," he said, resting his notepad against his leg and drinking deep. "It sounds like it's going to be a long one. Why don't you take my car and head back to Dare? I can hitch a ride home with someone."

She only shook her head. "I want to stay."

Those blue eyes took her measure once again. "Okay. There are a few people leaving who can let Maybelline know you're going to be with us for the duration."

"Thank you. She would have been worried."

"No doubt. Let's take care of that, and then we can talk to someone on the Rescue Team. See if they've heard any of the men's voices with their equipment."

Arthur found a woman who was leaving, and Harriet gave her the information she'd need to get in touch with Maybelline. After thanking her, Arthur took Harriet's elbow and led her away from Rescue Camp. Her skin grew tight as they walked toward the rope cordoning off the path to the mine. Harriet realized that if they hadn't heard any of the men's voices yet, the trapped men were either all dead or too deeply buried for the sound to travel.

She was almost afraid to find out.

Arthur took her elbow when she slipped on the dirty snow, his grip firm. She was glad he didn't tell her to turn back.

"Paul," he shouted when they reached the rope.

A man with an orange hard hat looked over his shoulder and then said something to the rest of the team before jogging toward them, his boots making huge muddy imprints in the snow.

The men shook hands. Arthur introduced Harriet and offered Paul a cigarette. The man took a long drag, his gaze searching over their shoulders for a moment, as if taking in the scene behind them.

"What can you tell me?" Arthur asked.

His eyes flicked to Harriet, a question in them.

"You can talk in front of her. She won't say anything."

"It's bad," he said. "We haven't heard anything from

the men, which means they're in deep. We're waiting for other rescue teams to show up and start shoveling, but there was a blizzard to the south and west of us last night. Crews are having trouble digging out of that, and the roads are shit."

"What about the men from the surrounding towns?" Arthur asked.

"I'm about ready to ask for volunteers."

Arthur handed her his notepad. "You're looking at one."

Harriet turned to stare at him. His mouth was a grim line of determination.

"I thought you'd gotten too fancy for any real work out East," Paul responded, his mouth tipping up. "I've heard you're even wearing loafers. A far cry from the days when you and I would face off across the center line on the football field."

"What I would say to you if a lady weren't present…" Arthur only responded. "Why don't you let me round up some other volunteers from the camp? You have plenty to do."

Paul clapped him on the back. "Fine. It's good to have you back, Hale."

"It's good to be back," he responded.

The man turned and ran back toward the mine.

"What about the story?" Harriet asked, totally confused. Journalists were supposed to stand on the sidelines, right? Observe? Analyze? Not get involved.

"There are twenty-one men down there fighting for their lives. The story can wait."

He strode off toward the camp, his arms pumping with new vigor. Trailing in his wake, she realized she was more than a little in awe of him.

Even though he was younger than all the men in the camp, he found an apple crate someone had brought and stood on it in the center of the camp.

"Some of the surrounding rescue teams have been delayed by the blizzard last night. We need volunteers to help get the men out. Who's with me?" He thrust his fist into the air.

There was no loud cheer, but his short and sweet speech was like a battlefield cry of old. Men moved toward him from all sides. He shook their hands. Slapped some on the back. Always looking into their eyes when he did.

Arthur was very good at inspiring people.

He met her gaze, and for a moment, the punch of that fiery blue stole her breath.

Then they set off, the old and even older, men whose sons and grandsons were buried alive. When Arthur reached the rope, he flung it aside, and they all approached the rubble-strewn opening to hell.

Paul gave them instructions, and then the men took the shovels they were given from a nearby truck and headed toward the mine.

No one wore a hard hat. They were just a band of men, willing to put their lives on the line for the men who were trapped below.

Arthur led the way, his natural leadership evident. Why hadn't she seen the full power of his charisma until now?

His shovel penetrated the earth first as he put his back into it.

The men dug for four hours straight, slowly carving a path through the rubble. Harriet and some of the other women stood waiting with coffee at the rope line, which was now back in place.

Every now and then, the men would dash over to take a gulp. Then they'd head back, determination in every step. The small team of rescue workers continued digging for hours and hours. Lumber beams were hammered in place to fortify the makeshift entrance they'd dug and to prevent another cave-in.

Arthur found her on the few breaks he took, his face bathed in sweat despite the cold wind pushing around them, ruffling the surrounding pine trees. She would hand him some coffee and try to give him a smile of encouragement.

His mouth would tip up in response, but he didn't say anything.

In those moments, neither of them needed to.

The other rescue teams finally trickled in by the truckload. The number of men digging grew. Inch by precious inch, the mess in front of the mine was finally cleared. Then they continued deeper into the tunnel, backs breaking, breaths like puffs of smoke as they speared the rubble and shoveled it aside.

When the sun went down, the temperature plummeted with it. Harriet's hands were numb in her gloves, and her trembling wouldn't stop. Darkness settled all around them, punctuated by a few lone cries of coyotes, and with it, the crushing fear that the rescue would come too late.

They weren't just fighting the cave-in. They were fighting the cold, and hypothermia was a danger now. She glanced at her watch for the hundredth time, counting the hours the men had been down there.

So long.

Too long.

How much longer would they last?

She and the women set up lanterns and torches all around the camp and brought the rest to the rescue workers, adding them to the ones that had already been set up on makeshift poles. The light cast an eerie glow on the bodies bending over and digging, their shadows being cast on the wall behind them. They looked bigger than they were. Like the Titans from Greek mythology, she thought, able to execute Herculean feats.

Like digging twenty-one men out of hell.

The men dug all night and past dawn, hands blistered and bleeding.

Someone cried out as the sun finally rose over the mountain's ridge, which was dotted with a few deer out foraging for breakfast. Everyone in the camp stilled, waiting.

"We can hear them!" a man shouted, his words audible this time.

Women dissolved all around Harriet. As she rubbed one woman's back, tears slid down her own face. Her knees felt weak with relief, and the exhaustion of staying awake all night finally settled in. *Thank God.*

She kept vigil with the women as the rescue workers picked up their efforts to dig through the remaining rubble separating them from the miners. One woman started reciting the rosary aloud, and more women joined her. Harriet wasn't Catholic, but the continued repetition allowed her to memorize the prayer quickly. She began to chant with the other women as the men came for coffee or to devour a sandwich or an apple—anything that was handy.

Looking for Arthur's lanky frame to emerge for coffee from the make-shift tunnel they'd dug became Harriet's obsession. Her stomach quivered with fear when she couldn't see him.

And for the first time she felt like she understood a fraction of what the other women were feeling for their men. Even if Arthur wasn't *her* man.

At noon, they pulled the first man out. He stumbled out of the horrible hole, shivering, his face black and grooved, his eyes stark white in contrast.

"Martin!" a woman screamed and took off running.

The man limped toward her, and she lunged into his arms. He staggered back, but buried his face against her neck, and they stood there swaying in the wind, just holding each other.

Harriet felt a pinch in her heart. She wondered what it would be like to love a man like that and be so loved in return.

The woman next to her took her hand, and in that moment, she felt like she was one of them.

It took another hour to bring all the men out. And when the last couple reunited, his wife in his arms, his mother and father crying beside them, holding each other, she saw Arthur emerge from the mine.

He was filthy, but he shared a smile with Paul, his teeth a startling white against his dirt-smudged, unshaven face. They embraced and pounded each other on the back. As Arthur walked toward the rope line, he hugged the other men who had been digging with him. Shook hands with others.

And then he located her in the crowd, those blue eyes locking in on hers.

Her heart was suddenly as full and warm as a hot water bottle.

One of the men yanked the rope aside, and it fell to the ground on the muddy snow. She stepped over the line and made her way to Arthur. His eyes were blood-shot, filled with grit and exhaustion.

When she reached him, she latched her arms around him before she could think. "I'm so glad you're safe," she whispered as his face rested on her shoulder, his body heavy with fatigue.

His arms came around her, and he pulled her against him. She ran her hand over his neck, pressing him even closer.

When he finally leaned back an inch, their arms still around each other, she tipped her head up and saw his gaze travel from her eyes to her mouth. Her fingers contracted on his skin, beckoning him, inviting him.

He finally took her lips, the dirt and sweat of him going unnoticed by her. Shifting her closer, he changed the angle of the kiss and took her even deeper, unleashing an unfamiliar sensation.

Primal desire.

Her heart rapped against his, and her nearly frozen body finally turned warm in his arms. Her lips opened when his tongue sought hers, and in that slow, yet impatient dance, she finally understood what lay between them.

He wanted her.

She wanted him.

The truth had been there since their first meeting.

Someone shouted his name and clapped him on the back, interrupting their kiss. His eyes bore into her, all flame and fire now, and then he turned to look behind him.

To shake the man's hand, he had to let go of her with one arm, but he still held her close with the other. He simply introduced her as Harriet. Not as someone who worked for him, like he had before.

They talked with the other couples, other families. Everyone was celebrating the return of the miners, thanking the rescuers for their role in bringing them out. She stayed by Arthur's side the whole time, his hand around her waist.

No one looked at her strangely or questioned why she was being held by a man who wasn't her husband, a man she worked for, no less.

In this camp, with the relief running through it like a thread of gold in the mine wall, there were no questions about who she was or what she was to him.

When they finally made their way back to his car, and he had to let her go so she could get in, she realized everything between them had changed.

They drove in silence. He seemed too tired to talk, and she realized she probably should have offered to drive.

When he arrived at her house, he reached for her hand.

"We'll have to talk," he simply said.

"I know," she replied, making herself release his hand and leave the car.

Chapter 10

Arthur slept for fourteen hours straight. When he awoke, every muscle in his body felt like it was bruised from the inside out, and his hands looked like he'd installed fence posts on his family's ranch all day without gloves. As he located some liniment, he remembered dreaming about kissing Harriet. Sliding into her warm, wet mouth after he'd felt so cold for so long in that black hole had felt like coming home.

Leaving her at her doorstep with so much unsaid had been difficult but necessary. He needed—no, wanted—all his wits about him when they talked about what had happened.

After getting dressed, he decided he deserved another shave at the Barber Shop. He wanted the tactile comfort of having his face steamed with that rough, white towel. Dave was buzzing with talk about the cave-in and about Arthur's role in the rescue. He just closed his eyes, not wanting to feed any talk about him being a hero. He had done what needed to be done. That was all there was to it.

The questions followed him when he popped into Kemstead's Bakery for a treat of coffee and one of their award-winning homemade cinnamon rolls. He relayed the stories of the men who'd been trapped, shifting the conversation away from himself. Everyone agreed it was by the grace of God that no one had been critically injured.

When he finally made his way to his office, he spotted Harriet's sedan on Main Street. Picking up his pace, he entered the building, only to see that she wasn't alone. Herman Smith was leaning over her desk, his hands resting on his tool belt. He was flirting, Arthur realized with a pang.

It was as creepy as *Invasion of the Body Snatchers.*

"I'll tell you, it was brave of you to go up there, Harriet," Herman said. "If I hadn't been out helping old Mrs. Henderson with her septic tank yesterday, I would have helped dig those men out."

Since Herman weighed about one hundred and forty pounds, Arthur doubted he could have lifted much dirt. Then he caught himself. Why was he being so nasty all of the sudden? Because he was jealous, he realized. Creepy flirting or not.

Harriet caught sight of him and dropped her pen. "Good morning," she said.

Herman slapped him on the back, making him wince. "Heard about what you did from Patricia Depay. She said you were a regular hero."

"I did what needed to be done," he responded briskly. "Good morning, Harriet."

She met his eyes, and then promptly lowered them. So she was feeling unsure this morning too. Well, then.

"Let me make you some coffee," she announced, rising from her seat, looking tired yet lovely in a pale pink cashmere sweater set and navy skirt.

Her gesture surprised him. After all, she'd gone out of

225

her way to tell him she would never make him any. She must be feeling the change between them too.

"No need. I just had some at Kemstead's."

"But I want to," she said softly.

The sweetness moved through him. "Then I'd love some. Thank you."

She gestured to the front page of *The Denver Post*. "When did you call this in?"

His article chronicling the whole event was featured in the upper right hand corner. "After I dropped you off."

"But you were—"

"Exhausted, yes, but I had to tell the story."

Her face fell, and he realized she was probably thinking about how he'd dropped her off and then come back here to hammer out the story.

Maybe she was worried his story was more important to him than their talk.

What she needed to understand was that he'd had the words for the story, but not for her. Not with the bone-crushing fatigue as heavy as an anvil on his chest.

"It took me five minutes to type it up and call it in," he added. "I composed the article while I was digging."

Her mouth changed into a small smile, one of her reserved ones. "It's an incredible piece, Arthur."

He nodded because he knew it was. He'd mentioned his involvement briefly, talking about what it had been like to dig next to men from his surrounding community, working against the clock to free the trapped men. How he'd felt when they heard the first shouts from the miners. How he'd almost gotten teary eyed seeing the first man stumble through the narrow hole they'd dug, face dark as pitch.

Herman rocked on his heels. "Well, I guess I'd better

226

be seeing to the radiator. Harriet, I'll take some coffee too if that's all right."

"Of course," she replied.

"Herman, I need to speak to Harriet about an urgent follow-up story." Frankly he didn't like the idea of Herman getting coffee the first time Harriet made it for him. Wow, he *was* jealous, and over something as banal as coffee. Yeah, the winds had changed, all right.

His friend glanced between the two of them. "Sure thing, Arthur." And there was speculation in his eyes.

Arthur could tell Herman had heard the story about his kiss with Harriet on the mountain. At the time, he hadn't thought about that news making the rounds.

He inclined his head to his office, and Harriet walked in. Studying her trim waist, he remembered how soft she'd been in his arms. Closing the door partially, he sat on the edge of his desk as she took her usual seat in front of him.

"Folks around here have heard about our kiss by now," he said, deciding the direct approach was best. "I'd like to take you out to supper tonight if that's all right. If not, do you want me to tell anyone who asks that it was a momentary reaction to a life-and-death event?" Thankfully no one at Kemstead's had alluded to it.

Her fingers stroked her throat. "You're asking me out?"

Why did women always ask questions like that? "Isn't that what I said? I kissed you, I want you, and that's that."

A slow smile spread across her face. "Aren't you going to ask me how I feel about it?"

He leaned forward. "I already know. I could feel it when you were in my arms."

The smile turned into a pucker, like she'd just tasted a fresh lemon. "You're arrogant."

He stood and caged her in with his hands on the arms of the chair. "No, my dear, I'm observant."

She leaned forward, and up close, he could see the kaleidoscope of different greens in her eyes.

"Are you wearing a new cologne?" she asked, her nose scrunching up.

He struggled not to laugh. The odor was horrendous. "That would be liniment. When I woke up, I felt like I was eighty years old. It took me two minutes to stand up straight. Every muscle hurt. Hands too. Typing last night hurt like hellfire. I had a flash of what a pain in the…posterior…getting old will be."

"You have a ways to go," she said, scanning his frame. "It doesn't surprise me you were so sore. What you did was one of the bravest things I've ever seen."

He cupped her face before he could stop himself. "No," he replied. "I'm from this town. I knew some of those people, if only by name. You were the brave one. I'll never forget how you stood there with those other women, giving us coffee and food all through the long, cold night. Harriet, you are nothing like I thought you were."

She ducked her head again. "Neither are you."

"So, will you go out to supper with me?" he asked again.

"Yes."

"Good." His hand dropped. "I need to follow up with some of the miners who were injured in the cave-in. Do you want to come with me?"

"That would be nice, but first, I'm going to go make you some coffee. You still look tired." She turned and walked to the door.

"Harriet," he called.

She turned.

"I thought you said you weren't going to make me coffee," he said, needing to ask.

And there was that slow smile again. How beautifully it offset her high pinkish cheekbones.

"Things change."

Yes, he guessed they did.

And with that, she spun around and gave him a view that men since Adam had coveted—the round backside of a beautiful woman.

***

He sent her home at five o'clock and told her he would pick her up at six sharp. Then he took off himself to change for their date.

Maybelline answered the door when he knocked, giving him the narrow-eyed regard of a suspicious sister. "I don't know that this is a good idea," she said with her unerring New England directness.

His brow winged up, and he shrugged. "As your sister said, 'Things change.'"

The click of heels on hardwood announced Harriet's approach, and boy did the woman know how to make an entrance. She stopped in the doorway of the parlor and propped her hand on the door frame, giving him the opportunity to take in the whole picture. Her body seemed like a lush valley rising and falling with the curve of her breasts and hips. Her red hair curled on her shoulders, down like it had been the night she'd met him in the black slip. *Don't go there, Hale.* It contrasted pleasantly with a green blouse. The black skirt fell just below her knees, accentuating the slow slide of her calf muscles into her black heels. Her lips were tinted a fiery red, and he knew if he ended up kissing her tonight—which he planned to—

he'd need a handkerchief to scrub off the paint, something he was all too eager to do.

"Arthur," she said, finally lowering her arm.

Suddenly he had a new understanding of the phrase tongue-tied. He inclined his head and stopped short of bowing.

"Harriet. Are you ready?"

"Yes," she simply answered, walking to the closet and taking out her coat.

He stepped forward and reached for it as she turned, their motions as smooth as if they were dancing a tango in Paris, the steps known to them both even though they'd never danced them together.

Since Maybelline was still watching, he didn't let his hands linger on her shoulders as he helped her shrug into the sleeves. She tugged on her navy gloves after fastening her coat buttons, which were the popular over-sized ones, as big as fresh-baked cookies. Then she turned to hug her sister.

"Be careful," Maybelline whispered, loud enough for him to hear.

"Don't worry. I'll be fine," Harriet assured her.

Arthur wondered if she were trying to give both him and Maybelline the same message.

"Night, Maybelline," he said and opened the door for Harriet.

They walked out into the dark, cold night dotted with a thousand stars. He took her elbow, leading her to the car, and opened the door for her.

He drove them to Nellie's Tavern. Though he liked the American Legion, the food wasn't as good, and he wanted Harriet to enjoy herself since she was used to finer restaurants back East. It was a Thursday night, but there was a good amount of cars on Main Street. As they walked in, people looked up. Some waved. Some even called out his name.

Everyone seemed to have a knowing glint in their eye as he and Harriet made their way to an open booth. He helped her with her coat and then dispensed with his own, hanging them on the nearby rack.

Seated across from her, the conversation swirling around them, he leaned back and blocked out everything but her. But it was hard, knowing what people were saying, thinking. God, he hated being the subject of gossip.

At least the muted light in the tavern and the dark wood imparted a sense of privacy, even if it was an illusion.

"Stop frowning," she ordered as Bertha Linglefield, their waitress, appeared with water and dog-eared menus.

Bertha chatted about the cave-in, as he'd known she would, but she didn't include Harriet in the conversation. After she left, he hung his arm on the back of the booth.

"I'm not frowning at you."

"I know," she said, "but we both knew this would happen if we went out together tonight."

"And after what happened at the mine," he added, his voice dipping into a lower octave.

Her eyes flicked up, and he saw desire in them for a quick second before she smiled. "Yes. That was a rather in-the-moment kind of thing."

Not for him. He'd been thinking about kissing her since the moment she sashayed into his office and asked him *not* to call her sweetheart.

"Do you regret it?" he decided to ask.

She folded her hands on the table. "I wouldn't be here if I did."

"Good," he said gruffly. "So, let's decide what to eat, and then we can talk."

"You aren't going to order for me?" she asked, surprise in her voice.

"Gads, no. I would never presume to tell you what to eat."

She raised the menu, blocking her face from him, but he could hear the smile in her voice when she said, "Good."

Bertha came back to take their order and wanted to chat more about the cave-in, so Arthur talked to her while Harriet patiently sat across from him. He'd known Bertha since he was in short britches, and she was the best waitress in Dare, but she sure could be nosy. And she clearly wanted to know why he and Harriet were eating at the tavern together.

"So are you and Harriet working on a new article?" she asked, fingering her pink apron with NT handstitched in the corner.

He didn't reply, and silence hung over the table for a good minute. "No," Harriet finally responded with a smile, asserting herself. "He told me Nellie's Tavern was the best place in town, and since I'm new to Dare, he wanted to bring me here to find out for myself. What's your favorite?"

So she hadn't been here before. He'd figured as much. Everyone said the sisters didn't venture out much beyond a couple meals at The American Legion.

Arthur hung back and watched as Harriet took over the conversation. He didn't interject that they were on a date, since Harriet hadn't seen fit to share that information. After Bertha said her favorite things were the roast beef, mashed potatoes, and green beans finished off with banana cream pie, Harriet said she'd have exactly that. After Arthur muttered, "I'll have the same," Harriet flashed Bertha another winning smile, and the waitress walked off, beaming herself.

"You're good with people," he observed, something he'd noticed in her interactions with everyone from Herman to Ernest, the mailman.

"And you're gruff when you don't like people asking questions about you," she observed right back.

"Hallmark of a good journalist." He almost harrumphed for good measure.

She took a sip of her water. "Asking questions of other people is okay, but not about you?"

"I'm an open book," he responded, spreading both arms across the booth all casual-like.

Her delicate rust-colored brows rose. "I doubt that."

"Ask me anything."

"So you played football. What position?"

"How did you—"

"The rescue worker mentioned it. I forget his name now."

Much of that night had become blurred in his mind from the sheer exhaustion of digging. "Oh. Well, yeah. I was quarterback. We didn't make the state championship, but we won eight to ten games a year. Not too bad."

Her posture was so prim, as if she'd just matriculated from finishing school. He had the sudden desire to see her mussed up.

"Did you play any other sports?"

"Sure," he replied. "Baseball. Basketball. There's not much to do in Dare, as you have probably seen, so it's pretty much sports, church, and family gatherings."

"That sounds nice," she responded. "Did you letter?"

He scoffed. "Of course. All sports. Okay, so now you know I'm a sportsman. What about you? What were your hobbies growing up?"

She tilted her head to the side, almost as if embarrassed. "Well, I played piano and took drawing and painting classes. A few singing lessons, but I was never accomplished enough to perform. That's Maybelline's expertise. She was a soprano in Wellesley's choir her freshman year."

And now that door is closed, he thought. "I don't know if Emmits Merriam has a choir, but I'm sure they'd be open to forming one." If they stayed, which he was starting to hope they would.

Her face fell, and he was sorry he'd brought it up.

"That's good to know. This is all a big change for her. She loved Wellesley as much as I did."

She didn't need or want pity. That he understood all too well. So he only nodded.

"Now that we're going to stay for a while, Maybelline wants to do something. She's tired of being bored at home, reading and playing wife to me." Harriet laughed self-consciously.

"What's she going to do?"

"She's going to volunteer at the library. She loves books."

"That sounds like a mighty fine idea. I'm sure they'll be grateful for the help."

"I'm lucky," Harriet continued. "I already have my degree. With Maybelline…well, she's resigned to going somewhere like Emmits Merriam perhaps, somewhere other than Wellesley. But it's hard. Our mother went there, you see."

Ah, another legacy broken, and Dare's new university

would be nothing like Wellesley. "I didn't know that. Harriet, I hope you can find a way to tell me about your past, even with what lies between us about your father."

Her chest rose as she took a deep breath. He knew he'd surprised her. "For example, should I be calling you Evangelina?"

"I never went by Evangelina," she said after taking another delicate sip of water. "Harriet is what everyone calls me. Except for my father."

Lowering his arms from the booth, no longer feeling casual, he leaned forward. "Will you tell me about him? What you remember? Was he a good father?"

She crossed her hands prayer-like, but her posture was brittle. "He was a very driven man, known for his excellence in science. He expected the same of me and Maybelline. When he was home, which was rare, he would always ask us about what we'd learned in school or what we thought about this or that current event. I remember when he first asked me what I thought about the war in Korea. I was in high school. I didn't have an answer prepared, and told him so. I could see he was disappointed. After that I read what I could. The next time he asked me, I had an answer."

The dissimilarity of their childhoods couldn't be starker. He'd been raised by simple ranching people, who loved the land and knew more about the animals they tended than current events. Growing up, he'd wanted to talk with them about what he was reading in the national newspapers he'd begged the library to purchase. The news might have been old by the time it reached him, but it made him feel connected to something bigger than Dare Valley, which he loved, but knew was only one small dot on a rather big map.

Then he met Emmits Merriam while doing some manual labor at his summer house, and his life changed forever.

He'd asked Emmits what he thought about establishing oil production in Iran, which Exxon (was it "Exxon" or "Esso"?) and British Petroleum were discussing with the Shah. Emmits had stopped what he was doing, stroked his chin—a stalling tactic Arthur had picked up from him—and then asked how old he was.

When he responded, "sixteen," Emmits laughed and told him to come inside. He'd brought him into his study, a room filled with photos of him with famous presidents like FDR and Truman. Ivory tusks hung on the wall, a relic from a safari in Africa. And leather-bound, gold-embossed books were everywhere. Arthur had decided then and there he was going to have a study like that some day.

They'd talked for two hours about the future of oil exploration in the Gulf. And from that day onward, Emmits would invite Arthur in for another discussion after he finished his chores. It had been heaven on earth to him.

"Emmits and I used to discuss current events when I was in high school," he simply responded.

"He was your mentor, wasn't he?"

"Yes," he said, still feeling that sense of luck and destiny or whatever the poets called it. "I did chores at his summer house up here, and one day we got to discussing current events. From then on, Emmits saw something in me. 'Potential,' he called it. He suggested I apply to Columbia University and take classes in everything to see what I wanted to do. He was on the board and supported the school, so that helped my application. Dare's education system is…well."

Something Emmits had a mind to improve, he

thought, but didn't say.

She nodded, her soft gaze on his face.

"When I attended my first journalism class," he continued, "within minutes, I knew I had found my calling." It was as if he had been given the key to an unknown cipher about himself. The feeling was exhilarating, but it had made him worry for the man who'd been raised in the simple town of Dare Valley.

"And Emmits opened doors for you," she added.

His mouth quirked up. "So I'm not the only one who knows how to investigate."

That bold green-eyed stare again. "I had to know as much as I could about you."

He'd leave what she thought she knew for another time. "Yes, Emmits got me the job at *The New York Times* and opened doors for me when it came to interviews. But he knew I would do a da—darn good job at it. It wasn't charity."

They had been very clear about that.

"You have your pride."

"Darn right," he responded, rapping his knuckles on the table for emphasis. A man's pride was important. Hadn't Harriet's father and so many others lost everything out of damaged pride?

"I worked at the paper throughout school to pay for rent and tuition." And got a little financial aid, which he didn't need to mention, in addition to what his parents had been able to contribute. "I didn't sleep much, but New York isn't that kind of a town."

Her mouth tipped up. "No, it's not. Do you miss it?"

He looked around the tavern at people he'd known all his life. He liked being known here. Being cared about. He hadn't felt that way in New York. "I like Dare for its strengths and understand what it's not able to offer me."

"And what's that?" she asked.

"Sophistication. I doubt I could get a decent Manhattan here, but I still ask Vernon, the bartender, to make one for me. And the anonymity. No one knew who I was in the city, and there's freedom in that. I was just Arthur Hale, and sometimes that felt nice."

"Yes, Dare's prying eyes are a little tiresome." She leaned against the booth, finally relaxing that prim pose. "Is everyone still staring at us?"

He glanced over and winked at old Mrs. Withers, whose mouth dropped open when she realized she'd been caught staring.

"You're terrible," she managed with a laugh, resuming her picture-perfect posture.

"Sometimes," he responded, his gaze resting on her face. That face with skin so bright and clear it reminded him of the clouds on a summer day in Wildflower Canyon.

They grew quiet.

Bertha finally brought their food. Harriet picked at her steaming roast beef while he went straight for the creamy mashed potatoes, his favorite.

"My mother died when I was eight," she said as she forked the green beans. "My dad dove into his work more after that. Before, I remember us all laughing, and him working less."

Reaching across the table for her hand would only cause more talk. He put his utensils down to show he was paying attention. "I'm sorry."

She smoothed some curls behind her ears. "Me too."

They continued to eat and talk, sharing stories from the past. He started to see a fuller picture of who she was and still knew there was so much more. But they had time.

She was staying in town until she and her sister decided on their next steps.

And even while he told himself to protect his heart from the woman across from him, somehow he couldn't. He'd always known when a risk was worth it, and there was no question that *she* was.

He stole looks at her often enough that he noticed when her eyes widened. He looked over his shoulder to see Vera Henry digging a toothpick into her front teeth like she was digging for clams.

"Ah, people around here like their toothpicks," he said, clearing his throat to cover up his laugh. So far as he could tell, no one used toothpicks out East, especially women and certainly not in public.

"Apparently," she managed and snapped her red-painted mouth closed.

"Just another difference between Dare and the big city." He fished a toothpick out of the white plastic holder next to the horseradish jar and extended it to her. "Are you sure you don't want to try it? My dentist swears by them."

Her mouth twisted like she was fighting a smile. "No thank you. My toothbrush seems to do the job just fine."

He shoved one into his mouth like his dad did after every meal and flashed her a smile. "You're missing out."

And then she laughed, the sound like a train whistle, bold and yet oddly sweet. "You're incorrigible."

They enjoyed the banana cream pie, and he discovered she liked to bake, especially around Christmas. She told him stories about learning from their maid, Joanna, who'd been like a mother to them after their own had passed. She still wrote a letter to her every week.

After he paid the bill, he escorted her through the tavern. None of the other patrons had left their tables, toddling over more than one cup of coffee. No doubt about it—they'd stayed to see if Dare's own Arthur Hale was under the lure of the mysterious city-spun outsider. Many wouldn't be happy about that.

Like he cared.

And wasn't that putting the cart before the horse?

He drove Harriet to Hawk's Point Bluff since the moon was nearly full, and he didn't want to take her home just yet. Even though it was cold, he asked her if she wanted to walk down the snowy path with him.

"I will if you make sure I don't fall," she replied.

He promised he wouldn't, hoping she realized he was also making a promise to be there for her.

With his arm around her, they walked the six yards to the edge of the bluff. The moon illuminated the snowy blanket covering the earth. The pine trees cascading up the side of the mountain waved darkly in the breeze.

He turned to her then, and the moonlight covered her face, starkly illuminating the angles of her cheekbones, which called out to be traced by his fingertips.

"Harriet," he murmured, caressing her delicate skin.

"Hush," she whispered and stepped closer.

He kissed her in the moonlight and let the moment be enough.

Chapter 11

Working with Arthur during the day and then going to dinner with him most evenings provided an ongoing opportunity for Harriet to discover that there was so much more to him than she'd first imagined.

As the weeks passed, winter still clung to the trees in the form of snow and ice, and the breeze felt like it was issuing from an automatic fan over a block of ice. According to the people she talked to at the market and the Five-and-Dime, the groundhog had seen its shadow, and sure enough, spring felt like a distant memory.

Arthur made the most of it on one Saturday in early March, agreeing for once not to work all day at the office. They were having an outdoor date since they'd already seen the new movie that had arrived in Dare, Frank Capra's *Pocketful of Miracles* with Betty Davis and Glenn Ford, which would be showing for the next month.

Their staff was growing, and Arthur was busy training the new hires and planning for the launch of the paper. They had five reporters now, Arthur's deputy, an advertising manager, a bookkeeper, a financial manager, a typesetter, and the head of distribution. The new printing press had arrived, along with the large news rolls and tubs of ink, and had been assembled in the old factory. Arthur and the typesetter were getting familiar with its quirks by doing dry runs. And the distribution manager, with Arthur's guidance, had been working out the best routes to get the papers out to Denver and other major cities. High school students in Dare had been hired to go door-to-door to ask for local subscriptions.

Arthur had also been making visits to Denver, Las Vegas, and San Francisco, talking with the bigger newspapers, hoping to run articles from *The Western Independent*, including his Sunday editorials, in theirs from time to time. With Emmits' connections, he was collecting national subscriptions right and left.

"I'm not sure snow-shoeing was the smartest idea you've had," she commented as her snow-shoe sunk into the powdery snow again, throwing off her balance for the hundredth time.

He looked back over his shoulder, his blue eyes twinkling. "You only need to walk faster. If you lug through the snow, you'll fall. You need to stay light on your feet."

Right. With two shoes that looked like large wooden tennis rackets secured to her feet with rawhide. Yeehaw.

He had to outweigh her by fifty pounds, and he looked a heck of a lot lighter on his feet. It was enough to make a girl jealous.

"This view had better be worth it," she complained, her face and lips becoming chapped by the wind.

"Have I steered you wrong yet?" he asked, his arms pumping as he walked across the snowy basin.

"No," and the words hung between them as he stopped and waited for her to catch up so he could hold her hand.

Then he stepped close and framed her face. "I can't wait. I have to kiss you. Right now."

His cold lips touched hers, and inside, she felt the now familiar desire race through her from head to toe. Suddenly the sun felt too hot, and she too warm. As his lips caressed hers and then shifted to kiss her cheeks and eyebrows before moving back to her mouth, she took a step closer and sank into the snow three feet in front of him. Her hands slid from his shoulders to his waist, and she was clinging to him out of something other than passion.

Laughter bubbled out easily. "What's with me? I weigh less than you do by a mile, and I keep sinking."

His hands fit to the outside curve of her breasts, and he slowly pulled her up. "Perhaps there's another reason you're sinking."

As she looked into his blue eyes, a blue that now reminded her of the ocean near her old home, she realized that no truer words had ever been spoken.

She was sinking. Into him. More and more every day.

And was more than a little afraid of it.

"So where were we before you fell to your knees before me?" he asked with a wink.

His tone was playful, but she'd heard stories from other students at Wellesley about what it meant to sink to your knees in front of a boy. But when she glanced up to meet his eyes, she could tell that he wasn't implying anything more. Part of her was relieved, the mere idea making her blush.

He'd kissed her and touched her through her clothes, but that's as far as they'd gone. She knew he wanted her, and she wanted him, but they weren't married, and she was terrified of getting pregnant. Which just showed how crazy desperate she'd been the night she'd tried to seduce him. Some of the girls she knew at Wellesley had gotten birth control pills in Boston, but even if she wanted to go that far with Arthur—which she wasn't sure of yet—there were no such provisions in Dare. He hadn't asked for more, but if the tight mouth he had when he pushed her away and said goodnight was any indication, she knew he was suffering.

"I think you were kissing me," she responded, ducking her face, suddenly shy.

His brows quirked up, as they always did when he was teasing her. "Ah. How could I have forgotten? Let me see if I can jog my memory."

His mouth leaned in and bussed her cheek.

"There's nothing wrong with your memory." In fact, it constantly amazed her. He was the most brilliant man she'd ever known.

"But I want to get it *just* right," he murmured against her mouth, nipping at the corners, making her clasp his back with her mitten-clad hands.

"Arthur." Even she heard the plea in her voice and was shocked by it.

She said nothing more as he pulled her against his chest and fit his mouth to hers. They'd perfected the art of kissing each other, since that's as far as they'd gone. He knew how to press his tongue against hers and then dance around it, inviting her to take the next pass with him. Once she did, he would edge back and change the angle of the kiss before coming back inside her mouth.

As she fell under his spell, the winter clothes she was wearing started to feel hot and suffocating. Her body turned liquid, like an icicle in the full sun.

When he edged back, he cupped her cheek and stared boldly into her eyes. As if he saw her and only her and wanted to look at nothing else for the rest of his life.

"Bingo," he said, his eyes twinkling.

She laughed shakily, trying to diffuse the desire shimmering between them. "That reminds me. I've heard you're a wicked Bingo player."

He laughed, the sound deep and infectious in the snowy basin. "I am. I find out all sorts of information there. Be good for the Metro section of the paper when we launch. You should come with me sometime."

Taking his hand, she stepped back and squared her shoulders to continue their trek. "I might just do that."

The townspeople were becoming more accustomed to seeing them together, and while they were still watched with curiosity, she was either getting used to the attention or immune to it. When she was with Arthur, time stood still.

"Maybelline just joined the church choir," she absently commented. "She has her first solo tomorrow."

"Wonderful! I can't wait to hear her," he responded in that easy-going way of his.

"She seems happier now that she has music back in her life," she continued and then paused for a moment as a bald eagle flew over them, casting its massive shadow across the basin, its stark cry full of both longing and boldness.

The awe she had for this place grew every day, from the deer she'd seen eating at the edge of the road to the moose that had lumbered across the path they'd been skiing on a few weeks back, prompting Arthur to laughingly declare that it was one beast he had no desire to mess with.

"And what about you?" he asked suddenly. "Are you feeling fulfilled here?" He stopped again, stepping in front of her so he could touch her shoulder. "While there's nothing wrong with being a secretary, I know it's not your dream. What *is* your dream, Harriet?"

Her head lowered, and she shifted on her feet. How could she tell him that she wanted to be a wife and mother? That she imagined spending her time helping out at her children's school, the church, and the local garden club. Perhaps that's why she liked Dare so much even though she still felt like an outsider. Her dad had wanted her to be a scientist, to pave the way for women in a male-dominated profession, and while she believed in equal rights, she didn't want to sacrifice her family for it—like her father had.

Her mother had stayed home, but Harriet didn't remember spending much quality time with her. She'd been too caught up in the society set to bother with her children. Their maid had raised them, and Harriet didn't want that to be true for her kids.

"What?" he said gently, tipping up her chin. "What are you having such a hard time putting into words?"

She cleared her throat, which felt like there was a frog in it. "Well, with a father who worked all the time, and a mother who was never home, I kind of dreamed about being a happy wife and mother and helping out in the community."

His smile started slow, but it soon spread across his face. "I don't know why, but you still manage to surprise me. That sounds like a wonderful dream."

"You don't think I'm wasting my talents?" she asked him.

"Who told you that?"

"My father," she confessed, wishing she hadn't brought him up.

The tension between them wasn't as intense as it used to be on this topic, but it was still there, on both sides. Hovering. Like waiting for thunder after a lightning strike.

"Whatever you choose to do for *you* is the best thing. My mother raised us and helped out on the ranch, and I can't think of one minute when she wasn't using her talents. Perhaps I'm old fashioned, but it all starts at home."

She wondered again about what his family was like. Though his mother had popped by the office a few times, he hadn't introduced her formally yet, and even she knew it was a big step. Especially since her background was still a secret.

"I like that about you," she said, her voice hushed.

He framed her face and kissed her smack on the lips. "And I like that about you. Now, come on. We have some tracks to lay, or we won't be back to the car before dark."

She rolled her eyes, not really caring if they reached their destination, but he really wanted her to see this surprise, so she trudged through the snow after him. About fifteen minutes later, a light bulb went off in her head. She realized that she sunk into the snow less if she made smaller steps with her shoes. Plus it helped her move faster. Modeling Arthur's long steps had seemed the way to go, but he was taller, and it wasn't her natural stride.

With her newfound knowledge, she passed him for the first time since they'd set out over an hour ago.

"Somebody's found their rhythm," he commented with a grin.

"You betcha," she added, using one of his favorite phrases, and kept moving forward.

They trudged on in the silence, the late afternoon sun shining like a golden orb of fire above them, the blue sky as vast as the ocean.

When they reached the edge of the forest, he took her hand, squeezed, and rubbed her cheek with his finger.

"Best follow me now. We're nearly there."

The cold penetrated her clothing more without the sun to warm them. A trio of deer darted off across their path, leaping through the woods with the grace of ballerinas departing the stage.

As they broke through the next copse, Arthur halted. Harriet's mouth fell open in awe.

"Oh, my gosh," she said, staring at the frozen waterfall ahead of them.

A rock face of one hundred feet rippled with ice, ending in a frozen pool. The twists and turns of the ice gave the sight its own artistic magic, rather like the whitest, most translucent candle wax dripping down a pillar.

"People climb the waterfall in the coldest part of winter," Arthur commented. "But that time has passed. Spring is coming, and even the mountain can't stop it."

She turned to him, placing a hand on his arm because she liked touching him that way. "Did you ever—"

"Some of my classmates might tell you I have, but I'm not confirming it."

Just thinking about him trying to climb that wall of ice terrified her. "I hope you have more sense now."

"I don't feel quite the need to prove myself like I used to," he said. "I've moved beyond that old George Mallory quote about needing to climb Everest 'because it's there.'"

"I'm glad," she replied, wrapping her arms around herself as the wind blew.

He stepped behind her and pulled her against him. "You cold?" he asked.

"Arthur, you are not normally a man who states the obvious," was her response.

Nuzzling her ear with his nose, he laughed softly. "Then let me state the unobvious."

"Is that even a word?"

"I don't care," he murmured, sliding his lips along her ear lobe, just under her stocking hat. "Do you want me to warm you up? How's that for less than obvious?"

Now she laughed. "I'd say, being a man and a woman, that couldn't be more obvious."

He spun her around. "Oh, really? You might be right there." Kissing her one more time, he grabbed her hand. "Then how about some ice skating?"

She jerked away and dug her feet into the snow. "There is no way I am going out on a pool of ice when you can see bubbles of water under the surface."

Letting her go, he walked toward the pool and tapped the frozen pond with his snow shoe. "It's still pretty solid. Folks stop walking across this pond come late March. We have a while yet."

"Arthur, please," she said, because she'd heard about people falling through the ice this time of year.

"Okay, Harriet. You win. But how about taking a closer look at the waterfall? That alone is a thing of beauty."

They walked along the edge of the pool, the snow covering the grass and wildflowers that would spring up again in another couple of months.

He put his arms around her again and kissed her cheek. Holding her, they stood gazing at that austere tower of ice. Harriet realized that's what she'd been when she had come to Dare, so determined to bring Arthur down and have her revenge.

Suddenly his arms tightened. "Harriet, I love you."

Somewhere deep inside, she'd known it was coming, known he wouldn't fear saying the words first.

"Oh, Arthur," she whispered, not exactly sure how to express how she felt about him or what he'd just said. For so long, everything between them had been so complicated. And staying here was supposed to be a temporary plan.

"Is that an 'Oh, Arthur, good,' or 'Oh, Arthur, bad'?" he asked with his usual directness laced with a hint of humor.

She stroked his hands, which were still resting on her stomach. "'Oh, Arthur, good,' I think."

"Then that's enough for now. I know we still have more to sort out, but I want you to know you can trust me."

"I know that," she replied easily. Arthur stood for integrity. It was the core of who he was.

And why, yes, she was a little in love with him.

"Let's head back," he finally said, nuzzling her neck through her scarf.

She turned in his arms and lifted her face to his. "Let's give it a while."

Next to that tower of ice that was slowly melting underneath just like she was, she opened her mouth and poured everything she felt into their kiss.

Chapter 12

Emmits Merriam had the barrel-chested body of a linebacker, even at eighty-one. His hair was shock-white now, yet he still had that same take-no-prisoners attitude Arthur had always appreciated.

"Well, now," he boomed out from Arthur's doorway, spreading his arms wide in the frame. "Doesn't this place look a sight better than the last time I saw it."

Arthur took a moment to catalogue the changes. Yes, the walls were all painted white now, and the space had been filled with more furniture now that his staff topped out at a grand total of fifteen. The artwork on the walls gave the office a pleasant ambiance. Harriet had a fine eye and had arranged all the framing. A photo of President Kennedy giving a speech in Washington hung by the wall near Harriet's desk. Other black and white photos lined the hallway, from FDR to Martin Luther King, Jr., and a world map graced the wall outside the break room.

"Yes, doesn't it?" he responded. "Good to have you back. Come into my office and sit a spell."

Emmits slapped him on the back and followed him.

"Happy to."

In his office, they'd hung photos of him with various congressman and business executives. And his two favorites: one of him and his old boss from *The Times*, Arthur Hays Sulzberger, and the other of him and Emmits in the Capitol Rotunda, taken when he'd accompanied Emmits on some political door-knocking.

When Emmits sat in the chair in front of Arthur's desk, he folded his hands across his belly and inclined his head toward the door. "Is that the pretty thing I've heard you're sweet on?" he said bluntly.

After going five months without seeing each other, he'd thought his friend would be eager to talk about the university and the paper. This question couldn't have been more surprising—or annoying.

"You're sitting in the office of *The Western Independent* for the first time, and that's what you've got to say?"

"You afraid to answer me, boy?" he challenged with his famous Oklahoma drawl.

That word made him feel like he was sixteen all over again. "No. That's the girl." He pushed aside the newspaper in front of him and reached into his bottom drawer for a bottle of Emmits' favorite bourbon, Pappy Van Winkle's, and two glasses, pouring them both a dram even though it was mid-afternoon. If he'd been in New York, drinking this early would have been commonplace. Plus, he'd been waiting for this moment. He felt like a proud papa over his baby, this newspaper. It was all coming together.

"My wife had one rule when we got married," Emmits mused, grabbing his glass and extending it in a toast. "She told me my secretaries had to be twenty years older than me and as ugly as a mud fence. Joanne is one smart woman."

"Amen to that," Arthur agreed, although the whole secretary thing made him uncomfortable. "How is the university going?"

"Coming along nicely, thanks for asking. Just had a meeting to tour more of the finished construction this morning. I knew Preston Sullivan was the man to set things up." He extended his glass again. "Just like I knew you would create a damn fine newspaper."

Arthur looked around. "It's not a newspaper yet. Takes forever to start up." He'd given himself plenty of time, but sometimes the waiting drove him nuts.

"Don't I know it? The university won't open its doors until this coming fall, but there's plenty of work going on now. Admissions are being finalized. We're setting up for the first board meeting. I have to remind myself that a good foundation can't be rushed," Emmits said. "Like yours. You have employees now. And you're getting more subscribers every day. We both know there's no point in putting out something no one's going to read."

"Your mobilizers are doing a fine job," Arthur said, picking up the recent folder of names from Chicago. "Thank you for the help."

"If there's one thing I learned in my failed attempt for the Oklahoma senator's seat, it's how to get the word out and take names. We're doing something big here, Arthur. Education and information—the hallmarks of this century."

Emmits never did anything by halves, something Arthur admired. Small acts never caused enduring change.

"I read the articles you wrote on the mine cave-in," he continued. "Your usual combination of gritty details with a human touch came across like a holiday post card. Might be a Pulitzer prize in there for you. Right now, I think you're a shoe-in for the Wentworth editorial. Be a big boon for the paper's launch."

His gut clenched.

Harriet.

He'd been trying to forget that Pulitzer winners would be announced May 1st. His excitement at the prospect of being elevated to that elite class of journalists was mixed with utter despair. It would stir up all the unpleasantness he and Harriet had been trying to move past.

How was she going to feel about that?

"You're looking a little green around the gills at the thought, boy, which makes not a lick of sense to me. It's your dream. Has a mule kicked you in the head?"

No, he'd fallen in love with a woman whose father had been destroyed by the very articles that might cement his reputation in journalism. If she stayed in Dare to be with him, Harriet couldn't keep going by her alias forever, especially if her sister enrolled in Emmits Merriam. Maybelline would need to transfer her transcripts from Wellesley. In her original name. He hadn't mentioned that problem yet, although they'd undoubtedly thought of it. He and Harriet didn't talk about her legal name.

Why pick up a stick of dynamite when it could blow off your hand?

Which is why he also hadn't mentioned the Pulitzer prospect. "It's nothing," he said, but he knew better.

How were they supposed to move forward as a couple when her father's disgrace was the reason they'd been brought together? Another conundrum had been rolling around in his head when he couldn't sleep at nights: If Harriet stayed and she wanted to share her real name, how were they supposed to explain why she'd come to Dare in the first place?

It looked damning. If the townspeople found out the whole truth, they would judge her harshly. He was one of them. The Hales had been in this valley since the beginning.

"You in a pickle, boy?" Emmits said when he remained silent.

Again, what the heck was he supposed to say? He couldn't lie to Emmits.

"Don't like your silence one bit." His mentor downed his bourbon and set it on the desk with gusto. "Come with me. We're going to get out of here for a while, and you can tell me all about it. Let's go shooting. That always clears my mind."

"Fine," Arthur said, realizing he badly needed someone's advice. Emmits could be boastful and bombastic, but he was trustworthy.

He hadn't told his family. Not even his brother, George, who was returning to Dare soon from his dig in Butte, Montana. They might think uncharitably of her, and he didn't want that. Which is why he hadn't officially introduced her to his parents, despite their many invitations. It was a step most thought led to marriage, and while his thoughts had been drifting that way, he wasn't ready to buy a ring yet. Not with all of this muck still between them.

He was in a pickle all right.

As they headed out of the office, they stopped at Harriet's desk.

"It was nice to meet you, Miss Jenkins," Emmits said as he shrugged on his coat. "Arthur and I are heading out early."

Harriet's gaze locked with Arthur's.

He tried to make his shrug casual despite the knots of tension in his shoulders. "He's dragging me off."

"You could use some time off. You've been working day and night," she replied, resting her current filing in her lap.

"See you soon," he said, a bit brusque. He already felt a bit guilty about sharing her secret, *their* secret. Oh, dag nab it.

As he and Emmits walked out into the blustery cold, he had a moment to think. Knowing Emmits, he was about to get some home truths he was pretty sure wouldn't sit well.

Part of him knew he deserved it.

***

"You're in the worst pickle I ever did hear, boy," Emmits growled in front of the fireplace in his study, where they'd come to warm up after skeet shooting.

The wind had been brittle, and Emmits had racked up the hits while Arthur had missed a fair share. He hadn't done much shooting after leaving Dare, and none since returning. He was rusty.

"How could you have let this woman get under your skin? A woman out for revenge isn't wife material."

Arthur didn't correct his assumptions. If he were honest with himself, which he needed to be, falling in love meant marriage, and since he was in love…

"Harriet doesn't want revenge anymore," he commented from his seat in the leather chair, holding his hands out to the crackling blaze for warmth.

"And how is that woman supposed to marry you, knowing why her daddy can't take her down the aisle? I tell you, boy, this is the fattest hornet's nest I ever did see."

"I didn't plan on any of this," he said, feeling the strong urge to defend himself. He hadn't expected to fall in love with her. Help her, yes. Be attracted to her, yes. But not love. Yet the cave-in had been a turning point for him, and since then, he'd fallen hard.

"Look, I don't like it any better than you do. I just don't know what to do about her fake name and secret past."

"Dishonest people aren't worth spit," Emmits raved, his mud boots wearing out the blue Persian rug in front of the fire. Usually the older man's colorful language made him laugh, but not today.

"If you're gonna be with her, this whole thing needs to be resolved honorably."

"I know it," he said.

"And that's what you want, yes?"

The truth had been there all along. "Yes, yes it is."

He stroked his chin, thinking. "Well, she can legally change her name to Jenkins. If she does, you can stick with what she's told everyone in town. I can arrange it with Judge Smithers."

Emmits and his connections could pretty much achieve anything, and usually Arthur didn't mind, but he was uneasy about embracing this solution. And, of course, they were assuming Harriet wanted to stay, which he wasn't sure about. He thought she loved him, but she hadn't said the words. And there was Maybelline and her schooling to consider…

"Even if she wanted to change it, which I'm not sure, *I* don't know how I feel about that. I don't want any longstanding lies in my life. Plus, her sister would have to agree, and Maybelline is even harder to read than Harriet sometimes."

His old friend paused in front of his chair. "There's a sister too? Wonderful."

His own chuckle was dark. "Yes, imagine that. She has a family. And you'll love the irony of what I'm about to tell you. The sister is considering enrolling in your university when it opens. She just finished her freshman year at Wellesley and was politely asked not to return."

The growl Emmits gave reminded him of the bear they'd once tracked up in Hudson Creek. "By jove, boy, I tell you what! I just don't know what to say. I always wanted you to settle down with a nice girl and raise a family, but this seems like a disaster waiting to happen."

"Listen." This time Arthur rose and squared him head on. "She *is* a nice girl. She was trying to defend her father and reclaim their family's reputation. I would think you'd admire her grit."

"Not when you want to marry her."

"Let's not put the cart before the horse, Emmits."

His friend strode over to him and thrummed his finger on his chest. "I know that look, Hale. Every time you want something, you have this same fire in your eyes. I saw it the first time you and I talked about oil exploration in the Gulf. You wanted knowledge and debate then. When you went to New York, you wanted to be the best damn journalist out there. And now this woman. You want her. *Forever.* If you're not aware of it, you're lying to yourself."

Putting his hands on his hips, he stared back at Emmits. "Fine. I have been thinking about marriage, but I also know Harriet is a tough case, so I've been trying to be patient. Even though her father was guilty, I'm darn well aware that I destroyed her life as she knew it. She and her sister shouldn't have to suffer for their father's sins."

"Don't confuse guilt with love, son," Emmits said, picking up a photograph of his parents from the mantel. "My father did that with my mother, and they were miserable. They made everyone around them that way too."

Emmits had told him the story of how his father had claimed eminent domain on a large tract of land, resulting in the removal of a ranch family who'd held it for a hundred years. He'd been attracted to the rancher's daughter, and since he felt guilty about taking her home from her, he offered his hand and pledged to give her a new one. It had been a disaster.

"It's not like that," he defended.

"Be sure," Emmits said. "Divorce is starting to happen in this country, but it's still a shitty way to gain your freedom, especially when kids are involved."

They both sat down again in the leather chairs in front of the fire. The embers glowed orange, and the wood logs popped as the fire raged.

"I can handle the sister's situation at the university since it's in-house," Emmits continued. "But you'll need to talk through what Harriet and her sister want to do long-term if they plan to stay. The truth has a way of getting out even if they do change their name permanently."

How was he supposed to bring it up? They'd refrained from talking about the reason she was in Dare, almost as if they were two generals who'd signed a short-term truce in secret.

But Emmits was right. It was time.

"Okay. I'll wait for the right moment."

"Don't wait too long, boy. People in this town are

curious about outsiders, and they'll want to know everything about the woman who seems to have landed Arthur Hale."

Didn't he know that? There'd been more than a few hints along that line lately.

"I'll talk to her, Emmits," he said and experienced that pinch of weirdness he always felt when he called the great man by his first name, something they'd agreed he'd do when he graduated from college.

"Let's go eat," Emmits said, patting his belly. "I'm famished after all that shooting."

As they walked out the study, Emmits slung a beefy arm around his shoulders. Arthur scanned the photos on the wall. All were of his friend with various notable figures, just like the ones he'd hung in his own office. As he left the room, he realized more was at stake than just his heart.

His reputation could be harmed if he and Harriet didn't do the right thing.

People might think he was a party to her lie, and truth be told, he was. They wouldn't like that. It would confirm their fears that he'd picked up a bad character while living in the big city.

Emmits was right.

They couldn't wait too long.

If they did, everything he'd built could be destroyed.

Chapter 13

Krotter's Bowling Alley was as packed as an opening for a Broadway show, but perhaps that shouldn't have surprised Harriet. It was a Friday night and still cold as the dickens outside, being late March and all. They were meeting Arthur's brother, George, who'd just returned to town, and she was more than a tad nervous. Arthur had picked her up, inviting Maybelline along too to be social. George had caught a ride into town with a friend for a drink at McGinty's Bar and was meeting them at the bowling alley.

Arthur cupped Harriet's elbow, urging her and Maybelline, who held her hand, through a sea of male and female bowlers who were hurling enormous black bowling balls down brightly polished wooden lanes. The crack of ball meeting pin sounded off all around them, punctuated by the shouts of the players and onlookers. The smell of burnt popcorn made her wrinkle her nose, and she stepped on something sticky and winced, certain it was bubble gum. Wonderful.

A trio of kids side-swiped them like an old Buick to a Cadillac and then raced off. People all around called out greetings to Arthur and stared at her and Maybelline. Yeah, they had clearly dressed up a little too much for this place. A matching pearl necklace and earrings might have been a bad choice in hindsight, but this was a date with Arthur and her first time meeting his brother. She'd wanted to look her best. She had forgotten she'd have to trade in her lovely heels for rented shoes and that people would be wearing bowling shirts, which looked like a uniform except for the different colors of each team, prison gray being the worst of the lot.

"Arthur," a younger man shouted as they reached the final lane of the bowling alley. He rushed up to them.

"George," Arthur said and punched him in the shoulder. "Harriet. Maybelline. This is my younger brother, George."

The blue eyes were the same, but George had a crew cut and was about three inches shorter. She knew he was two years younger than Arthur and had graduated from the Colorado School of Mines last year.

"It's good to meet you both," George said. "I've been out on a dig and just got back today, so I told my big brother here that I had to meet the newest ladies in town, especially the one my brother's been seeing so much."

Because he was smiling so earnestly, it was easy to return it. "What dig were you on?" she asked even though Arthur had told her some of the details.

"There's a new mine being considered outside Butte."

It made her think of the mine in Blisswater Canyon and the cave-in. "Sounds interesting."

"What were you doing up there?" Maybelline asked.

"Some work for the company that owns the land. I'm a geologist."

"Oh," Maybelline said, taking off her coat. "You

study rocks and the layers of the earth's crust. I've always thought that would be fascinating."

George stepped forward and helped her and then set her coat on one of the seats in front of the bowling lane. "Arthur said you recently finished your freshman year. What are you studying?"

"I was studying theater," her sister responded, her pink-painted mouth tightening a little.

"Cool. Not a lot of that around here," George said, reminding Harriet again that Maybelline would have to change her concentration if she decided to go to Emmits Merriam. The thought saddened them both.

Arthur helped her with her coat and then shed his own, dropping them on the other empty chairs. "Have you two ever bowled?"

"Of course," she responded, working off her tan gloves and adding them to the heap of coats. "Our bowling is a bit different though."

"Right," Arthur said. "I did some Candlepin bowling when I …"

And then he paused. He had almost said "when I was back East," but he couldn't because that's not where people thought she was from.

"Well, I'm sure you just need a refresher course," he added, trying to smile through the awkwardness of the moment.

His brother was studying them intently. Her stomach twisted into a sailing knot, and she wondered whether coming here and meeting him had been a bad idea.

"George, why don't you and I go get sodas for everyone?" Maybelline suggested, giving Harriet a knowing look.

Arthur passed his brother some money. "What do you

want, Harriet? They have a pretty good cherry coke here."

Yeah, he knew she liked that, and with a real cherry too. "Sounds lovely."

"I'll have a root beer, George," Arthur said. "And bring us some popcorn and peanuts too. If we're going to bowl, we should do it properly."

George and Maybelline headed off, her sister's forest green pleated skirt swaying as she walked.

Harriet turned to look at Arthur. "I'm sorry."

His mouth tipped up, but it couldn't be mistaken for a smile. "I know. Me too. There just aren't a lot of places to go in Dare. If it were summertime, I would have suggested the drive-in, but that won't be open until summertime."

Harriet hadn't thought that far ahead. She and Maybelline had agreed to hold off on any decisions for a few more months. Her sister's schooling wouldn't start until the fall anyway, and they both wanted to act a little like ostriches right now and bury their heads in the sand.

Both of them had nurtured the hope that it might be easier to return to their old lives as time passed, but neither of them really believed it was true.

Plus where would that leave her and Arthur?

As she looked into those familiar, understanding eyes, she still didn't know. She liked being with him. Working with him. Okay, and she might be a little in love with him, but this wasn't her home.

And she'd lied to the whole town. How could she possibly make a life here?

"I feel bad," she admitted. "About all of it."

He squeezed her elbow and met her gaze. "Don't. I'm a grown man, and I agreed to keep quiet. Now, why don't you let me run you through the differences between the two types of bowling?"

Keeping her mind focused was difficult with all the activity around her. One team was cheering at the top of their lungs when their partner hit a strike, the crack of ball and pin reminding her suddenly of a homerun she'd witnessed at Fenway Park when her father took her and Maybelline to a game.

They'd never attend another Red Sox game with their father, she realized.

Oh Daddy.

"Hey," Arthur said suddenly, touching her arm. "Where are you?"

In the past, which could never be repeated. Even if she wished on every falling star she saw in the mountains.

"Right here," she responded. "This is going to be awkward, trying to hurl a larger bowling ball."

"The holes are supposed to make it easier." He hefted one of the giant spheres up like Hercules himself. "You want to try it out?"

She looked at the holes, and then her new pink manicure from Miss Ivy's Beauty Shop. One of her nails was going to break for sure. When she nodded, he put the ball down and gestured toward a different one.

"This is the one the ladies use."

Well, it was a little smaller, but not much. She gingerly inserted her fingers into the holes and tried to lift it. "Whoa! That's heavy." Using her other hand to balance it only helped a little.

"You're a lightweight," he joked, taking the ball from her. "Maybe we'll need to find you a junior ball."

She narrowed her eyes at him. "I'll get the hang of it." Maybe.

The bowling lane was the same as the ones back home, thankfully, maple surfaced with the embarrassing gutter just waiting for her to make a fool of herself. She'd played when she was younger. Her father had taken them to Perry's Lanes every once in a blue moon. He'd let them drink too much soda, she remembered, and his laughter had been much freer. Even her father had needed a break from the scientific precision with which he ran their life. Those times at the bowling alley hadn't been about winning or being excellent. They'd been about fun.

"You went bowling with your father, didn't you?" Arthur asked by her side.

"Yes," she replied.

"Are they good memories?"

A smile formed at the corner of her mouth as she turned to him. "Yes."

"Then hold onto that, Harriet."

The screams and chatter from the people around her seemed to drop a decibel level as she stared into his eyes. She was glad he hadn't suggested leaving the bowling alley because of her memories. Another man might have thought she was acting like a girl.

But, then again, Arthur wasn't like other men.

George and Maybelline returned with drinks and snacks, interrupting the moment. She broke eye contact with Arthur, scanning the rest of the room. Many of the players were watching them. As usual.

Lovely. Another Dare outing with the invisible scarlet letter "O" for Outsider on her and Maybelline's chests.

"Were you thinking about Dad?" Maybelline asked as George walked up to the lane to start their game.

"Yes. You?" She took her sister's hand.

"Hard not to. It was one of the few times he ever really relaxed."

"Yes," she agreed. "I miss him."

Her sister's hand tightened around hers. "I do too, but the man we knew is gone, and somehow we have to make peace with that. Otherwise we'll never be happy."

Turning, she took in her sister's ponytail and shining green eyes. "When did you get so wise?"

"I just finished *To Kill a Mockingbird*, that book by the new author, Harper Lee. I told you about it, remember?"

She nodded. Maybelline had raved about it without giving too much of the plot away.

"The main character in the book lost her mother like we did, and it got me to thinking about how we choose to act when we lose someone. Scout—that's the young girl—doesn't lose her enjoyment in people or life and can still laugh, but her father sits on the porch swing after she goes to bed and doesn't laugh anymore. He's perpetually sad."

Harriet could feel tears brimming in her eyes, so she blinked fast.

"Daddy became like that when Mom died. He worked harder and laughed less. I don't want to turn into that."

Harriet hugged her sister then, not caring that they were in the middle of the bowling alley or that half the bowlers were paying more attention to them than to their own games. "You won't be, Maybelline. I know you won't."

And as she said the words, she said a little prayer for herself too. Perhaps it was time for a new beginning for them both.

They broke apart and laughed, blinking away tears, and walked over to join the Hale boys, who had clearly been watching the scene.

"Who's up?" she asked, wanting to break the silence.

"You, my dear," Arthur said, and somehow the

endearment was sweet beyond words.

She lugged the ball up to the red line of demarcation on the lane, and yes, she broke a nail as she hurled it as far as she could in her outfit. Her black skirt was too tight, and she couldn't bend over without thinking about it hiking up a few inches more than was proper. The ball fell into the gutter and rolled and rolled, slowing down until a three-year-old on a tricycle could have passed it with a blur. Then it stopped three-fourths of the way down the lane.

Not reaching *one single pin.*

Her cheeks flamed, and inside, she was sure everyone in the place was watching and judging her incompetence.

Then she heard Arthur's piercing *I need a taxi* whistle, something he must have picked up in New York.

"Good job, first timer." He rose and grabbed her shoulders, shaking her playfully. Took her hand and examined her nails. "Well, you'll have battle scars for sure."

Then he made a production of getting her ball out of the gutter and staggering like it weighed as much as an elephant.

"Beginner," he called out to the people watching. "Let's cheer her on. It's her first time."

And the truth was, in this place, with this differently shaped ball and pins, it *was* her first time.

Men whistled then, and the women started cheering too.

"You'll get the hang of it, Harriet," Alice from Kemstead's Bakery called out.

"Just imagine you're trying to hit your boss' face," Herman yelled out from the next lane, making his whole blue-shirted bowling team guffaw with laughter.

Over the next three series, she learned just how much

magic Arthur had over people. In one sweet gesture, he'd managed to get the whole town on her side. They cheered as she finally hit one pin finally, then four more in the next pass.

Maybelline somehow did a lot better. Harriet told herself it was the freedom of her skirt, but she knew better. Maybelline had always taken to new things easier than she had.

Because she didn't have the oldest child's desire to do everything perfectly running through her head.

Harriet slowly relaxed over the next hour. The two additional nails she broke were badges of honor.

Her hair fell from her bun—another not-so-bright idea—and she was sure her mascara was smudged.

When she bent over to hurl the ball again, determined to hit six pins this time, she heard her tight skirt rip. She dropped the ball and arched her back to look, gasping in horror. The tear exposed a few inches of her inner thighs. Oh no.

Arthur laughed and jumped to his feet. "Can't see anything, darn it. Maybe if you do that again, Harriet, you'll give us all a real show."

Everyone laughed. Including Maybelline.

Grabbing his long coat, Arthur tugged her into it. Her cheeks were on fire now.

"Ah, don't worry. Herman once split his work pants down to his thighs. Right, Herman?"

"Right," Herman called out, slapping his knee. "I think Mrs. Hemshaw might have fainted at the sight."

People continued to laugh, like there was nothing untoward about a lady tearing her skirt bowling.

She couldn't imagine anyone in Beacon Hill laughing.

Arthur's coat enveloped her, and he rolled the sleeves

up as much as was possible with the wool. His spicy aftershave settled around her, providing a measure of comfort.

"Your coat is too short to hide the tear," he murmured. "You can bend over in mine without worrying about it."

She sighed again, and he tapped her on the nose. "Relax, sport. You're doing great."

And then he gave her a nudge toward the lane.

Facing it down was like stepping back up to the plate with two hideous strikes on her record. God, she didn't want to fail at this.

Herman darted forward and grabbed her ball out of the rack, presenting it to her in a courtly fashion. "Just let her rip, Harriet."

She realized he meant let loose even if it was a terrible pun after what happened to her skirt. Well, it seemed she'd reached a turning point. She could play like a sissy or play with the wild abandon she'd seen in the other players, forgetting about what was proper or presentable.

She did what Herman suggested, or at least what she thought he meant.

She let it rip.

Closing her eyes, she drew her arm back as far as she could and took three steps forward before hurling her arm forward and throwing the ball as hard as she could.

Her shoulder popped.

Her last two nails broke.

But she still didn't open her eyes.

A resounding *crack* echoed in her ears.

"Yes!" Maybelline yelled.

People cheered.

Whistles pierced her ears from all sides.

"I'll be darned," she heard Arthur say.

She opened one eye and then the other and saw her nemeses—those darn pins—scattered along the end of the lane like overturned toy soldiers after a rowdy Christmas party.

All ten of them.

Jumping up and down in rented shoes, she thrust her hands up in the air like she'd just won the World Series. She jogged in front of the lane, and then Arthur spun her around, his hands on her shoulders, and grinned at her.

"Imagining my face when you threw that one, were you?"

Everyone laughed again.

As she stared into his eyes, she realized how different she felt when she was with him. How light. How free.

"Always," she whispered.

His eyes darkened, and his smile dimmed before spreading across his face again. Then he took her in his arms and executed a flawless fox trot down shiny maple lane.

When they danced back to the end of the lane, Arthur whispered into her ear, "I like you this way."

"Me too."

And she did.

When they finally broke apart, Herman was standing next to George and Maybelline—all three of them with big grins on their faces.

"Wow, Harriet. When you let her rip, you really let her rip."

The townspeople of Dare laughed, and standing there in Arthur's oversized coat, her manicure destroyed, her hair in clumps around her face, she finally felt like she was one of them.

And not like an exiled Wentworth from Beacon Hill.

Chapter 14

Arthur and George dropped Harriet and Maybelline off at their house. As the motor idled, he studied Harriet as she left the car. She looked mussed and messy, but she was all the more beautiful because of it. George rolled down the passenger window.

"Thanks again for the evening," Harriet said, tucking her hands in her short winter white wool coat.

Maybelline waved next to her. "It was fun. We're going to practice, so we can take the Hale brothers next time."

George rubbed his hands together. "Can't wait for that. See ya."

"Good night, Arthur," Harriet said, ducking her head.

Yeah, she was thinking the same thing he was. No goodnight kiss.

Dating in a small town had its drawbacks.

"I'll see you tomorrow," he said and then waved.

As they pulled away, his brother turned to him. "Are you going to tell me what's going on between you and that woman?"

Crap. He hung his wrist loosely on the steering wheel.

"We're seeing each other."

"I know that. What I don't know is what you're helping her hide."

He slowed when they came to another street even though it was as black as pitch, and there wasn't another car in sight. His brother was too smart by half. "Let's leave this be. So tell me about the dig."

"Mr. Journalist is changing the subject?" George asked, turning in his seat. "Not this time. Mom said Harriet and Maybelline arrived from Denver and aren't related to the local Jenkins family. Oh, and Denver isn't where they play candlepin bowling."

Yeah, and they'd made that slip all too easily. "George, I'm asking you to let this go."

"Why can't you talk about it? Her sister studied theater, which I'm pretty sure isn't offered at any of the schools in Denver. Plus, they fairly scream upper class with all that polish. Maybelline is easier going, but seriously, Arthur, nothing about them adds up."

Lying to the town for Harriet was one thing, and if anyone asked about her roots, he evaded. Lying to his brother was something else entirely.

"There are things I can't tell you yet, George. Please drop it." He jerked on the shift and put it into fifth as he crested out of town to their parent's house to drop his brother off.

"Are they in trouble?" George asked, finally turning down the radio station playing "Are You Lonesome Tonight?"

Yeah, Elvis, he thought, *I am. I'd rather be with Harriet than* my brother right now.

"Look, I can't talk about it, okay?"

Even though he'd told Emmits, he knew the family

code. If he told George, his brother would tell his dad, or his mom would wheedle it out of him. It's what she did best.

"*Now* I understand why you haven't brought her to the house for supper. I don't like this, Arthur. You've just gotten back in town after being gone five years, and you're trying to set up something that most people here think makes you too big for your britches. And you're dating a mysterious woman and hiding things for her. No, I don't like this at all."

Arthur's pulse started pounding, and he eased off the accelerator and pulled off the highway at the next scenic point. Turning in his seat, he glared at his brother.

"Look, I know people think I've picked up some strange ideas out East, but dammit, I hoped you of all people would understand why I left and why I came back."

George slumped in his seat and kicked out his legs. "I do. You know, I didn't think you were coming back when you left for New York—neither did Mom and Pop—but when you said you were opening up 'The New Voice of the West' in Dare, I wasn't sure Dare was the right place for it. People here don't like change and big ideas, Arthur. And with Mr. Merriam starting a university, people—"

"Dammit!" Arthur slammed his hand into the steering wheel. "What's so wrong with big ideas? It's what this country was founded on. Emmits has a vision for higher learning out here, and I have one for putting out a newspaper that represents *these people's* thoughts. I would think I'd have their support."

The sigh his brother gave was long and deep. "People fear what they don't know. People think you and Emmits don't think Dare is good enough as it is, and that's why you're trying to change it."

274

"I love Dare, for cripes sake, but after trying to date Harriet here, I can say I support change. People need to mind their own goddamn business. I can't even kiss her goodnight, for heaven's sake, without the news being spread across Dare by lunchtime."

"More like breakfast," his brother tried to joke, elbowing him for good measure.

But he held himself stiffly. Knowing people were talking about him bothered him plenty, but hearing they doubted him burned like a boil on the skin.

"The newspaper and Harriet are a lot to accept after all the time you were gone. Mr. Franklin thinks she was your secretary in New York, and you're only pretending not to have met before."

"Wonderful!" he harrumphed. "Why would I orchestrate such a thing?"

"Perhaps she's having your baby."

He growled, making George throw up his hands in surrender.

"Come on. You have to laugh a little. Folks like to tell tall tales. Did you lose your funny bone?"

He turned and faced his brother in the muted light from the dashboard. "You wouldn't be laughing if they were saying these things about you."

"No, you're probably right. But you've changed, and people need to get used to the new you." His brother shook him playfully. "You're not the same boy who left Dare."

No, he was a man now, and he lived life on his own terms. "So what do I do?"

"Well, first, I'd suggest that you start inviting people over to the newspaper for coffee."

His brows bunched together. "What? I'm working."

George held up his hands. "I know, but seriously,

people have said you're not friendly anymore, that you're not even willing to take a coffee break. You know how people around here do it throughout the day."

He hit the steering wheel again. "Yeah, and it lasts too long. I'm starting up a business, for cripes sake."

"Arthur, even Mom said she's stopped dropping in because you seemed too busy to talk to her."

"Oh, crap," he said. That made him hang his head.

"She and Pops have been giving you space—they know you're trying to get your bearings and start a business—but it's hurt them, not having you come around as much."

He gripped the wheel. "I come for Sunday dinner."

"They want to see you more than that. And they *are* hurt you haven't introduced them to Harriet. They're more than a little confused by that, Arthur."

Oh, no. Not that. "I don't know what to do." In trying not to lie to the people who meant the most to him, he'd hurt them instead.

"Slow down for one. You can't become 'The Voice of the West' overnight. Despite what Mr. Merriam says. And ask Mom and Pops to drop by when they're in town." He turned up the heat since the car had gotten cool while they were idling. "As for Harriet...I don't know what to tell you without knowing the full story."

Emmits was right. They had to deal with Harriet's past. This could not go on, not when it was hurting his family. "I'll handle it."

"Okay," George said.

"You just get back today, and you already know this much?" he asked, putting the car in gear and easing back onto the highway.

"I had coffee with Mom and Pops earlier."

276

"And how long did that take?" he mused.

George snorted out a laugh. "About two hours."

"Figures," Arthur muttered. "How long are you staying?"

"I don't have my next site visit for a couple of weeks, so I'm around if you need anything."

"Do you have ink in your veins?" he asked as a joke.

In his peripheral vision, he saw his brother turn his hands over and stare at his arms. "Gads no. Why?"

"My kids will and their kids too," he said, knowing he was building something for his family, something future generations could take part in with pride.

"You always did dream big Arthur."

As he drove down the snow-covered lane to their parent's simple ranch house and dropped his brother off, he made himself a promise.

He wouldn't stop dreaming just because he was back in Dare.

Chapter 15

The zing of Arthur's typewriter and the chatter of the staff swirled around Harriet. The bookkeeper was friendly and liked to joke. His wife had baked an apple pie, and she'd enjoyed a piece along with everyone else, standing around the newly installed water cooler in the break room. People were still curious about her, but it was bothering her less.

Except when they asked where she was from.

Trying to utter 'Denver' had become harder, like she was losing her voice.

At five o'clock, everyone grabbed their coats off the shiny brass coat rack that Arthur had installed by the front door at her insistence. Harriet hung back since Arthur was taking her to supper tonight. Reaching into her purse, she pulled out her compact and eyed her hair in the mirror, smoothing back an errant curl that had escaped near her ear.

"I like seeing your hair a little mussed," Arthur said from behind her.

She jumped a mile and snapped her mirror shut with a clack. "It's not nice to sneak up on people."

His blue eyes were twinkling. "I couldn't help it. I like knowing that you're prettying up for our date."

"Then shoo," she said, motioning her hand like a scythe. "I need to put on some lipstick."

"I like the red one," he said and chuckled. "Okay, I'm going. Just holler when you're ready."

Like she'd ever holler. Ladies didn't holler.

She took her time, and ten minutes later, she leaned against the doorframe of his office. Arthur's back was to her, his fingers moving across the typewriter with his usual intensity and urgency, as if the words he had to write were a matter of life and death.

"I'm ready," she said, and even to her ears, her voice sounded husky.

He swiveled in his chair and leaned back. "Well, well. Now that was worth waiting for."

Pursing her lips to fight the smile that wanted to spread across her face, she didn't move from her place at the door. "I'm glad you think so."

Rising slowly from his chair, he strolled toward her. "You don't mind if I kiss you, do you? I don't think I can wait until after supper."

They'd never kissed in the office before. Part of her had felt it was too tawdry, the boss and his secretary fooling around at work. The other part knew people in Dare walked into the office all the time, especially now that they had a growing staff, and wouldn't that be embarrassing?

A blush slid across her cheeks. "Let's wait. I just put my lipstick on."

His hand eased into his pocket, and he dangled a handkerchief in front of her like the line judge at a horse race. "I always come prepared."

Her heartbeat pounded against her ribs, and her gaze fell to his lips."Someone could walk in."

"They already know we're dating," he volleyed back, his voice dark and tempting.

She cleared her throat. "I want to, but I…I don't want them thinking we're…" Her hand made an impatient gesture.

His face softened, and he tucked the handkerchief away. "Fooling around at the office. I understand. Let's go."

For some reason, she'd expected him to push, and then perhaps condemn her for being a prude.

Edging out of his doorway to let him pass, she touched his arm. "Thank you."

He winked that mischievous wink of his that raised her blood pressure. "Sure thing." Then he walked forward and looked over his shoulder. "Sweetheart."

Her mouth dropped open, and she darted across the floor and gave him a playful punch in the back. "I told you not to call me that!"

His shoulders shook as he continued ahead and grabbed his coat from the coat rack. "I couldn't help myself. Just this once. Seeing your reaction was worth it. Plus, you hit like a girl."

She grabbed her purse and shrugged her navy coat on. "I *am* a girl, so there's nothing offensive to me about that comment."

His hands helped her with her coat and then spun her around, doing up her buttons. "And I'm glad you're a girl." She could hear the smile in his voice. "You ready for supper?"

"Yes," she said.

When they arrived at Nellie's Tavern, their favorite

haunt, Bertha greeted them with a smile and led them to a table.

"We're going to take the one in the back, if that's all right. Big story to discuss," he told Bertha conspiratorially and waved to Vernon the bartender.

"Of course," she replied and gave them menus as soon as they were seated.

Harriet lifted an eyebrow. "What big story?"

"Let's order first," he said, picking up the menu even though they both knew it by heart.

Watching him, she realized he seemed a bit nervous, his hands hadn't stopped moving, like they missed dancing across the typewriter.

She settled her own menu in her lap, and they gave their orders when Bertha arrived. He asked for a Manhattan, and she decided to go with a vodka tonic.

"Okay, let's hear it," she said when they were alone again.

His fingers continued tapping the table. "Hmm…I don't know how to bring this up." His laughter was self-conscious.

Self-conscious? Arthur Hale? Her guard immediately went up. The back table. His nerves.

"You're breaking up with me," she said in shock.

His head whipped back. "What? No. Good God, Harriet." He reached for her hand and gripped it. "No, that's not what this was about."

The heart that had just taken a swan dive in her chest, settled back in place. "Okay, then what's going on?"

Arthur was usually Mr. Cool or Mr. Charming. Not Mr. Nervous. Her heart hustled to the diving board again when another thought occurred to her.

He's not going to ask me to marry him, is he?

"It's about your name," he said and blew out a breath.

And any thoughts of rings and flowers subsided, replaced with darker thoughts. The ones that kept her awake nights.

"The real one. And what you've told people here, and what's the real truth. It was awkward…the other night at the bowling alley."

Acid burned in her stomach.

"My brother suspects something," he informed her, gripping her hand. "And I've talked to Emmits about this too. If Maybelline wants to go to the university here, he can handle the transcript issue. The difference in names."

She bit her lip. Hadn't she and Maybelline discussed the same issue without any idea how to resolve it?

"I see," she said, trying to keep her voice even.

"Emmits also said he could arrange for your name to be permanently changed to Jenkins if that's what you want."

Inside her, her heart finally took that swan dive, and instead of water, it encountered the hard ground. A name change? Wentworths had been in this country since 1756. "How?"

"He knows a judge who would keep it quiet." He gripped her hand again, hard, making her aware of each individual bone, and how fragile they all seemed right now.

It would be a huge, final step. "I don't know," she whispered.

He patted her hand suddenly. "Bertha's coming."

The waitress arrived with their drinks and Arthur's smoked ham, steaming mashed potatoes and gravy, and canned corn—one of his favorite meals here. The chicken breast, wild rice, and broccoli she often ordered usually delighted her, but today, it only made her nauseous.

"Thank you," she said, keeping her eyes on her food, praying Bertha wouldn't stop to chat like she usually did.

"Thanks, Bertha. This wonderful food will help us figure out what to do with the story. I'm sure of it."

She beamed, the lines on her round face lifting from the compliment.

How he could pull off charming anyone right now baffled her. Then again, it wasn't his name they were talking about changing.

When Bertha left, he reached for her hand instead of his utensils. "Talk to me."

A headache was developing at the base of her skull, and all she wanted to do was close the door to her bedroom and have a good cry.

"Arthur, I don't know. Changing my name..." It would be like disowning her father, wouldn't it? And saying she wasn't her mother's child, even though she had passed.

"I know it's a big step, but I don't know how to make things right here. We can't just tell the town it's not your real last name. It begs too many questions. If you'd come here with your real name, with only me knowing about your past, things would be different."

Right. They'd have to explain why she'd used a different name, which would mean her real reasons for coming to Dare would get out.

Suddenly the sunny walls of the tavern seemed to turn black and ominous around her. It was like she was in a cage...and worse, one of her own making.

His blue eyes were the only source of light around her. She focused on them.

"I've told you that I want you to stay, and I mean it,

Harriet. I love you. But this is a major hurdle." He lowered his head, as if suddenly tired, his thumb stroking the back of her hand. "I don't want you to get hurt, Harriet. Or your sister."

And they could. People didn't easily forgive deception—and certainly not of this kind. The bold truth was that she'd come here to wreak revenge on Dare's favorite son and had instead fallen in love with him.

"Even if you decide to leave Dare and resume using your real name, people could still find out about what happened."

And be as unforgiving as they'd been in her community back East. Yes, she and Maybelline had concluded that as well. If they reassumed the name of Wentworth, they might become pariahs again no matter where they went. And always, always there would be questions and lies.

Continued exile seemed the only future.

Suddenly the years she had left in this life seemed too long, too heavy to bear.

"I'll do anything you want, Harriet," he said, squeezing her hand. "Help in any way."

"I know," she whispered, staring at her plate again.

The simple food reminded her of how different her life was now. The old life was fading the longer she stayed here, and sometimes, she felt like she was fading with it. Like the initial scent of perfume first sprayed in the morning that wears off by the end of the day.

"I want you to meet my family. I want to take you for supper, but I've been…" He sighed long and deep. "I didn't know how to handle the questions about where you've come from. As an outsider, people are curious, and you'll be the first girl I've brought home."

Even though she knew he couldn't have brought any of his New York girlfriends home, the sweetness of it still blew through her.

"My mom has an inner radar about things being off. George and I never could get a single thing past her. I don't want—"

"To lie to them," she finished, finally realizing his full dilemma.

He was in love with a woman who had lied about who she was, and he was trying to protect her. Who said all the knights in shining armor had died with the Crusades?

"I need to think about it, Arthur. And talk to Maybelline. We've…discussed this situation a lot. But we weren't sure how to get out of our current…predicament. Thank you for providing a possible solution."

"I love you, Harriet, and I do want you to meet my family."

This time she clasped his hand tightly. "I want that too, Arthur."

"Okay, then," he said. "Let's eat before this dinner gets any colder."

And he winked, but it didn't hold its usual sparkle. Her mouth lifted, but it wasn't a real smile.

They picked at their food. Arthur managed to convince Bertha that the story they'd been discussing had ruined their appetites as he paid the bill.

When he drove away from the tavern, she turned in her seat. "Let's go up to the Bluffs," she whispered, not wanting to go home yet, not wanting the unavoidable conversation with Maybelline or the long, sleepless night ahead.

"Okay," he said, glancing over at her.

When they reached the bluffs, the half moon looked

like the piece of chocolate meringue pie she'd turned down at the tavern.

"Kiss me," she whispered, sliding as close as she could, minding the stick shift, needing comfort, needing the connection with him that always made her feel like everything was perfect even when it wasn't.

He pulled her toward him, angling his body on the seat to press them as closely together as possible. His arms left her, and she gasped when the entire bench seat squeaked back a few inches. Then he leaned back and pulled her on top of him.

They'd never been this close, and her body thrummed with a darker passion than she'd even known.

She poured all her fear and passion into the kiss. His mouth was hot and demanding, and she was shocked to hear a moan erupt from deep inside her. His hands slid down her back, his fingers tickling her waist through the wool coat.

She eased back and dealt with the three buttons holding her coat in place. His hands slid inside, one brushing her stomach, causing every hair on her body to stand up straight. He pulled her back onto his body, and now that her eyes had adjusted to the darkness, she could make out his heated gaze.

"I love you," she whispered, knowing it was true, letting at least one part of her be honest and free.

He squeezed his eyes shut for a moment, and then his hand cupped her face. "I wasn't sure you were ever going to tell me."

A slight sob—a combination of relief and naked vulnerability—rushed out. "I didn't know if I should. Things have been…so complicated, and I didn't want to hurt you."

"The only thing that could hurt me is not being with you, or seeing *you* get hurt. I don't want anything to hurt you anymore, Harriet."

It was something he couldn't control any more than she could, but she pressed her face to his chest just the same.

"I know it," she whispered. "Touch me, Arthur. I want you to touch me."

His fingers tickled the baby curls at her neck, and he tried to roll them over so that she was under him. It was awkward in the cramped space of the front seat, and her knee banged into the glove compartment.

"This is the last place I want to touch you, but it's our only option right now. It's at times like these that I miss New York."

Her head was pressing against the door, and she had to raise her knee against the seat to get comfortable, but that was an overstatement since she felt every spring in the seat against her back. She tried to ignore the embarrassment of her skirt hiking up her thighs.

"How far are we talking here, Harriet?" he whispered in the dark, cold seeping into the car now that the heat was no longer blowing.

Warmth spread across her cheeks. "Just some," she whispered, unable to say more. A lady *never* said more.

His chuckle was deep and dark. "So I'm just supposed to know what 'some' means?"

"Arthur, you're a smart man," she said as he leaned over her, his head near the steering wheel.

Bracing himself with one hand on the floor, he traced the line between her breasts. She swallowed thickly. When he reached the hem of her pink sweater, she held her breath as he inched it up slowly, his fingers tracing her skin.

Her flesh cooled as he exposed it, and their mingled breath could be seen in the dark car.

When he reached the underside of her breast, he swiped his finger across her ribs. "Is this some?"

"Arthur, you're embarrassing me," she whispered.

"We've never talked about it, but now might be a good time. You told me that night that you're a virgin."

She huffed out a breath at the reminder of that horrible incident. "Yes."

His hand covered her breast, and then his fingers dipped inside her white bra to stroke. She shifted on the seat under him, the sensation like lightning across her skin.

"I know it makes me old fashioned, but I'm glad you are."

He eased her bra up, and she shifted to try and help him.

"Let's just touch *some,* Harriet."

And then he lowered his head to her breast.

It was a shock, having his mouth tug on her nipple. She'd never done anything but kiss a few boys before. But as he nipped and sucked, she didn't care. Her body arched off the seat, the springs digging into her back, but it only heightened her sense of wanting to be closer to his warm, wet mouth.

His hand journeyed lower and touched the edge of her bunched up skirt, pushing it up to her waist on the right side. Sliding under her bottom, he pressed her against him, and she felt it, that hard line of his desire.

With his mouth sucking strongly, she tilted her head back, reaching out to tunnel her fingers in his dark thick hair. He shifted to the other breast, and this time, she couldn't hold back the moan. It shattered the silence of the dark night around them. And in response, he lifted her still closer and moved his hips against hers—a question, an invitation.

It felt shocking, yet so good that she used her raised leg to press up against him. And he responded in kind, moving his hips against hers again. Oh sweet heavens.

Then he pressed his mouth to her bare stomach and rubbed his forehead against her cold skin. "Okay, we'd better stop now."

He leaned up to kiss her on the mouth, but didn't linger, and then eased off her and opened the car door, exiting awkwardly.

"I'll give you a minute to straighten up," he said and shut the door.

She righted her bra, wincing at the sensitivity in her breasts. Is this what people called unfulfilled desire? A few of the girls had talked about it in school. Every part of her body throbbed, almost like it was in pain, but it wasn't like the pain that came from hitting an elbow or scraping a knee. It was an urgent pain in her belly, and since those same girls had told her so, she knew Arthur was experiencing it too.

In the darkness, it was difficult to smooth her hair back into place, so she did the best she could. There would be no finding the bobby pins in the dark. Hopefully Maybelline wouldn't say anything when she got home.

She slid to the passenger side and waited for Arthur to return. He was smoking a cigarette, something unusual for him, the red tip illuminating the trail of smoke in the darkness.

Should she go out and join him, or did he need some time to settle too? She decided to wait.

He finally returned to the car and turned to glance at

her.

"You all right?" His voice was gruff.

Her cheeks flamed, but she nodded.

"Good. Let's get you home then."

And as he drove, she realized there was one more thing she was looking forward to. Telling him she loved him when she said goodnight and went inside.

She might not know what to do about her name, but at least she knew how she felt.

Somehow that seemed more important.

Chapter 16

Working and playing became Harriet and Arthur's rhythm as April arrived, and excitement grew over the May 7th launch of the paper. She finally went to his parents' house with him for supper, and they got through the night all right, his family talking more than she did. Fortunately no one had asked questions about where she was from. It was almost like they knew not to go there.

The trap had seemed incredibly tight that day.

The Bay of Pigs captured everyone's attention mid-month, especially Arthur, whom she heard speaking Spanish on the phone in raised tones one day right before he pounded out his latest editorial on the typewriter. When she asked about him knowing the language, he absently remarked that he'd learned enough to get by with the help of a classmate from Puerto Rico when he lived in New York. A man of hidden talents for sure.

While Arthur rushed to keep up with current events surrounding Cuba and the launch, she and Maybelline agreed not to hurry into any decisions. Changing their name would be a big step, and the guilt they felt over considering it was huge.

Her old life continued to slide away, almost like the ice blocks around Dare's Snake River that were breaking away with each passing day, disappearing from view as they became water again.

One night, she made the decision to put her mother's pearls back in the jewelry box and don simpler jewelry. And when they went to Krotter's Bowling Alley, she wore a looser skirt. Everyone had smiled knowingly at that the first time. Arthur suggested a bowling shirt for *The Western Independent* in a dark green that matched her eyes. The first time she wore it, her self-consciousness was so acute she was sure she was blushing from head to toe. If only people back home could see her now.

But as she fell more in love with Arthur each passing day, a niggling fear grew inside her. With each day they waited, it would be harder and harder if they finally decided to tell the truth. It was like a trap was tightening around her.

A snowstorm swept across the valley on May first, the weight of the snow as heavy as the burden on her heart. She donned her snow boots and shoveled the driveway and sidewalk with Maybelline before heading to the paper. It was a heck of a way to start the work week. Cold weather this late in the year made her grouchy. Snow just shouldn't be allowed to happen in May. It threw her off, and she and the other staff complained about it all day. Even Arthur was in a bad mood and spent most of the day out of sight.

"Harriet," Arthur called as he stepped out of his office as she was about to change her shoes so she could head home. In the snow.

"Yes?"

"Can you come in?"

His tension worried her. Arthur was working brutal

hours again in preparation for the launch. He'd done about twenty drafts of his first Sunday editorial for the paper and still wasn't happy with it.

When she entered his office, he shut the door behind her, something he rarely did. Her stomach immediately knotted up like a ball of yarn. "What is it?"

He sighed, long and deep, and ran his hand through his hair, causing a stray lock to fall across his forehead. "I'll just spit it out. I've been awarded the Pulitzer for the first editorial I did on your father."

Pressing her hand to her stomach, she concentrated on breathing. The news stole her breath. A Pulitzer? It was an astonishing honor, especially given his age.

And all because of what her father had done.

The trap was so close around her it was digging into her limbs.

"Congratulations," she uttered, and even to her ears, her voice sounded brittle and cold, like one of the old matrons on Beacon Hill.

He crossed the room and put his hands on her shoulders. "I don't know what to say to you. It's the most bittersweet news I've ever received."

Those blue eyes beseeched her, and she made the corners of her mouth tip up. But inside she felt dead. He was being honored for something that had hurt her family, and the injustice of it was impossible to bear.

"It's great news, Arthur, and I'm glad for you. Truly. It's quite an honor." Stepping back, she clenched her hands into fists at her side, feeling the need to flee.

"Harriet, please let's talk about this. I can't imagine what this—"

"Arthur," she interrupted, her voice harsher than she'd intended. "If you don't mind, I'll just go home now." She stared at the floor, eyes dry and unblinking, reaching for control.

While he stepped closer, he didn't touch her, and for that she was glad. If he did, she might dissolve right in front of him.

"This is dredging up everything we've put behind us, isn't it?"

Clearly it wasn't behind them. They'd only put a tincture on the wound.

"Arthur, I'm still here under false pretenses. I don't think *anything* is behind us." She hung her head, suddenly as sad and tired as she'd been when she first read the award-winning article one Sunday morning in their Beacon Hill townhome. She hadn't left the house for three days.

"Harriet." This time he did touch her back lightly, drawing her in for a sweet embrace.

Tears gathered in the corners of her eyes, and she had to blink them back.

"I love you. We'll figure this out."

This couldn't be figured out. And in that second she knew the truth. "I can't change my name, Arthur."

It would be the ultimate betrayal of herself. She wasn't willing to pretend she was something she wasn't, not even if it gave her distance from everything that shamed her. Oh God, why couldn't she have figured this out before she fell in love with him?

His fingers caressed her cheek, and then tipped her chin up so she'd meet his eyes. "I know, baby. I guessed that all along, and I love you for it. We'll find a way to make it work."

Her heart gave a cry of utter defeat. With her past, they could have no future. Suddenly she had to get out of there.

"I don't think…Maybelline and I can stay here anymore, Arthur."

"Harriet…" His face fell. "Please don't say that."

She shook her head. "This story about my father is *never* going to go away, don't you see? And after lying to the townspeople and dragging you into it…"

His hands grabbed her shoulders. "Stop this. Stop this right now. I won't hear any talk of you leaving."

And the hoarseness in his voice finally brought the first tear sliding down her cheek. Oh, God, this was too much.

"You can't keep running away, Harriet. We have something here." He shook her lightly, like he was trying to imprint his will on her.

"Arthur, please," she pleaded.

"The people in town like you now. It will work itself out."

His head was buried as deeply in the sand as hers had been. Well, she was seeing clearly now. "I've lied to them, Arthur. How forgiving do you think they'll be?"

"I forgave you," he said.

Her lip trembled. "Oh, Arthur."

"And your actions affected me more than anyone else in town. Have a little faith, Harriet."

She thought of the way the people she'd grown up with, her friends, her own extended family had turned on her. They'd known her, liked her, even loved her, and yet they'd abandoned her all the same.

"You're wishing on a star, Arthur."

His brows slammed shut. "Fine, don't trust them." He took a breath. "We don't need to tell them. We'll find another way."

He was as stubborn as an ox, and his refusal to see the truth hurt her more than anything. "I *told* you," she ground out, clenching her teeth to keep from crying. "I can't abandon who I am, and things can't continue this way forever."

"I know, dammit," he said, yanking her against his chest. "Harriet, just trust me. We'll figure it out. Just don't, for cripes sake, leave."

His voice broke, and she wrapped her arms around him.

"I don't see how this is going to work anymore," she whispered, another tear falling.

Edging back, he stared straight into her eyes, the intensity of his gaze pinning her in place. "Harriet. Do you trust me?"

"Arthur, I—"

"I said, 'do you trust me?'" he asked with more force, his hands tightening on her skin.

"Yes," she whispered, her heart breaking. "But this is getting too complicated, and it could have negative repercussions for you, for the paper."

"Like I give a flying flip."

Shoving away from him, she stood her ground. "Don't you *see?* I can't even be happy for you, and it's a *Pulitzer,* Arthur."

His brow knotted. "Harriet—"

"You're being willfully blind about this, Arthur, as blind as I was, and that's not like you. Aren't you the one who's all about seeing things clearly and calling a spade a spade?" Her body started to tremble.

Those blue eyes stared into hers. "What I see is the woman I love, who was hurt by something I did, but can still see me for who I am and love me for it. Do you think that kind of love is normal? We've been tested in fire, Harriet, and I'm man enough to know that's as rare as it comes. The other stuff doesn't matter."

She swallowed thickly, the pressure to cry squeezing her chest. "I don't think I can stand any more testing, Arthur. What if we get married? What are we going to do, hide the award in the basement?"

Her hand pressed against her mouth when she realized she'd brought up marriage—something the woman was never supposed to do. Something she'd been terrified to think about.

His shrug was almost Gallic. "I don't know. I don't give a damn about the award. All I care about is you."

"No," she said with force. "Don't you see? That's a problem. You *should* care about this. It's an enormous honor. I'm dragging you down."

He framed her face in his hands. "No, baby. You make me happier than I've ever been. Nothing can compete with that."

Closing her eyes, she pressed her lips together, wondering how she could make him understand. She pulled his hands away from her face and stepped back. "Arthur, when I met you, your career was the most important thing to you."

"That's changed," he said, his voice thick.

Her heart bled at the hurt in his voice, which was usually so sure and strong. "This paper is your dream, and a Pulitzer is an incredible feather in your cap."

"I know that, dammit," he said suddenly, control snapping. "Do you think I like this? Do you think this isn't tearing me in two? I've wanted a Pulitzer since I knew what it was, and now I get the goddamn good fortune of winning one for the very editorial that ruined your life and brought you here in your quest to ruin mine. Life's not always fair, Harriet, but when this kind of stuff happens, it shows you what matters. It shows you what you're made of. And Harriet, I know without a doubt that you're made for me, just as I am for you."

Her heart pounded in her chest when he thrust a hand out toward the phone.

"When I got that call, I didn't have one moment of happiness over it. All I could think about was how this would hurt you, hurt us. I thought about it all day, how to tell you. Don't you understand? I love you. The rest of it doesn't matter. Who gives a damn about an award if you're not by my side?"

She'd never heard him swear this much, and it was as shocking to her as the emotion rolling through him.

Lips trembling, she crossed her arms over her chest. "Arthur, we're not going to settle this today, but you need to think this through. People are going to be happy about your prize, and you should be too. As for me and Maybelline…well, it's our problem."

He was across the room in a second, his hands gripping her shoulders again. "No, baby. Your problems are my problems, especially this one."

Hadn't he compromised his integrity to protect her? It had to stop somewhere. She lifted her chin, realizing she still had enough Wellesley spirit in her to carry her through this. "I'm a grown woman, and I'm not your responsibility."

"I admire and respect your independence," he said softly. "But it's the two of us now, and that changes things."

They weren't going to reach any agreement today.

"Like I said, let's both think about it." And because

his eyes narrowed and the pulse beat wildly in his temple, she leaned forward and kissed his cheek. "Go celebrate with your family."

"Why should I? I don't feel like celebrating."

Making her way to the door, she clenched the knob. "Because it's expected."

He shook his head. "I thought you knew me better than that. I don't give a flip about what's expected, and neither should you. If there's one thing you should let die from your days at Beacon Hill, lay that one on the altar."

Her breath caught at his comment, but she firmed her shoulders. "Congratulations again, Arthur," she said formally and opened the door.

Fortunately everyone was gone when she walked to her desk, stuffed her feet in her ugly, clunky boots, and collected her things, trying not to cry.

Arthur was wrong.

Sometimes the only thing that kept you going was doing what was expected.

Chapter 17

When Harriet entered the parlor, Maybelline was sliding a tube of pink lipstick that matched her shirt over her lips.

"What's the matter?" she asked immediately, twisting the lipstick and snapping it shut.

Her lips trembled.

"Maybelle," she said, using her sister's old nickname.

"What is it?" she asked, her face tensing. "Is it Father?"

"Indirectly. Arthur found out he's won the Pulitzer prize for the editorial he wrote about Father."

Her sister dropped onto the mauve settee, her red hair tumbling around her shoulders. "Oh, no."

"Oh, yes," she answered, taking a seat next to her.

She'd cried on the way home, but had tried to compose herself before coming inside. Part of her felt like that crackled glass made by European glassblowers, their spidery fissures adding gravitas to the piece. Held together, but still broken, the lines visible and far reaching.

"Is he happy about it?" her sister asked, a tear streaking down her cheek.

Harriet put an arm around her, and Maybelline rested her head on her shoulder. "No, he's not, which is sad, don't you think? I mean, if not for me, he would be overjoyed."

"I figured he wouldn't be happy. Arthur had to know how much this would hurt you. Us. Oh, Harriet, when is it ever going to go away?"

Wasn't that what she'd been asking herself for the past half hour? Could it ever go away while they were living a lie in this small town? Hurting the man she loved and being hurt in return by a past they couldn't seem to escape?

"I told Arthur I can't change my name. It feels—"

"Disloyal," her sister finished for her. "I want more than anything for things to be the way they used to be, but they can't. Sometimes at night, I wish with all my heart that when I wake up we'll be at home again and none of this has happened. Just like when mom died."

Her heart pulsed with remembered pain. She'd cherished the same wish, but their mother had never come back.

"I know," she whispered, tears appearing again in her eyes.

"If Arthur weren't here, what would you do?" Maybelline asked her, sniffing.

"I'd leave," she said honestly, and handed her sister her clean handkerchief.

Her sister's hand fell open, and she stared at the cloth. "That's mother's, isn't it?"

The W embroidered in the corner had been commissioned by their mother. They'd had a collection of linens sporting the W for Wentworth around their house in Boston. "Yes."

"I'm just starting to feel settled in Dare, but we can't escape what happened, can we? Not when Arthur's so connected to it."

Eventually he would resent Harriet for taking away his joy in achievements like the Pulitzer. Her motivation in coming here had been sordid, and like a poisoned well, there was nothing she could do to change that.

"I think we should leave," she told Maybelline. "We can go to a bigger city, one with a good college for you. Use our real names and only share our real story with the people we trust. I don't want to hide who I am for the rest of my life."

Maybelline straightened and turned toward her. "But what about you and Arthur? You love him."

She rocked in place for a moment, struggling not to cry. "Yes," she whispered, "but I don't think we'll be able to overcome how things began. I'll just have to get over him."

But she couldn't imagine doing that. Was it possible to get over the love of your life?

"Oh, Harriet. I'm so sorry. For both of you. I like Arthur."

What wasn't there to like?

"He won't like this one bit," Maybelline whispered, wrapping her arms around Harriet and rocking them both like their mother had done when they were little and scared during a thunderstorm.

"He's strong, and he'll move on." She knew it was true. A mountain wouldn't bend, not even in the strongest wind. "Nothing can stop Arthur Hale, not even a little thing like love."

But it hadn't been little.

Not to her.

Not to him.

A sea of tears slipped down her face, and she had to

302

grab the handkerchief from her sister.

No, it hadn't been little at all.

Chapter 18

"Why aren't you out celebrating, boy? You just won a Pulitzer, and you look like someone put down your prize bull," Emmits said the moment Arthur opened his front door. "Or do I even need to ask?"

That's why he hadn't called to tell him the news. Or anyone. He just wanted to be alone at home. Isn't that why he'd left the office early even though the launch was a week away?

As Emmits barreled into the foyer, Arthur stepped aside, knowing the man had no compunction about mowing down anything that stood in his path.

"Did you really expect me to be overjoyed?" he asked. "I love her, Mr...Emmits."

"Well, that slip of the tongue shows me how little your head is working right now." He held up a bag. "I brought a forty-year-old bottle of Pappy Van Winkle's to celebrate with."

He followed Emmits into his den. "I don't feel much like celebrating."

The older man slapped his belly. "Well, then, you can get drunk over your woman, and I'll do the toasting.

Where do you keep the glasses, boy?"

The crystal highball glasses Mrs. Merriam—he still couldn't use her first name—had given him for a house warming present radiated rainbows when he snagged them from his makeshift bar.

"How'd she take it?" Emmits said, twisting out the bourbon cork and sniffing it.

"About like you'd expect," Arthur replied, dropping onto the couch.

"You can set the scene better than that," Emmits said, pouring them both a double. "You're a journalist for crying out loud."

"Fine," he replied tersely and proceeded to lay out their discussion—well, their fight—in journalistic efficiency.

Emmits nursed his bourbon while he studied his crossed feet. "I have to admit, I would have been disappointed if she'd agreed to change her name and forsake her heritage. Now I actually respect the girl."

Truthfully, Arthur would have been too. "I never really liked that solution, but I don't know where that leaves us now."

"Sure you do," Emmits responded. "With a major stumbling block between the two of you, which has been there all along. The girl's right. You do need a woman who can be happy for you and stand proudly by your side when you receive your prize at the award dinner in New York."

His mind wouldn't even conjure up that vision. Not when he was convinced he was going to lose Harriet.

"She's going to leave town," he mused, downing his bourbon, the fire burning his throat.

He knew it in his gut.

"Well, that might be for the best," Emmits said in his usual sing-song Oklahoma drawl that usually came off charming.

Today it only annoyed the crap out of Arthur.

"You could walk away from the love of your life that easily?" he growled, reaching for the bottle Emmits had placed on the nearby lamp stand.

"We're not talking about me. The question is what do *you* want to do?"

"I want her to stay here."

He tossed down another shot, and his gaze found a picture of his parents on the fireplace. They had their arms wrapped around each other after the spring calving. His mother was beaming, and even his dad was grinning, a rare sight. He wanted what they had, and he'd found it with Harriet.

"I want to marry her, Emmits." He knew it with the same surety he'd felt about becoming a journalist, about moving back to Dare and starting his own newspaper.

Wouldn't that resolve the name issue? They could marry somewhere else, and no one would be the wiser. She wouldn't have to change her last name to Jenkins. Of course, he didn't know what Maybelline wanted to do. And while Harriet was his primary concern, he couldn't disregard her sister. They were family. Well, they could figure it out.

"I thought you might," Emmits said, setting his highball aside. "But you need to think about being with her for the long haul, boy. Can you see that? Because trust me, in fifty years—hell, even five—there will be moments when your wife annoys you. When they come, you need to have a heck of a long list on the other side, reminding you why you put up with her starching your socks or making you pot roast, even though you've hated it all your life."

"Starching your socks?" he scoffed. That was it?

Emmits drilled him with a stare, the kind he'd seen him give to congressmen who hadn't been inclined to support a bill that favored Emmits' businesses. "How about this one? You're as old as I am—or heck, even ten or twenty years younger. The sex with your wife has slowed to a snail's pace. Her body is sagging, and she just isn't as passionate as she used to be for you, or you for her. And a woman in her twenties, the most beautiful woman you've ever met, approaches you and tells you that she wants you."

Of all the things they'd discussed, they'd never discussed sex. "Is she a hooker?"

The old man barked out a laugh. "Trust me, boy, that's the last thing your body will be asking you." He poured another bourbon for himself and gestured to Arthur, who shook his head.

"So, you've never—" Arthur waved his hand.

"Cheated on my wife?" He gave a slight smile. "No, boy, but I can tell you there were moments when it was tempting. Not because I didn't love her, but because the body didn't really care about things like vows and children and our life together. It only saw the beautiful woman offering herself to me. When you have money and power, women are a dime a dozen. I've always tried to remember that. Lucky for me, my wife loves me for who I am. I'm not going to throw that away for a woman who's after something else. You need to think about the women you'll meet at the fancy parties you'll be attending and how you'll feel about them when you have a wife. Can you imagine saying no to them like I have?"

Yes, he could. In a strange way, the fact that he'd

managed to turn Harriet down in her fake seduction attempt confirmed it. He couldn't ever imagine wanting anyone more than he had her in that moment. "Yes, I love her enough."

"Good, because if you don't know now, you're easy prey."

"I'd always wondered about the women around you," Arthur said, meeting his friend's steady gaze. "I saw them flock to you at parties in New York and when we went to D.C."

Shaking his head, Emmits laughed again, loud and deep. "I knew you did. If you'd been man enough to ask me back then, I would have told you. Guess you're man enough now, and it seems like Harriet might have helped you get there. I'm starting to think she just might be a good match for you."

He liked hearing that. Emmits' opinion meant the world to him.

There was a knock on the front door. It was only half past seven. Part of him hoped it was Harriet.

"If you'll excuse me—"

"Go," Emmits said and set his highball aside.

When he opened the door, his family stood on the front steps. His mother had a casserole dish in her hands.

"Emmits told us the Pulitzer prizes were going to be announced today," his mom said, staring at him like she could read his mind. "Did you hear?"

His mouth tipped up, but it just wouldn't stay. "Yes. I won."

"That's great!" George said, barreling forward to hug him.

His body was stiff, and the hurt inside him started to rise. George must have sensed it because he gave him a light shove. "What's the matter with you? This is a huge honor."

His dad laid a hand on his shoulder, and he fought against the pain tunneling up in his chest.

"Everything all right, son?"

George turned somber next to their father, and their mother's eyes were narrowed like when she was trying to figure out what was wrong with him. Suddenly he couldn't keep the secrets he'd been carrying anymore. It was time to trust the people he loved.

"Why don't you come in?" he said, stepping out of the way. "I have something I need to share with you."

And he didn't mean the Pulitzer. He was going to tell them about Harriet. Tell them he wanted to marry her. Trust they would support him, like they always did, and stand by him.

In the grand scheme of things, a Pulitzer seemed insignificant in the face of that.

Chapter 19

When Arthur saw Harriet's face the next morning, his stomach plummeted.

She'd reached the decision to leave, just like he'd suspected. Her greeting was a little too cool, and her beautiful, blood-shot eyes evaded his gaze. He closed the door to his office for privacy.

Well, he wasn't accepting that. No, not one bit. It was time to execute the next part of his plan.

He picked up the phone and called his brother. "Everything ready for noon?" he asked.

"Yep, called in a few of the guys. We'll hang the banner ten minutes till."

His family had taken the news of Harriet's background like champs. They'd been concerned at first, but Emmits had voiced his approval, telling them "the girl has spine," and they'd gradually relaxed. When he told them he planned to marry Harriet, Emmits said "you'd better move fast, boy," making them all laugh. His parents had offered their support and George had asked him when he was going to make his move.

He'd decided to ask her as soon as possible, since he

didn't want her to up and leave without a word. And when he thought about where to ask her, the answer had floated down to him like leaves on a fall day.

Dare's town square.

He could tell her there how much he loved her and wanted her to be a part of his life and this community. That he would give her his name.

She wouldn't have to give up her heritage because the people they trusted would know who she was and where she'd come from.

And to show her how much support they had in Dare, he and his family had invited the townspeople to come out at lunchtime, spreading the word through the great web connecting everyone in Dare.

He'd also decided to make up a banner. They didn't have billboards in Dare like they did in the big city, but he had the freshly pressed newspaper rolls. Using the paint his parents had leftover from their work on the barn, he and George had painted the bold red phrase: *Harriet, will you marry me?*

It was the most public way he could ask her, which was intentional. He wanted to remind her how much she'd acclimated to Dare. And to send a message about the kind of life they could have together here.

Fortunately, the sun had come out today after the horrible snowstorm yesterday and was shining bright. The temperature was supposed to be fifty degrees by noon.

Emmits had called a Denver jeweler late last night, because he was Emmits Merriam and could get away with that. The man would be arriving in Dare at ten o'clock. Arthur was going to meet him at Emmits' house to pick out a ring.

There was no way he was proposing to Harriet

without a ring.

He might not be able to take her to Tiffany's in New York, but by George, he was going to do his best to make this the most memorable proposal in Dare's history since Frank Summers had asked Nancy Peters to marry him by the old Kissing Tree in 1941 before he went off to war.

His chest grew tight, and he sat back in his chair. He was proposing to the woman he loved at noon today in front of the whole town.

What if she didn't say yes?

Shaking himself, he stood and decided he was going to head over to Emmits' house early. His friend would keep him occupied until the jeweler arrived.

There was no way he would get any work done today, a crazy thought with the launch fast approaching.

He opened the door to his office and gazed at Harriet. The funny truth hit him again in the gut. He really didn't care if he got any work done today. It was true what he'd said to her yesterday. She'd somehow managed to become even more important to him than his life's passion.

Because she was his heart.

"I'm going to see Emmits," he told her, stopping briefly by her desk. "If anything comes up, you can reach me there."

She lifted her puzzled face to meet his eyes. "Okay. When do you think you'll be back?"

"Around noon. I'd like to take you to lunch. Would that be all right?"

The corners of her mouth lifted in that infernal polite smile he remembered from their first days of working together. "I don't know…"

"It's important," he said, using Emmits' play book. Never let them say no. "I'll come by for you. Have a good morning."

He made himself walk away without letting her respond and waved naturally to the rest of the staff. When he stepped outside onto the sidewalk, he glanced at his watch. Noon felt like eons away.

Just as he'd hoped, Emmits helped distract him with conversation. When the jeweler finally showed up at the house and handed Arthur the first ring he recommended, he fumbled it. The simple setting flew into the air, causing his heart to palpitate, but the jeweler's hand shot out and caught it.

"Don't worry," the man said. "Happens all the time."

Emmits just laughed, his arm wrapped around Mrs. Merriam's waist.

"That one's not...right." He handed the other ring back and scanned the black jewelry case, running his gaze across the rows, looking for the perfect ring for Harriet. When he reached the third row, bottom corner, he pointed.

"Let me see that one."

"An excellent choice, sir," the jeweler said.

The ring was gold, featuring a simple lone diamond surrounded by a sea of rubies. They had fire, just like his Harriet did.

"Mrs. Merriam?" he asked shyly, holding the ring. "What do you think?"

She and Emmits exchanged a look—one he'd seen between his parents—and then she walked forward for a closer look at the ring, her white hair all soft and curly around her round face. "From what you and Emmits have told me about her, I think it would suit her perfectly. She doesn't strike me as a conventional woman."

He smiled his first easy smile since learning about the Pulitzer. "No, she's not. And that's what I love about her."

As he glanced at Emmits, he remembered what he'd said about imagining what it would be like to grow old with the woman you wanted. In that moment, he knew he'd always love Harriet, want her, and that she would never bore him.

"This one," he told the jeweler.

After conducting the transaction, they saw the jeweler to his car. Emmits slapped him on the back. "You ready?" he asked.

Arthur took a deep breath and nodded. "I am."

"Good," the older man replied. "We'll follow you."

He felt his mouth drop open a little at that. "You're coming?"

Emmits snorted. "Of course, boy. Didn't you want the whole town there? Plus, I need to make sure you don't muck it up."

"I won't."

He headed to his car and sat inside, watching Emmits take Mrs. Merriam's elbow as they walked to their navy sedan. When the older man opened the door for her, Arthur turned the ignition. He'd remember this lesson too. You never stopped treating a woman like a lady. Even if you'd been married for more than fifty years.

He put the car in gear and drove off.

It was time to claim his lady before the whole town.

Chapter 20

When Arthur returned to take Harriet to lunch, he was acting strange, as if he'd drunk too much coffee up at the Merriams' house. His foot tapped with impatience, and he wouldn't meet her eyes.

Had he come to the same conclusion she had?

Would he call it quits between them over lunch? Well, she was of the same mind, even though it broke her heart to even think about it.

"I'm ready," she called out, picking up her black clutch after donning her winter white colored coat.

"Okay," he said, taking her elbow. "Let's go."

That simple touch had her blinking back tears. Oh God, this was going to be hard. Deep down inside, she wished they'd made love. That way she'd have at least the memory of that forbidden passion.

The sun was harsh to her eyes, so she reached inside her purse and pulled on her black sunglasses. Arthur squinted beside her.

"I want to show you something before we have lunch. Okay?"

She nodded, and he led her in the opposite direction of

the tavern. Fortunately, it was warmer today, something she'd heard was a regular occurrence in early May—snow one day, spring weather the next.

"Where are we going?"

"The town square," he replied, his hand gripping her elbow a little tighter than usual.

It seemed like an odd destination, and she wondered if he was looking for a private enough place to end things between them. He wouldn't do it in the office, she knew that, not now that there were other employees. This way, she could go straight home to cry. Hadn't her girlfriends said it was easier to break things off in a public place during the day? And Nellie's would be too cruel after all the time they'd spent there.

Blinking back tears, she noticed a few people giving them sidelong glances before darting ahead and around the corner. It seemed like all of them were heading to the square too. Well, perhaps it was more popular than she'd thought.

When they turned onto the brick path that led to the square, she firmed her shoulders. She could do this. She was a Wellesley graduate after all. Weren't they part of the modern generation? They didn't go to pieces over a man.

Her heel caught in a small hole in the brick path, and she leaned down to pry it out when it wouldn't budge. It finally came loose and as she rose, her gaze swept across Dare's classic brick town square. She gasped with shock as she took in the scene. Hundreds of people standing there, almost like they were waiting for a speech.

And then she glanced up and saw the sign in bold red letters fluttering in the wind, hung from the courthouse's second floor.

Harriet, will you marry me?

Her hand flew to her throat, and she heard Arthur clear his throat. Her heart pounded in her chest as she took it all in: him, the crowd, the banner.

Oh no. Not this. She couldn't bear it.

Then he lowered to one knee before her.

When he looked up at her, the sun caught his face, and all she could see were the twin flames of his blue eyes, so familiar, so dear, staring straight into her soul, ripping her heart to shreds.

Her breath caught, and she was certain she'd fall into a dead faint right there on the brick path.

"Harriet," Arthur said, his voice strong and true. "I love you. I want to marry you. I want to have children with you and grow old with you. I want to make a legacy with you here in Dare. I offer you my life, my family, and my hometown." His hand swept out in an arc as he gestured to the crowd.

She bit her lip to hold back the tears. Heavens if he hadn't gone and shocked her speechless.

"But most of all, I offer you my name. So we can start anew."

His name. So she wouldn't have to forsake her own. Just take a new one. His.

Her face trembled. He was still trying to protect her, still trying to shield her from what she'd done.

His hand reached into his coat pocket and drew out a black box. It popped open with the flick of his finger. The sole diamond shot rainbows, and the rubies surrounding it looked like a ring of fire.

Her hand flew to her tight throat. The beauty of it stole her breath. How had he known she'd want something unconventional?

"When I saw this ring, I knew it was yours." Then he

held it out. "Harriet, will you marry me?"

Not a single sound carried across the square, everyone waiting in silence for her answer.

The little voice inside started crying, knowing what she should do but so desperately didn't want to. Still, being strong was the only way to make this right. She couldn't take the coward's way out, which is what taking his name would be.

She turned her back on the crowd. "Oh, Arthur, I can't," she whispered, stepping back. "I can't start our life on a lie."

Oh why couldn't he have done this in private? The crowd only made it harder. Everyone in town was going to see her turn him down, and he was a proud man.

He grabbed her hand urgently. "Harriet," he whispered. "I've told my family because I don't want that either, but it doesn't have to go any further. They're the people who matter the most to me."

Hadn't she said a poisoned well?

"And our *children?* What are we supposed to tell them?" Her voice broke, and she was conscious of the crowd watching from behind her.

Arthur finally rose, and she had to look up to see his dear face.

"We'll tell them that you were a very tenacious woman, and that once I met you, there was no one else for me. That's the God's honest truth."

The weeping in her heart ceased, and with it, a new emotion arose. Courage. It spread through her chest like a forest fire. In that moment, she knew what she needed to do. It was the only way they could be together.

"I can't do it," she whispered hoarsely. "I *can't* keep lying to everyone." And then she moved away from him and toward the crowd.

"Harriet!" he called urgently, his steps echoing on the brick behind her.

The faces she saw in the crowd looked uniformly puzzled. Some people were whispering, others casting sad glances at Arthur.

"Marry him, Harriet!" someone called out.

A few others shouted "Say yes, Harriet!"

When she stood before them, she took a deep breath. Scanned their faces. So many people she knew by name now—Bertha from the Tavern was frowning at her, and Herman was smoking a cigarette, his eyes narrowed.

"I need to tell you something," she called out as the wind gusted. "I…"

She stopped. Oh God, if she said this, she'd be lucky they didn't throw stones at her. Suddenly her courage evaporated.

Her sister moved toward her from the edge of the crowd. She hadn't realized Maybelline was there. She approached Harriet with a soft smile on her face, and grabbed her hand, strength flowing through their connection.

"Go ahead, Harriet."

When their eyes met, Harriet had to scrub tears from her cheeks. Her sister nodded. Maybelline knew what she was going to do and was supporting her, even though it would affect both of them.

"Time to face the music, right?" she whispered to her sister. Feeling bold again, she took her sunglasses off, wanting the crowd to see her eyes.

Arthur reached for them, stuffing them in his coat pocket, and then grabbed hold of her other hand. She jerked her gaze to his, and in them, she saw understanding and a love that shone brighter than the diamond and ruby ring.

"Go ahead, sweetheart," he urged, and his mouth tipped up at the corner.

George walked forward then, Arthur's parents following, until his whole family stood beside her too. Then Emmits and his wife stepped forward and joined their group.

Her heart swelled and broke free of the cage constructed of her lies.

"I don't know where to start," she began, forcing herself to raise her voice to be heard, "but it means the world to me that you came out here today to support Arthur. There isn't a finer man in the world, and I love him." Her voice broke, and his hand clenched hers. "But I can't say yes to him without telling you who I am or why I first came to Dare."

Harsh whispers punctuated the square.

"My name is Harriet Wentworth, and my sister and I are originally from Boston. My father—" A sob erupted before she pressed her lips together. "My father is Dr. Ashley Wentworth, and if you've read the newspaper, you'll know that he was the scientist responsible for the deaths of seven infants across the United States."

A few gasps broke out across the crowd, and she saw several of the townspeople's faces contort with shock. She dug her toes into her shoes to stay strong.

"I'm not making any excuses for what my father did, but I will tell you that he's a good man who made a terrible mistake. What's worse is that he tried to cover it up, and that's been hard for me and my sister to believe— and forgive."

She glanced over at Maybelline. Tears were running

down her sister's face, but she tightened her grip on Harriet's hand, like she was urging her forward.

"At first, I didn't believe my father was capable of such a crime. The whole idea was abhorrent to me. He's my father, you see, and I just…didn't imagine it could be true. It *had* to be a mistake, and I nurtured that belief as my world fell apart. I came to Dare Valley determined to prove that Arthur Hale, the man who had written the story, had gotten it all wrong. I lied about my last name when I arrived. I…"

The faces in the crowd were frowning now, and one by one, the spectators crossed their arms across their chests, like they were shutting her out.

She took a deep breath, gathering her courage again. "I accepted the position of his secretary in a desperate attempt to find new evidence that might clear my father. And when that failed—"

"Harriet!" Arthur called to her right, his tone harsh. "Don't."

She bit her lip. "And when that failed, I decided to ruin his reputation."

A few women gasped and put their hands over their mouths.

"But I couldn't do that because he's just too honorable for words."

Finally she turned her head to look at him, tears trickling down her cheeks. "You are, you know. You always have been."

His Adam's apple moved thickly in his throat.

"Well, Arthur figured something was wrong after that. He discovered why I was here, and then he showed me the evidence he'd compiled against my father."

Her sister gripped her hand hard, like she too was

feeling the pain of their father's betrayal.

Harriet raised her chin. "It was all there. Arthur had been more than thorough, and I felt ashamed for what my father had done, for those little babies who drank the bad formula, for the parents who lost them, and for what I had done to Arthur.

"And because he's so darn noble, Arthur tried to help me. He asked me to stay on as his secretary and take more time to figure out what Maybelline and I wanted to do. The more time I spent with him, the more I saw him for the man he was, and I fell in love with him."

She glanced over and met his mother's gaze. The woman smiled softly at her, and the compassion in her expression encouraged Harriet to take the next step.

"I'm sorry for lying to all of you. I'm sorry that I came here under false pretenses. My sister had nothing to do with my actions. She only came because my alma mater and her college wouldn't let her come back to school. You see, the two of us are exiles now. From our home. From our family. And for a while, from ourselves. I don't want to start a life with Arthur based on a lie. He deserves better than that, and after all this heartache, I'm starting to believe that I do too."

Bertha from the Tavern nodded to her, and she took that for encouragement.

"I don't know if you'll ever be able to come to terms with what I've done, but I had to come clean and tell you. Dare is a close-knit town, a special community, and I've been grateful for the acceptance you've shown my sister and me while we've been here. And if that can't continue now that you know the whole story, we'll be sad, but we'll understand." She made the corners of her mouth tip up. "Thank you for coming today."

AVA MILES

Then she lowered her head, her emotions zigzagging in her chest—hurt, relief, and fear.

Someone patted her on the back, and she turned around to see Emmits Merriam smiling at her. "You done good, girl."

"Well said, my dear," his wife voiced, her quiet presence a comfort.

Arthur's mom touched her shoulder. "Oh, you poor thing," she said, and pulled her in for a hug.

Harriet had to let go of Arthur and Maybelline's hands to return the embrace. His mother was shorter than she was, and had a spine of steel.

When Mrs. Hale stepped back, she nodded in a crisp fashion that was reminiscent of Arthur. "Welcome to the family, Harriet."

Arthur's father also nodded, and in his bright blue gaze—so like his son's—she also saw acceptance.

Then George barreled forward and hugged her, calling out, "Oh, come on, everyone. Let's show Harriet and her sister what a great town Dare can be."

"Yeah," a little girl with braids said. "She said she was sorry."

A few people chuckled at that.

When George let her go, Arthur stepped close and caressed her cheek. "For a moment there, I thought I'd made a mistake, asking you in public, but I can't imagine loving you any more than I do right now. My, you're brave. We're going to make one hell of a family."

Her laugh came out more like a sob. And then someone tapped her shoulder.

She turned. It was Bertha, whose eyes were wet. Her hand reached out for a shake. "Welcome to Dare," she said, "I'm Bertha Linglefield."

Harriet had to bite her lip a moment before responding. "Good to meet you, Bertha" she replied as she shook her hand, another tear falling down her face. "I'm Harriet...Wentworth. And this is my sister, Maybelline."

"Good to meet you both," she said, and then winked at Arthur. "Welcome to Dare Valley."

When the waitress stepped aside, Herman Smith introduced himself just like Bertha had, giving his full name. And then Alice York from the bakery. Soon the crowd made a line to introduce themselves.

When the last person shook her hand and Maybelline's, she wiped away more tears and hugged her sister.

"It's going to be okay," she whispered into her ear. "It really is."

Maybelline rocked her back and forth. "Yes, Harriet. It will be. I'm so proud of you."

When she let her go, Arthur put his arm around her. "Okay," he said, the hint of impatience in his voice. "Will you marry me *now?*"

A few people laughed.

As she looked up into his blue eyes, she smiled. "I'm sorry, but have we met?"

His brow rose.

Then she extended her hand. "I'm Harriet Wentworth. And you are?"

His mouth twitched. "Your future husband," he responded, yanking her to him and then swinging her in a circle.

As the crowd started to clap, she simply held on, knowing her anchor was sound and would never let her go.

Chapter 21

The citizens of Dare Valley packed into the church one Saturday in June to watch Arthur Hale marry his beloved Harriet Wentworth. When the minister announced her full name, people smiled, remembering her impassioned speech in Dare's town square on May Day and how everyone had become reacquainted with her then.

There had been talk, no two bones about it, but the couple had weathered it, largely because they only had eyes for each other and a whole lot of support. His family and Emmits made sure of that.

As Arthur slid the wedding band on Harriet's finger, she leaned close and whispered, "I still say you should have chosen sapphires so it could remind me of your beautiful eyes."

He snorted, something totally inappropriate at a wedding, especially theirs. But she didn't care. "Tomfoolery," he blustered, but his eyes twinkled, and she couldn't look away.

He said his vows with the same intensity that he did everything else. She responded with the new confidence she'd felt since delivering her speech before the town.

It had saddened her that her father wasn't there to walk her down the aisle, but Emmits Merriam had asked for that honor. My, how she was growing to love that man.

When the officiant pronounced Harriet and Arthur man and wife, she turned to look at her new husband.

"You may kiss the bride," the minister said.

When Arthur leaned in, he waggled his eyebrows. "I thought he'd never get to that part," he whispered before putting his sweet lips on hers. He took her hands when they separated and simply looked at her. She beamed back.

"Shall we, Mrs. Hale?" he asked, nodding to the aisle.

Wow, Mrs. Hale. She was a Mrs. It would take some getting used to, but it sounded great.

Maybelline, her sole attendant, smiled as they passed. Her transcripts had transferred easily to Emmits Merriam, and she would begin in the fall when the university opened. She'd decided to study English literature, thinking she might want to become a librarian some day after all her volunteering in Dare's public library. The church choir indulged her love of singing, and she was already planning to form a theater group at the university. She'd live with Harriet and Arthur until she moved into her dorm. Both sisters were thrilled with the arrangement. It seemed like the Wentworths were all settled now.

The reception was packed, and she was kissed and hugged until she was sure her makeup had been rubbed off. When she asked Arthur about it, he just winked and said, "If there's any left, I'll be sure to rub if off later."

Later.

Oh yes.

Finally.

They took their first dance, and her mouth parted in

surprise. "You're pretty good at this," she commented.

"I'm a man of many talents," he said, leading her with a firm, but gentle touch.

"Mmmhmmm," she only responded and laughed when he spun her in a circle.

As the night continued, their eyes kept coming together like magnets, from across the dance floor when she was paired with someone else, when they were cutting the white Lady Baltimore cake and feeding it to each other for the first time, and the embarrassment of the whole garter toss as the men fought to catch the white lace band with the baby blue bow, her something blue.

Though she knew this was a celebration to be enjoyed, she couldn't stop thinking about what the celebration later would be like.

She was talking to Maybelline when Arthur's unmistakable hands slid around her slender waist. Leaning back, she felt his warmth.

"Are you ready to go?" he whispered near her ear. When she nodded her assent, he took her hand. "Then go throw that bouquet, and let's get out of here."

Maybelline called the single women to follow them to the center of the dance floor. But Harriet threw the bouquet with so much gusto that it leapt over the women and hit George in the chest like an arrow.

He immediately threw it away like it was poison ivy. "Get that away from me!"

Arthur slapped him on the back. "You're next, baby brother."

"Oh, no," he said, dancing back, holding up his hands. "One marriage this year is plenty."

"I just have one piece of wisdom for you when you propose. Don't ask the lucky lady in public. If she ends up balking, you're going to be embarrassed beyond words. I had a moment there…"

"Yeah, looked like she was going to hang you out to dry in front of the whole town."

"But she didn't."

As the brothers continued bantering about George's future nuptials, Harriet turned to Maybelline. "It's time for me to go."

Her sister blinked away tears before enfolding her in an enormous hug. "I know you'll only be gone a week for your honeymoon, but I'll miss you."

"I'll miss you too," Harriet whispered.

When her sister leaned back, she smiled. "If Mom and Dad could have been here, they would have been so proud of you. I know I am."

Her eyes grew wet. "Thanks, Maybelle." She grabbed her again. "I love you."

"I love you too," she whispered. "I won't tell you to be happy because I know you already are."

"Yes," she said. "Yes, I am." And it felt really, really good.

Arthur was saying goodbye to his parents and the Merriams when she joined him. Emmits slapped him on the back. "You did good, boy," he said. "Real good."

"I still feel a little bad about leaving the paper for a week."

"Trust me," Emmits said. "Everything will be fine. Your deputy seems up to the job."

Harriet agreed, but Arthur had only consented to taking a week off. The timing of their wedding hadn't been the best, but neither of them had wanted to wait.

Harriet's hand slid into his after she said goodbye to his family, and together they walked out the front door and into a shower of rice. He pulled her along as the small pieces pinged off her face and body, causing her to laugh.

Then he was opening the door and pushing her into the passenger seat. After shoving her train inside after her, he ran around the hood and lunged into the driver's seat, laughing beside her.

"It's everywhere," she cried, brushing grains of rice off her dress.

"Well, if we run out of food, we'll know where to find some."

He honked the horn twice and took off through a sea of faces, the metal cans tied to their bumper clanging together as he increased the speed.

Then he headed to his house.

No, *their* house.

They'd agreed to spend their wedding night there before driving to Yellowstone for the rest of their honeymoon. She'd never seen that part of the country, and after all George's praise, she'd told Arthur she wanted to see it for herself.

He held her hand while he drove, letting go only when he had to shift.

When they reached the house, the front lights were on, almost as if the house were waiting to welcome them.

He came around and helped her out, and she scooped up her train as best as she could. Then he lifted her into his arms, and she laughed.

"I was hoping you'd do this," she said, leaning against his chest in total trust.

"Well, of course. Didn't I marry you proper?"

"You did," she agreed and turned the handle when he reached the front door.

The door opened, and he carried her inside.

"Welcome home, Mrs. Hale," he whispered.

His face lowered, and she caressed those beloved cheekbones. When he kissed her, his mouth gentle and firm, like they had all the time in the world, she wrapped her arms around his neck.

"I love you," she said.

"I love you, too," he said back.

"Make love to me, Arthur," she whispered before she could lose her courage.

He drew back and smiled. "It would be my pleasure, Mrs. Hale, my sincerest pleasure."

When they reached their bedroom, he set her down and reached for the twenty-odd cloth buttons over her spine. About halfway down, he sighed. "This could take a while."

"But you're a determined man. A few little buttons won't stop you."

"Be lucky I *am* determined, my dear, or I might consider finding some scissors to hurry this along."

His hands slid inside her dress, caressing her shoulder blades and then the length of her spine. She shuddered at that first delicate touch. When he finally freed all the buttons, she slid the dress off and stepped out of it, standing before him in her white corset, panties, garter belt, hose, and heels.

"You're stunning."

When he reached for his bowtie, she stepped forward. "Let me."

His eyes sparkled, and his mouth twitched. *"Now* look who's determined."

She gave a slow wink, something she'd never been bold enough to do before, and his mouth parted in surprise.

"Well, well, I think I'm seeing a new side of you."

330

So was she. Standing in the intimate soft glow of their bedroom, she felt like a new person.

"This is Harriet *Hale."*

"Nice to meet you, Mrs. Hale." He traced her cheek. "My wife."

She took his hand and laid it on her breast. "My husband."

Their mouths met, and they caressed each other's bodies. Neither rushed, knowing they were building a sacred foundation, one that had begun in the church and would end in them coming together tonight.

When he shed his clothes, she blushed slightly, but held her ground.

"Will I do?" he asked, taking her into his arms.

"I think so. Yes." She turned her head as his lips met her neck.

"Let me know when you're completely sure." There was laughter in his voice.

When he lay beside her, his mouth on her breast, she said, "Okay, I'm sure now."

He lifted his head and grinned. "Glad to hear it."

Then he kissed her long and deep, preparing her body, acclimating them both to these new sensations. It hadn't been easy to wait for tonight, but they'd both agreed to it, wanting this night to be as special as possible.

When he finally entered her and broke through the final barrier between them, she gasped at the sensation, the heat, the size, the tightness. He held himself still, waiting for her to adjust. As he took his mouth to her breast, she felt her body relax. Her back arched toward him, and the initial pain became but a memory.

"Arthur," she whispered.

"I know, love," he only responded. "I know."

Her body, while new to pleasure, seemed to know when to rise and fall with his. His eyes never left hers, beckoning her, loving her. She kept her gaze on his as her pulse quickened, as her body grew more urgent, as the pace increased.

She gripped his waist, wanting to chain him there, wanting a release. His hands lifted her, and he lunged, and she cried out, the pleasure cresting across her, fanning out deep inside her body.

She heard him call out above her, and then felt him lower until he rested completely on her, his harsh breath hot in her ear.

Gulping in air, she marveled at the clenching in her body, at the heat, at the sweat.

At the connection. And the soft pink glow, almost like she was floating on a cloud.

When he lifted his head to gaze at her, her whole heart seemed to expand in her chest.

"I never imagined," she whispered.

He pressed his brow to hers then. "Me either."

When he rolled them to the side, still keeping that new and tenuous connection, she pressed her face against his chest and tried to take it all in. No one had ever told her it could be like this between a man and a woman.

They didn't speak other than to whisper words of love.

And when the peach rays of dawn crested through the window, he awoke her and rose over her again.

"We're going to make something together, Harriet. Not just the paper. But a family. One where we all support each other no matter what."

Hers hadn't been like that, and she was determined not to make the same mistakes as her parents. She linked their hands. "I like the sound of that."

"Emmits said to try and imagine how I'd feel about you in fifty years, and I have to say that right now, fifty years doesn't seem like near enough time."

Tears spurted into her eyes. "Oh, Arthur, that's the sweetest thing you could ever say. I hadn't thought of us all old and gray."

"And you a grandma. I bet you'll be good at it."

Resting her head on his chest, she eyed her ring. "Well, I know one thing. I want to give our oldest grandchild my wedding ring when it's her time."

He caressed her back. "Oh? I rather like that idea."

"But I still say you should have gone with sapphires for your eyes."

"My love, all you ever need to do is look into my eyes. Now what else do you want for our family?"

She thought about it for a moment. "Well, women are becoming more independent. By the time we have grandchildren, they might even own their own businesses. I want to set aside some money for them, so that they have a nest egg to do something bold once they graduate from college."

"Oh, I love that idea. Empire builders in the making."

Stroking his chest, she said, "Yes, like their grandpa."

He laughed. "I'll probably be curmudgeonly when I'm old. I have no patience for anything slow."

"I can't wait to see you like that. In the meantime, how about let's concentrate on being young and newly married?"

He looked down into her face, a slow smile spreading. "How would you like to start our first morning together?"

Her brow rose. "Oh, I think you know."

His grin was a mile wide. "I knew rubies would be

just the thing for my passionate wife."

"Wait. That reminds me. I have something for you."

She'd seen the red hots in the Five-and-Dime, and they'd reminded her of rubies. With their ongoing joke about him selecting rubies instead of sapphires, she'd thought it would be a fun way to tease him. Grabbing a throw, she wrapped herself in it and ducked over to her suitcase, a little embarrassed at her nakedness. After locating her gift, she snuck it behind her back and walked toward the bed.

"Since you bought me rubies, I wanted to give you these to chew on."

"Okay," he said, taking the metal tin wrapped in a red ribbon. He opened it and laughed.

"I couldn't find any blue ones, but I rather liked the idea of a candy that looked like rubies to remind you of me when we're apart."

He popped one in his mouth and rolled it around. "Like I could forget about you. Mmm, I like these. Spicy."

She eased onto the bed. "Plus I thought cinnamon kisses would be…"

Yanking her forward, he settled his mouth onto hers, proving his mouth was even more tantalizing with the candy.

"What do you think?" he asked when he drew away.

"I think I'm going to like this. I'll make sure you're well stocked in red hots from now on."

His eyes twinkled. "Now are you glad I didn't buy the sapphires?"

Would he always want the last word? Well, he wasn't going to get it. "Yes, but I still contend that sapphires—"

As he took her mouth with his cinnamon-coated one, and they welcomed their first morning together as husband

and wife, she realized the ring didn't matter.

What mattered was their love, and they had that in abundance.

Chapter 22

"So that's how your grandma and I met," Arthur finished, focusing once again on baby Violet in his arms. He almost chuckled at all of the parts he'd left out, the saucy bits between him and Harriet that were stored in his memory, reserved only for himself.

Meredith and Jill were wiping tears away, and Peggy's mouth seemed frozen in a permanent O.

"No wonder you said you understood tough women," Peggy said.

"Oh, Harriet softened up," he murmured, remembering. "Just like you have with Mac."

Violet stretched then, her little arms punching out of her swaddle, and he smiled. He'd been telling the story for over an hour, so she was probably about ready to wake up and eat. Thank heavens Meredith had gone downstairs to gather some snacks, or he'd have to start worrying about his infernal blood sugar.

"You know," he continued. "She gave you girls that money just like she said she would the night we were married. She wrote it down in her wish book, a journal she kept that tallied all of the things she wanted to do in her life."

"And I have her ring," Meredith said, lifting her hand, the rubies and single diamond shining as brightly now as they had when he first put it on Harriet's finger in the town square.

It was good to see it there, and it always made Arthur smile. Meredith and Tanner had a love like he and Harriet had shared. She'd be proud that their ring had gone to such good use.

"And I used the money she gave me to start Don't Soy with Me," Jill said.

"She'd love your coffee shop, Jill. I know she's smiling down from heaven at you two. I just know it," he repeated, coughing a little, feeling a bit misty eyed.

My God, how he missed his sweetheart.

"And I might as well tell you that she had something in mind for her great grandchildren too," he told them.

"What is it?" Jill asked, tucking Mia close when she gave a cry.

"She was worried about the pace the forest was being cut away, so we bought some land up in Meadowlark Canyon in the 80s. She wanted to turn it into a preserve, but that's for the great-great grandkids to do if they so choose. For now, the Hales own it. And I'll put all of the kids you girls have on the deed when it's time."

Jill sniffed. "Oh, Grandpa."

"That's the loveliest present ever," Meredith said, tearing up. She stood, eyes shining. "This moment is so perfect... I know Tanner won't mind if I share our news. We're having a baby."

Giving a cheer, Jill ran over, Mia giving another cry to protest the sudden movement. "You are? Oh, Mere, I'm so happy for you! Did you hear that Mia and Violet? You're going to have a cousin soon."

They hugged awkwardly with the baby between them, and then Meredith walked over to him and knelt by his rocking chair.

"Oh, sweetheart," he said, "you make this old man so happy. Your grandmother would be too, if she were still with us."

A tear slipped down her cheek. "I love you, Grandpa."

"I love you too, little miss," he said, irritated at the wetness in his eyes.

His granddaughters were making him cry like a girl. He looked over at Peggy. "What about you? Are you pregnant yet?"

Her mouth dropped. "Ah, no. But it's under discussion."

No surprise there. Peggy was a great mother. Keith had wanted a sibling for years, and Mac would be a wonderful father. "You'll get there."

"Congrats, Mere," Peggy said with a big smile. "I'm going to be an aunt!"

"Hey," Jill called. "What about my kids?"

"They can't call me that yet. They can barely open their eyes and look around."

"Haha," Jill replied. "So tell me more about this land for the next generation, Grandpa. My mind is already churning out ideas."

He gave them more details, bouncing Violet gently in his arms. When he finished, he said, "Who knows what will happen down the road? It will be nice to know the Hales are preserving the beauty around Dare Valley as the town continues to grow."

"And it *is* growing," Jill commented. "It's becoming

the place to be."

"Emmits had a big part in that. He'd be mighty proud of how everything has turned out."

Dare Valley had changed so much in his life, but some things had remained the same: family, community. The important stuff.

"My time is coming to a close," he continued. "Now it's time for you two to write in your own Wish Book about what you want for your lives and your families. You may have taken new names, but you'll always be Hales. What do you want for your children and grandchildren?"

Meredith gave a slow smile. "We're just getting used to the news. I'll have to think about it."

"Good coffee," Jill replied, making them all laugh. "I would just hate to think the planet might become so overcrowded down the road that we can't even grow any coffee."

"Always my practical one." Arthur turned to Peggy. "What about you, my dear?"

"Well, even though I know I'll sound like a softy, I'm just going to come out and say it. World peace. I don't want my kids or grandkids—wow, there's a mind twister—to have to worry about crime and violence."

"An admirable wish, especially for someone in law enforcement, Peggy," he said rising from the chair, still cuddling Violet close. "Well, if you'll excuse me, I need to stretch these old bones."

Meredith took the baby from him, her eyes shining, and he grabbed his cane and walked to the door, a bit stiff, but feeling that glow in his chest that always came in warm moments like this one.

"Regardless of what you choose, girls, choose well. Your grandchildren might be sitting in a room like this someday, talking about you."

He walked down the hall to the far window. Pushed back the curtain until he could see the endless sky and the sea of stars.

They all looked like a bunch of diamonds to him, and he knew Harriet was up there somewhere.

"Did you hear that, Harriet? Our Meredith's giving us another grand baby. But you probably already knew, didn't you?"

He sighed deeply, missing her so very much.

"I'll see you soon, my love," he whispered.

And as he said it, a reddish star winked in the darkness and then disappeared. He smiled slowly.

So, she'd found a way to be a ruby, after all, even up in heaven.

Well, she always had been a determined woman.

Thanks for reading!

If you enjoyed this book, I would really appreciate it if you would help others enjoy it too. I would love for you to let me know what you think by posting a review. You can write one on Goodreads. If you do post a review, kindly email me at ava@avamiles.com and let me know so I can personally thank you. This book is also lending-enabled, so feel free to share it with a friend or family member. Please also consider recommending it to your book clubs and discussions boards.

And In case you missed my other books, keep reading. I included brief snippets of them all as well as Coming Soon and an excerpt from COUNTRY HEAVEN, the first book in the new Dare River series featuring Rye Crenshaw from THE GRAND OPENING and THE HOLIDAY SERENADE.

Also please consider signing up for my newsletter and liking my Facebook page to keep up with all of my exciting news and enter my fun giveaways. Happy Reading!

Coming Soon
The Dare Valley Series continues…
Book 6: THE PARK OF SUNSET DREAMS
Jane Wilcox and Matthew Hale's story
Available Spring 2014

Also Coming Soon
The Dare River Series continues…
Book 2: THE CHOCOLATE GARDEN
Tammy Morrison and John Parker
McGuiness' story
Available Summer 2014

Other Books By Ava

All books can be enjoyed as a stand-alone if this is your first time reading. Enjoy!

Dare Valley Series
NORA ROBERTS LAND
Meredith and Tanner's story

A journalist returns to her hometown to debunk the Nora Roberts' romance novels her ex-husband blamed for their divorce only to discover happy endings exist when she falls for a hero straight out of a bona fide romance novel.

FRENCH ROAST

Jill and Brian's story

A small-town girl mixes business and pleasure with her childhood BFF until his own Mrs. Robinson returns, making her question their friendship and their newfound love.

THE GRAND OPENING
Peggy and Mac's story

A cynical single-mom cop discovers she can't bluff her way out of love when a mysterious poker-playing hotel magnate shows her it's worth the gamble.

Dare River Series
COUNTRY HEAVEN
Tory and Rye's story

A down-on-her luck cook uses food's magical properties to tame a beastly country singer after he hires her under false pretenses to restore his image.

And please enjoy this excerpt of COUNTRY HEAVEN. Available Now.

Obligations make my stomach hurt.

They're no fun.
Make me want to run.
Feel too up-pity.

Don't make me go.
Forget about the show.
I'm not for display.

Obligations just aren't for me.
No more obligations please.

Rye Crenshaw's first Top Twenty Hit, "No More
Obligations"

Prologue

Nashville's Disadvantaged Children's Association's Annual May Day Charity event at one of the city's finest country clubs didn't have a whiff of disadvantage, in Rye Crenshaw's opinion.

Ice sculptures of unicorns and cherub-faced children were dripping in the hot sun on the plush buffet table. The silver flatware fairly blinded him, and the plates gleamed so brightly they looked like they'd been shined with furniture polish. At least the food appealed to him, the succulent beef tenderloin and slow-roasted pork being sliced delicately by black-tie waiters while others carried around silver trays with champagne, mint juleps—this was Nashville, after all—and delicate canapés of crab and caviar. An assortment of European cheeses from bleu to goat caught his eye, and his stomach grumbled. Food was one of Rye's greatest pleasures in life, and he loved indulging in it.

Thank God the only thing the chairperson of the DCA wanted from him today was his presence, his pocket book, and for him to take some pictures with the disadvantaged kids they'd brought to the event. No live performance singing songs from his new album, *Cracks in the Glass*

House, which continued to rise to the top of the charts.

His had been a wild ride to stardom after a childhood spent without any autonomy. Now, he did exactly what he wanted, went where he wanted.

Except on days like today, when his manager, Georgia Chandler, arranged for him to attend a hobnob charity event. He liked giving back to the community and hated seeing kids treated poorly, but he didn't like being put on display like some zoo animal.

And he downright hated hoity toity events like these, having had his fill of them growing up in blue-blood Meade, Mississippi, before breaking the family tradition of being a lawyer in the family practice to pursue country music.

Of course, his family hadn't liked that one bit. And events like these made him think about them…and how they'd disowned him when he stepped out of line.

Georgia made her way toward him, wearing a leopard-print mini skirt, a black blouse, a black cowboy hat, and five-inch black cowboy boots that left punctures resembling bullet holes in the finely manicured lawn as she meandered through the crowd.

"Are you ready to work your magic?" she asked when she reached him.

"Yes," he said, and joined her to stroll through the crowd of Nashville's finest, being stopped for an occasional autograph or a more personal proposition from some of the elegant ladies in attendance.

He had just finished shaking hands with the mayor when his cell phone vibrated in his jeans, and since Georgia was busy chatting with the politicos, he stepped away. He dug his smart phone out of his pocket, and his heart just about stopped…

It was the number from his family's house, which he hadn't stepped foot in for five years.

A spear of fear drove straight into his heart.

"Hello?" he said, hurrying away from the crowd, the sun beating down on his black cowboy hat.

"Rye, I hope this is a convenient time to call," she said.

Mama? The reason she was calling must be dire. She must have gotten his number from his sister, the only person in his family with whom he still communicated. And just as he remembered, Mama's tone was so cold it could have kept the ice sculptures from melting.

"Of course," he woodenly replied. Manners must always be observed.

"Good. Well, then. I've learned that you plan to attend Amelia Ann's graduation from Ole Miss, and I'm calling to tell you not to come."

Anger sparked inside him, hot and fierce. "She's my baby sister, Mama, and I'll come see her graduate if I want." It wasn't like he'd planned on sitting with them anyway.

A brittle laugh echoed on the line. "I thought you might say that. Rye, when you left this family and turned your back on everything we stood for, your Daddy and I made it crystal clear you were to have no contact with any of us again. And wasn't it a surprise to hear that you've been secretly in contact with Amelia Ann for some years now. Well, I forbid it."

One of his songs suddenly erupted from the speakers, and he had to put his finger in his ear to hear her. "Too bad. She's an adult now, and I'll see her if I want."

Amelia Ann had reached out to him five years ago when he'd been disowned, sending him an email, and they'd kept up a secret correspondence ever since. When she started at Ole Miss, they began talking on the phone now and again, and Rye had even visited her periodically. But they'd been careful, both of them well aware that Mama wouldn't approve.

"Rye, I won't have my baby sullied by your lifestyle or your unconventional belief system. Amelia Ann will take her rightful place back home in Meade after graduating, and she'll marry a fine Southern gentleman and have babies, just like Tammy has done."

Yeah, his older sister, Tammy, had toed the line. She was so much like Mama they might as well be twins.

"Mama, I'm going to that graduation," he said, an edge in his voice.

"If you do, Rye, or if you have any more contact with her at all, I will disown her too."

The punch of that threat rolled across his solar plexus.

"I won't tolerate another rotten apple in my barrel."

"You wouldn't," he said, even though he knew she would. Mama was the kind who would eat her own young at any provocation.

"Try me, Rye. You didn't use to underestimate me."

No, he hadn't. Her weapons were sharp and unforgiving. And he had the scars to prove it. "Fine," he said. "I won't go to her graduation." It cost him to consent, but he couldn't bear to see Amelia Ann hurt. She had a gentle, loving heart, which is why she loved her black sheep brother against the family's wishes. They would find a way to be in touch.

"And no more phone calls," Mama added, as if reading his mind. "I'll be monitoring her phone bill in the future."

Christ.

"Don't mess with me on this, Rye. I've spoken to Amelia Ann, and she has accepted my dictate. You'd best do the same."

His sister had caved? The hurt of never again seeing her bright smile or hearing her laugh on the phone almost brought him to his knees. "You're a goddamn mean-spirited bitch," he spat.

"I love you too, son. Bye now."

The phone went dead, and he fought the urge to hurl it across the yard. Goddammit! He punched the air instead, wanting to strike out at something, anything.

He didn't often feel helpless in his life anymore, but he did now. And it was pure hemlock, hearing the utter hatred in Mama's voice again, like he was a whelp she'd brought into the world and hoped would simply disappear from existence.

Getting out of this charity event was the first order of business. He didn't care if it was early. Georgia could write them a fat check to smooth over any complaints.

He texted her to say he was leaving and that he'd explain later. As he reached the side entrance to the country club's lobby, a heavily built man grabbed his arm.

"Leaving so soon?" the man drawled, his mouth an ugly sneer. "A hot shot like you can't even stay to help disadvantaged kids?"

Since he'd been harassed by strangers before, he knew better than to reply. He tried to step around the guy without comment, but the man was bold and blocked him. Rye could guess at the reason for that boldness when the stench of alcohol wafted over him.

"Best get out of my face today, boy. I'm not feeling too nice today."

"You're just some country whelp." Little did this man

know how thick the blue blood ran in Rye's veins, even if he went out of his way to conceal that fact. "You don't belong among good family folk," he continued.

"Your opinion."

The man only scratched his fat belly with his other hand. "You're a good-for-nothing son of a bitch, and you don't deserve to be here."

The words echoed in Rye's head, but this time it was his mama's voice he heard. The towering inferno of rage erupted inside him, spewing like a dormant volcano that had just come awake after sleeping for years. He shoved the man out of his way, and the man fell to the side and started howling.

Rye immediately reached to help him up, but the guy jerked away and yelled, "He hit me! Rye Crenshaw hit me."

Of course, a crowd gathered at the noise, the man yelling about how violent Rye had been. How he wasn't fit to be around children. And wouldn't you know it, a few of the disadvantaged children the association had brought for the event teared up and cried like in some frickin' Dickens novel.

Camera phones flashed everywhere.

He was screwed.

Striding out of the country club, hounded by the man's shouts, he waited for his truck to come around to the valet stand and called his lawyer on the way home to tell him what had happened so he could call the police and give Rye's account. He'd bet the farm the man was going to press charges. Good God, the whole rigmarole made his head swim.

By the time he made it home to Dare River, Twitter had exploded with pictures of the fat man writhing on the floor, Rye standing over him looking dark and foreboding. And then there were the accusations.

Rye Crenshaw Punches Innocent Man at a Charity Event.

Rye Crenshaw Mean to Children.

Rye Crenshaw Violent Around Kids.

He threw his phone against the wall of the den, the crack of it breaking doing nothing to comfort him. Georgia would be wild to talk to him, as would the rest of his staff, but he couldn't handle that now. Grabbing a bottle of Wild Turkey, he headed out to the river and stood by the bank. But the usual delight he took at seeing the water turn to diamonds in the light was gone.

His reputation had just taken a devastating blow. He might cultivate a bad-boy image, but what was being said in the media would shock his fans. And it wouldn't matter if the police didn't press charges. Like the old phrase went: a picture is worth a thousand words.

Even he knew that.

And just as he was starting his tour at the end of the month.

His career could be in trouble, but all he could think about was that his baby sister, his precious heart, was lost to him.

He hung his head and sank to his knees by the river.

About the Author

USA Today Bestselling Author Ava Miles burst onto the contemporary romance scene after receiving Nora Roberts' blessing for her use of Ms. Roberts' name in her debut novel, NORA ROBERTS LAND, which kicked off The Dare Valley Series and brought praise from reviewers and readers alike. Much to Ava's delight, *USA Today* Contributor Becky Lower selected it as one of the Best Books of the Year. Ava continued The Dare Valley Series in FRENCH ROAST, which Tome Tender says "raised the entertainment bar again" and then THE GRAND OPENING, which reviewer Mary J. Gramlich says "is a continuation of love, family, and relationships." The next books in the series, THE HOLIDAY SERENADE, was met with high praise and her ode to the early 1960s, THE TOWN SQUARE, what she calls *Mad Men* in a small town with a happy ending, melted reader's hearts.

Ava based her original series on a family newspaper, modeled after her own. Her great-great grandfather won it in a poker game in 1892, so Ava is no stranger to adventurous men and models her heroes after men like that—or like Tim McGraw, her favorite country music singer. Now Ava shares the Dare River series, set in the deep South, telling the story of a country singer and a beautiful cook. A former chef herself, Ava used her culinary background to infuse the story with family and personal recipes, but she also used her love for music to write country music songs to set the stage in the novel, creating a unique book experience. Ava—a writer since childhood—now lives in her own porch-swinging-friendly community with an old-fashioned Main Street lined with small businesses.

Made in the USA
Middletown, DE
13 January 2015